'You are in contempt of this court.' The Judge spoke in a voice like thunder.

'I'm contemptuous of you,' said Carla in defiance.

'Strip her!'

'No!' cried Carla. 'Not in front of all these people.'

But hands were already at her throat, loosening the cape which was all that shielded her naked body from the burning gaze of a room full of people.

The cape fell away and a gasp rose from the watchers. Carla blushed scarlet and looked down at her plump, jutting breasts and the thrusting curves of her hips and belly. What a sight she must make, she thought, imprisoned aloft on the punishment dais, the chain pulled taut between her slim nude thighs . . .

The Trial

Samantha Austen

HEADLINE DELTA

First published in 1997
by HEADLINE BOOK PUBLISHING

A HEADLINE DELTA paperback

10 9 8 7 6 5 4 3 2 1

ISBN 0 7472 5517 2

Typeset at The Spartan Press Ltd
Lymington, Hampshire

Printed and bound in Great Britain by
Cox & Wyman Ltd, Reading, Berkshire

HEADLINE BOOK PUBLISHING
A division of Hodder Headline PLC
338 Euston Road
London NW1 3BH

The Trial

Chapter One

Carla knew immediately that the long black limousine that purred around the corner was coming for her. There was something both stylish and sinister about it. Something that told her not only was she to be its passenger, but also that the dark figure sitting in the back was Phaedra. She stepped away from the curb as, sure enough, it glided to a halt beside her.

She glanced about to ensure nobody was watching. The gesture was unnecessary, and she knew it. The wide, tree-lined street in which she was standing was deserted, as it always was at night. People who lived in this neighbourhood were not pedestrians. If they went out, it was by car, the gates outside the mansions whirring open automatically to allow egress. Even the servants were dropped off from minivans, the intercoms attached to every gatepost making sure that only they and welcome visitors were ever granted access to the fortresses behind.

And this was where Carla lived, an inmate of one of the huge Georgian edifices that crouched behind the high walls, where the rich and the good could feel certain that their privacy was in no danger of being invaded.

Carla shivered, unable to rid herself of the sensation that she was being watched. At that moment, the rear door of the car opened. She glanced into the gloomy interior, but could discern nothing. Taking one last look about her, she stepped into the waiting car, fumbling for the seat and settling into the thick cushions as the door clicked shut behind her. Then the note of the engine rose slightly and the vehicle slipped away from the curb.

Despite the lack of illumination, Carla was now able to discern the figure sitting to her right, her long, slim body stretched out across the seat. Even if she had been unable to see her companion's face, the scent of expensive perfume would have told her it was Phaedra. She turned to the woman.

'What is it tonight, Phaedra?' she asked quietly. 'You sounded very insistent.'

'Patience, my dear.' The woman's voice had an oddly husky tone to it. A tone that was undeniably sexy. This, coupled with the heavy Eastern European accent made her sound like some sinister Mata Hari from the steppes.

'It's lucky that Eric is out tonight,' went on Carla. 'I could never have got away otherwise.'

'Kneel on the floor.'

The order cut short Carla's small-talk instantly. It was as if the woman had not heard a word she had said. Carla stared at her for a moment. She had never heard Phaedra talk like that. But she recognized the tone of authority in her voice as she gave the order, and somehow she knew not to disobey. At once she rose from her seat and dropped to her knees on the thick carpet, facing the tinted window, through which she could just make out the shape of the driver's head as they made their way through the darkened streets. At the same moment a light came on inside the passenger compartment, illuminating its plush interior.

'Take off your dress.'

A familiar feeling of pleasure ran through Carla's body as she heard the command. Clearly this would be no ordinary social evening – evenings with Phaedra seldom were. Her fingers trembling slightly, she reached for the zipper that ran down the front of her dress.

She pulled it undone in a single movement, holding the material close to her for a second before letting it fall open. Then, with a shrug, she pulled the flimsy dress over her head and allowed it to fall to the floor of the car. She wore no underwear, her lovely young body looking pale in the car's soft lighting. Behind her she heard a rustle of material as Phaedra took her dress.

'Put your hands behind you.'

Once again Carla obeyed instantly. There was a clink of metal and cold steel bands closed about her wrists. She experimented with moving her arms, but the cuffs held them locked behind her. Then something was placed across her eyes. Something soft and velvety that obscured her vision completely. Still she made no complaint, kneeling patiently whilst her companion secured the blindfold.

'Sit.'

She rose awkwardly, ducking her head to avoid banging it on the ceiling of the car as she eased herself back into her seat. It was uncomfortable to have her hands secured behind her, but she said nothing. She knew instinctively that when Phaedra spoke to her like this, the only response was complete obedience.

She settled back into the seat, enjoying the feel of the soft leather against her naked flesh. The car's motion was smooth and silent, almost lulling her to sleep as they travelled through the night. She wondered where they could be going. It was unlike the escort agency to call her out at such short notice. Normally she was the one who called them to say she was free. Even when they did make the initial contact, she was usually given at least a couple of days to invent an excuse and cancel any social engagements that prevented her answering their summons, but tonight the phone call had come completely out of the blue.

She had recognized the dark brown tone of Phaedra's voice at once.

'I'm calling on behalf of the agency. They need you tonight.'

'But why are you calling? It's normally someone else.'

'Be outside in thirty minutes, suitably attired.'

'What if I can't . . .'

But Phaedra had already rung off.

As usual the call from the agency had sent an odd thrill through Carla's body, and she had found herself shivering as she made her way up to her bedroom. The maid had followed her up, asking if she could be of assistance, but Carla had shooed her away, preferring to be left alone as she prepared for whatever Phaedra had in store for her.

Carla's wardrobe was large. Extremely large. If there was one thing to be said about her husband Eric, it was that he was a generous man. Rows and rows of designer dresses hung before her as she had begun the search for the right outfit, discarding those that she thought too dressy, or not sexy enough. She had eventually chosen a short, black dress of plain design, which she had laid out on the bed.

She had stripped and hurried into the bathroom, stepping into the shower. Soon she had been luxuriating in the warmth of the spray as it played on her skin. Once clean, she'd pulled one of the thick towels from the rack and dried herself, then strode naked into her bedroom once more.

On the door of her wardrobe was a full-length mirror, and she'd paused before it, critically examining her body.

Carla Wilde was twenty-three years old and stunningly beautiful. Her face was perfectly proportioned, with high cheekbones, a small, elegant nose, a pretty mouth and lips that cried out to be kissed. Her eyes were a deep green with long lashes and an apparent innocence that would have melted the heart of any man. She wore her dark hair down to her shoulders, so that it formed a perfect frame for her features.

She was not tall, no more than five foot four in her stockinged feet, but her body was perfectly proportioned, and she'd gazed approvingly at her full, round breasts. They were the shape and size of ripe grapefruits and jutted from her chest, firm and plump with long, luscious nipples that, even when soft, stood out prominently. Below them her body tapered to a slim waist, with a flat stomach and neat navel, then widened to full hips. Her pubic hair was dark and trimmed to a neat triangle, the tufts so short that her sex lips showed thick and inviting beneath. Her bottom was pert, the tight flesh wiggling deliciously as she moved, and her long, tapering legs completed what was an almost perfect body.

Carla had lingered in front of the glass, eyeing herself with satisfaction. She'd thought of the evening to come, and once again a shiver of pleasure had run through her. She'd had no idea what Phaedra had in mind for her, but if her previous experiences with the agency were anything to go by, she was glad that she was looking good.

She had turned away from the mirror, and her eye had

alighted on a picture that stood on her dressing table. It showed her on her wedding day with her husband. Taken two years before, it depicted a happy, smiling young bride on the arm of a man who was clearly some years older then her. In fact Eric was more than ten years her senior, looking very distinguished in his morning suit. She'd studied his features. There was no doubt that he was extremely handsome, and she remembered how she had been bowled over by his rugged looks. The fact that he was a successful Harley Street surgeon had also been an attraction, not just for the money, but for the prestige and the lifestyle he led. At the time it had all seemed so glamorous to her, a recent graduate seeking a career.

She'd smiled wryly to herself. Some career! Barely had she begun work than she had found herself wed to this rich, influential man, with no need to do anything except attend cocktail parties, play bridge and lounge beside their private pool.

At first it had seemed a wonderful life, with no worries and a dutiful husband. She would rise late, swim in the pool, breakfast on the terrace and then attend to the usual round of engagements. In the evenings there were innumerable social occasions which she would go to with Eric, meeting the great and the good. Carla had found herself at the centre of a world where money seemed no object, and where the pursuit of pleasure seemed the major priority in life.

It wasn't long, though, before the lifestyle had begun to pall. Her husband began working longer hours, arriving home late at night, sometimes not coming home at all. The house began to feel more and more like a prison, and she would sit for long hours at her bedroom window gazing at the high walls that surrounded her, wondering whether their purpose was to keep the world out, or to keep her in. Suddenly the social round seemed trivial, the people shallow sybarites, and she found herself longing for something more exciting in her life.

Then came the party where she had first encountered Phaedra, and where her life had changed forever.

And now here she was, seated in the rear of this long, luxurious vehicle, naked, blindfolded and shackled, with no idea where she was going, or what awaited her when she got there. She thought of the driver, whose shape had been so clearly visible to her through the glass, and imagined his eyes upon her body as they drove along. The idea sent yet another shiver of pleasure through her body and, on a sudden impulse, she moved her knees apart, lying back and pressing her hips forward so that she knew her sex would be on full view to him.

She sensed the woman beside her move slightly, and she knew her overt action had not gone unnoticed by her companion. She didn't care. She wanted to draw attention to herself.

Carla was beginning to feel very aroused. It was something to do with her nudity and the proximity of the other woman. She thought of making love with Phaedra, imagining the woman's fingers caressing her flesh, and she gave a little sigh. She wanted to ask Phaedra to masturbate her, as she had done in the past, but she knew the older woman would call the shots tonight, and that all the initiatives would be taken by her. It was clear that Carla's role was one of obedience. She didn't mind, though. There was no doubt in her mind that, whatever lay in store for her that evening, there would be no shortage of sensual pleasure.

Her mind swimming with erotic thoughts, Carla rested her head against the back of the seat and relaxed as the car moved on through the night.

Chapter Two

The journey took about fifteen minutes. It was impossible for Carla to gauge where they were going as the car twisted and turned through the dark streets. Occasionally they would come to a halt at what she guessed were traffic lights. She wondered if people could see in, and what they would think to see the naked girl, her charms on display as she was driven through the night in the long, mysterious vehicle. The idea of being seen excited her, and she spread her legs still wider as she imagined men's eyes upon her.

At last the car took a left turn, and she heard the unmistakable sound of gravel beneath the wheels. Then they swung to the right and came to a halt. For a moment there was silence, then a click as the driver opened the door beside Carla.

'Get out.'

Once again Phaedra's tone brooked no disobedience, and Carla climbed from the car, suddenly embarrassed by the display she had put on for the driver during the journey. Then he had seemed a remote figure, separated from her by the barrier of the glass. Now he stood beside her, so close that she could smell him, could almost touch him. She wondered if he thought her a slut.

'Is this her?'

The voice was a woman's, and Carla jumped as she realized they were not alone. Its tone was formal, hard even, reminding her of her teachers at school.

'This is her,' replied the chauffeur.

'All right.'

Carla heard the door through which she had just come close behind her. Then the driver was no longer beside her as boots crunched across the gravel. Another door closed, then the engine revved and she heard the car move away. She gave a gasp of dismay as she realized she had been abandoned. Suddenly she felt very alone and rather afraid. Here she was, naked and shackled, in a strange place and in the company of someone she did not know.

She was filled with an urge to run away. But to where? She didn't know where she was or which direction was home. Slowly it dawned on her how hopeless was her position, and that she was trapped, by the simple inexpediency of her nudity.

'Come with me.'

A hand was placed on her arm, and she found herself being led away. Phaedra had allowed her to keep her shoes, slim black stilettos, and she tottered slightly as they walked across the gravel together.

'Three steps ahead.'

Carla moved tentatively, anxious in case she should trip, but the woman's grip was firm and she negotiated the steps without difficulty. Suddenly she found herself inside a building, her heels ringing on the hard marble floor. The echoes that came back to her told her that she was in a large room, probably some kind of reception area, with a high ceiling.

Then there was carpet beneath her feet and she was being

led down a corridor and up a flight of stairs. They walked on a little further, then stopped and she heard a doorhandle turn. The door creaked open and she was led through.

'Here she is. You have forty minutes. See to it.'

'Yes, Ma'am.'

There were two voices this time, both female and both sounding considerably younger than her escort. Carla stood quietly as she heard the woman exit and close the door behind her.

She sensed the two women approaching her, then a hand went to the back of her head and released the knot in the blindfold. She blinked as the bright lights hit her, trying to focus on her surroundings.

Slowly things became clear. She was in a large room, with a thick carpet on the floor and heavy drapes at the windows. The only furniture was a dressing table, surrounded by mirrors, and what looked like a barber's chair set on a pedestal. She turned to look at her two companions.

They were young, no more than eighteen or nineteen, and dressed in maids' uniforms with short black dresses and white aprons. One was blonde, the other dark. They were both extremely attractive and were eyeing the naked captive in a way that made Carla blush.

'Where am I?' she ventured.

'Quiet,' said the dark-haired girl. 'You are not permitted to speak. If you do, you will get us into trouble. Anna, the cuffs.'

Carla stood quietly whilst her wrists were freed. Then the two girls took a hand each and led her through a door on the far side of the room. As they stepped through, Carla realized that it was a bathroom. In the centre was a dais on which the bath was placed, already filled with steaming water.

Carla opened her mouth to tell them she had already showerd, then closed it again. After all she had had her orders.

They led her to the dais, which stood about a foot above the floor. A set of steps ran up to the edge of the bath and Carla was made to climb these. When she reached the top, her two companions slipped off her shoes and gestured to her to enter the bath.

The water was warm and sweet-smelling, and Carla lay down in it, allowing it to lap up around her breasts. She stretched her arms out along the sides and leaned her head back, enjoying the relaxing feel of the bath.

At once the two maids set about bathing her, rubbing expensive perfumed soap onto her skin and rinsing it off with soft sponges. To Carla the sensation of their hands on her naked flesh felt wonderful, and she sighed with pleasure as her breasts were caressed by them, the nipples hardening to points as their fingers drifted over them.

The girls scrubbed her back, working the soap deep into the pores and massaging the muscles in her neck. Then they were moving lower, their hands drifting over her stomach and combing through her pubic hair.

'Ah!'

Carla was unable to suppress the exclamation as two small fingers slipped into her vagina, causing the muscles to contract about them as a surge of pleasure swept through her body. She wanted the girl to keep her fingers there, to rub her clitoris and stimulate her sex, but she merely soaped and rinsed as she had the rest of Carla's body, leaving the hapless girl aroused and frustrated.

When at last they were satisfied that their charge was clean, the pair helped her from the water, standing her beside the bath and towelling her body, dabbing at every nook and cranny, whilst Carla tried her best to suppress the emotions the two youngsters' touches were kindling in her.

Once dry, Carla was led into the dressing room. They took her straight to the barber's chair, and gestured to her to sit down.

Carla obeyed, shivering slightly as the hard plastic material of the chair came in contact with her bare skin. Then the maids took over once more, laying her arms on the arm rests and, reaching underneath, pulling out thick leather belts. Before Carla knew what was happening they had secured these around her arms, holding them in place. She struggled for a moment with these bonds, but in vain. She was trapped. She looked fearfully at the pair, realizing how vulnerable she now was, but they remained impassive, crouching down at the foot of the chair and fiddling with something there.

All at once, to Carla's surprise, they pulled a pair of metal arms out from the seat of the chair. These two steel poles projected about three feet, stretching out parallel in front of the chair on either side. Then the two girls swivelled round the top part of each, effectively doubling their length. These extensions locked into place at an angle to the originals, so that together they formed a sort of Y shape. Next the maids took hold of their captive's ankles and hauled them apart, attaching each to the ends of the extensions by straps that hung from them.

Carla found herself in an extraordinary position, her arms held fast at her sides, her legs forcibly spread wide, leaving her sex gaping. It was a perfect position to be fucked in, she realized with a start, and if anybody chose to take her now, there was nothing she could possibly do about it. The thought sent yet another spasm of lust through her as she sat eyeing her captors, her mind a whirl. Had she been brought here merely to be raped? But what would be the point of that? Phaedra knew that no bonds were necessary for a wanton young woman like her. She had already demonstrated her willingness by allowing herself to be stripped and chained. Still, it was with some trepidation that she watched as the two girls approached her.

There was a small case beside her chair, and the blonde girl stooped down and unlatched it. From it she produced a comb and a pair of scissors. Then she moved round behind Carla's head and began running the comb through her long, dark locks. But it was the other girl who caught Carla's attention now, as she too delved into the case. She emerged with a cut-throat razor and a can of shaving foam.

Carla watched as the young woman moved between her legs, her face reddening as she realized what a sight she must make with her legs spread so blatantly. Her eyes widened as she saw the girl squirt a blob of shaving foam onto her palm.

'Ah!'

Carla was unable to suppress the exclamation as the girl began to rub the white foam into her pubic hair, applying it liberally about the lips of her sex, her fingers brushing over Carla's already swollen clitoris and making her gasp at the intimacy of the contact. The maid was thorough, coating Carla's sex lips and working the foam in right the way around to her backside. Once she was satisfied with that, the girl opened the razor and ran it up and down a strop that hung from the side of the chair.

She began to apply the razor to Carla's flesh, sending shivers through the helpless girl as she scraped away the hairs about her nether lips in smooth strokes. Meanwhile the blonde began to snip away at the hair on her head, trimming it to a uniform length and combing it straight.

The hairdressing took no more than ten minutes. By the end Carla was surprised to see that her pubic triangle was still intact, though all the hair below it was shaved away, leaving the thick lips of her sex completely clear. Carla's face glowed as she thought of how she must look. She wondered what Eric would say when he saw her thus. However, she was certain that he would not be the first man to see her newly shaven slit, and the thought sent a surge of wetness through her as she contemplated what might happen next.

The blonde girl must have noticed the way the muscles of her sex had convulsed, because she paused, staring at Carla's sex.

'You're turned on, aren't you?' she asked.

Carla nodded, blushing.

'Would you like me to do something about it?'

Carla closed her eyes, unable to meet the girl's amused stare. Then she nodded again.

'Come on,' said the blonde to her companion. 'Let's have some fun with her.'

'The Mistress will be back soon,' cautioned her companion.

'With her in that state, this isn't going to take long.'

Carla watched as the maid pulled open a drawer. Her eyes widened as she saw what she pulled out. It was a phallus, shaped to mimic an erect penis, bulging with thick veins. The youngster brought it across and held it in front of Carla's face, still grinning as she watched the trapped girl's expression.

'You fancy this?' she asked.

Carla nodded once more.

'Say yes please.'

'Y-yes please,' she gasped in a small voice.

'Suck it.'

Carla hesitated for a second. Then she opened her mouth and took the thick object between her lips. It had a bitter, rubbery taste, but she didn't care, sucking hard at it as she would a real penis whilst her two companions looked on.

At last the blonde withdrew the object.

'That should be wet enough, I think,' she said, and moved down between Carla's legs.

'Oh!'

Carla's entire body jumped, straining against her bonds as the girl began to press the phallus into her vagina, twisting it as she did so. She pressed it home until only the base was projecting from the helpless girl's love hole. Then she flicked a switch and the object began to vibrate.

'Ahhhh!'

Carla's body squirmed and wriggled as the most delicious sensation flowed through her. The two girls simply stood back and watched as she pumped her hips back and forth, her backside rising clear of the seat in the most blatantly sexual gesture.

'I think she likes it,' giggled the blonde. 'My god, she's on heat.'

'Better get a move on,' said her companion. 'The Mistress will thrash us if we're late.'

'You're right,' the blonde replied. 'Right sweetie, let's hear you come.'

She took hold of the vibrator and began moving it back and forth, simulating the motion of a lover. Carla gasped aloud, her head shaking back and forth as her body was engulfed in lustful pleasure.

The girl manipulated the vibrator expertly. It was clear to Carla that this was not the first time she had frigged a woman with such a toy. She looked at the dark girl and wondered if she had received similar treatment in the past. The phallus felt wonderful, sending shocks of pleasure through her as it slid in and out, making a small squelching sound as it forced out the juices that filled her cunt.

Carla was ecstatic. She wanted the sensation to go on forever, but she knew that, such was her arousal, she would not be able to last long. In no time at all the pleasure was so intense that all she could do was moan aloud as she pressed her hips up at the humming object of her desire.

Then she was coming, shrieks of joy ringing from her lips as she pumped her hips back and forth. It was all the blonde girl could do to keep hold of the dildo, so violent were her movements. If not for the straps restraining her it would have been impossible.

At last, Carla began to calm down, her movements slowing as the passion ebbed from her. When she was finally still, her breasts rising and falling as she gasped for air, the girl removed the object from her.

'That feel better?' the girl asked.

'Mmmm.'

'Time to get you out of here, then.'

The girls began to release her, unstrapping her ankles and folding the leg restraints back into the chair before removing the bonds from her arms. They pulled the naked beauty to her feet, guiding her across to the dressing table. Carla allowed herself to be led without complaint, her mind concentrated on the odd feeling between her legs, the cool air feeling strangely arousing as it wafted over her newly-shaven sex.

They sat her down before the mirrors and began to make her up. Carla sat compliantly as the eye shadow and lipstick were applied, though she was somewhat surprised when they rubbed a light colouring into her nipples, making them harden once more as the soft young fingers rubbed her sensitive flesh. Her surprise was doubled when they made her spread her legs and carefully applied a line of lipstick around her sex, an action that she knew must draw attention to her lack of hair in so private a place.

At last the pair seemed satisfied with her appearance and pulled her to her feet once more. Carla paused before the mirror, eyeing herself critically. There was no doubt that the two young women were experts. Her face and hair had never looked better, and her breasts and sex were, if anything, even more prominent after their ministrations. She knew that any man seeing her now would want to fuck her at once, a thought that thrilled her anew.

The dark girl approached her carrying the handcuffs and Carla obediently placed her hands behind her, shivering at the coldness of the metal as it closed about her wrists. The blonde then produced a collar. It was made of leather, with shiny studs round its circumference, and she fitted it about Carla's neck. The inside was lined with velvet and it fitted snugly against the girl's throat. From it hung a long silver chain, about the thickness of a dog's lead, which dangled down between Carla's prominent breasts to the floor. Finally the blindfold was placed across her eyes, once more plunging her into darkness.

They led Carla to the centre of the room, then left her on

her own. She heard them exchange a word, giggling together, then the door opened and closed and there was silence.

Left alone, Carla's mind was filled with thoughts about her fate. Why had she been brought to this strange place? What were Phaedra's intentions in having her prepared in this way? There could be no doubt that something unusual was planned for her, and the more she speculated on what it might be, the more her arousal increased.

It was nearly a quarter of an hour before she heard the door open again. Somebody entered the room. It was a woman, the same one who had brought her into the house in the first place. Carla recognized the footfalls, and the scent she wore. She stood, tense and silent as the woman walked round her, clearly inspecting the job the youngsters had done.

Something was placed about her shoulders. A cape of some sort. It felt as if it was made of silk, and it caressed her naked flesh deliciously, hanging down and clinging to her contours. It was fastened by a single drawstring at the neck and hung almost to her ankles. She knew that when she moved it would billow open, offering almost no cover for her modesty, but at least it was some form of clothing, and she was glad of the fact that her shaven sex lips were, for the moment at least, hidden from view.

There was a soft clink as the woman took hold of the chain attached to Carla's collar. Then a hand reached inside the cloak and cupped her breast.

'Beautiful,' murmured the woman. 'Absolutely beautiful. And so wanton.'

She gave a tug on Carla's chain.

'Come on, my dear,' she said. 'They're waiting for you.'

Chapter Three

The woman led Carla out through the door she had come in by and back along the corridor, occasionally tugging at her lead if she failed to keep up the pace. The girls had returned Carla's shoes to her before leaving, and the job of walking blindfold in a strange house wearing high heels was not an easy one. On more than one occasion she momentarily lost her footing, but managed to stay upright.

They descended to the ground floor once more and headed off down yet another corridor. As she walked Carla's cloak trailed out behind her as she knew it would, so that anyone she encountered would have a clear view of her naked breasts and crotch. She wasn't certain whether they did pass anyone. Once or twice she fancied she heard a footstep or a whispered remark, but there was no way of knowing for certain.

The passageways twisted and turned, completely disorienting the girl. The woman walked ahead of her at a fast pace, and Carla had to almost trot to keep up.

Suddenly a sound met her ears. A faint hubbub of voices far ahead. Carla strained to listen. There was no doubt about it. Somewhere in front of them was a group of people talking together. She began to hear the tinkle of cutlery as well. It seemed to be some kind of dinner party, a very large one by the sound of it.

A sense of fear began to permeate Carla's mind, a knot forming in her stomach as she wondered what lay in store for her. Who could these people possibly be? And what did they want with her? It was obvious she was to be no ordinary guest, since the party had clearly been going on for some time. She wished that her hands were free so that she could at least pull the robe closed in front of her.

The sound was very loud now. There seemed to be dozens of voices. More than a hundred even, the volume increasing to a dull roar as they came closer to it. The woman brought her to a halt, and Carla heard a door being opened. At the same time, the full noise of the crowd reached her and she knew that this was the door to the very room in which the dinner party, if that's what it was, was taking place.

Once again Carla hung back, terrified of who might be there and able to see her. All at once the cloak seemed very scant covering indeed, and she shook her head as the woman pulled at her lead.

'No,' she said.

'What's the matter, girl?' demanded the woman. 'I thought I'd demanded absolute obedience.'

'I can't go in there. Not like this.'

'Why not? You surely knew that something of this sort would be required of you.'

'But so many people. What if somebody recognizes me?'

'What indeed? You should have considered that earlier. Now come along or it'll be the worse for you.'

'But . . .'

'Listen. Nobody can see you at the moment. After all,

we've been standing at the open door all this time, yet the conversation hasn't faltered at all.'

'I suppose not . . .'

'Nobody will see you until I am ready. You will be screened by a curtain. Now follow me.'

The woman tugged hard at Carla's lead and the hapless girl was forced to follow her into the room. It was as she had said, though. There was no break in the hubbub of conversation, though it was clear that she was no more than yards from where the people were sitting. Reluctantly, her heart thumping against her chest, Carla allowed herself to be led further and further into the room.

'Steps here,' said the woman.

Carla trod carefully, feeling for the edge of the steps with her toe and climbing slowly. There were five steps, then she found herself on some kind of platform.

'Stand there.'

Carla stood still, then suddenly felt hands grasping her ankles on each side, pulling her legs apart. She almost fell as her legs were spread. Something metal closed about each ankle and she realized with a shock that her legs were held apart by shackles. She tried to move them, but she was held fast. She gave a cry of dismay. There would be no escape now, that was for certain. Whatever was planned for her in this room was now inevitable.

She felt the presence of a person standing beside her. Then the lead, which the woman had relinquished when Carla had climbed the steps, was suddenly grasped again. To Carla's surprise she felt it being pulled between her legs, the cold metal sending a shiver through her as it came into contact with her open sex lips.

'Ah!'

Suddenly the chain was pulled tight, the links pressing hard into her slit and rubbing against her clitoris. Then there was a snapping sound and she realized that it had been fastened to something behind her.

The sensation of the rough chain against her freshly shaven sex lips was electric, and a shudder of lust shook her young body as she fought to keep her hips still, the slightest movement sending a wonderful sensation through her. Now she really was trapped in the most devious yet delicious way, and she bit her lip as she struggled to keep her emotions under control.

A hand slid under her cloak, running up her ribs and closing over the firm globe of her breast. The arousal brought on by the chain had caused her nipples to harden, and she sighed as the woman squeezed and caressed her sensitive mammaries, her touch light, yet firm. Carla was suddenly more turned on than she had thought possible, and the sound of voices beyond the curtain that she knew to be in front of her reminded her that it would not be long before her aroused state would be seen by the dinner guests.

The woman removed her hand, and Carla felt her rearrange the flimsy cloak that was her sole garment, pulling it across in front and smoothing the back, where it was lifted by the chain that passed between her legs. Then Carla heard her footsteps descend from the platform, and all of a sudden she was alone, blind and helpless as she listened to the chatter in the crowded room.

For the next ten minutes nothing happened. Carla remained where she was, standing silent and alone amidst the throng. As she waited her thoughts once more concentrated on what was to happen. Since she had fallen under the spell of the enigmatic Phaedra she had done many strange and often outrageous things, but never before had she been in quite such a position as this, and she trembled slightly as she contemplated what fate had in store for her.

All of a sudden there was a banging sound from beyond the curtain, like someone striking the table with a mallet, and the chatter immediately began to die away. Before long the room was silent. Such was the contrast to the hubbub that had preceded it, that Carla felt certain that the pounding of her own heart must be audible to all.

A man began to speak. His voice was sonorous, with an air of authority about it. He spoke slowly and deliberately, pausing occasionally for effect, and Carla strained to catch his every word.

'Ladies and gentlemen,' he began, 'the time has come to move on to the serious business of the evening. As you know, this is not simply a social affair. We are here to listen to a story and to judge whether there is a case to answer, ultimately we may even be asked to pass sentence. The time has now come to introduce you to our protagonist.'

There was silence for a moment, then Carla heard the swish of curtains. She had evidently been obscured on three sides by the drapes, and as they parted the murmur from the crowd suddenly became less muffled, indicating that they had been made of thick material.

She stood as still as she was able, her head held high as the hubbub of voices reached her ears. She wondered at the sight she must make, standing there above the crowd, her legs trapped apart, her only covering the thin cloak that hung from her collar. She knew it would be clear to all that she was naked underneath, but she could only guess at how they would react if they could see the chain that was trapped inside her cunt.

The gavel banged again and once more the talk died away. Then the voice continued its monologue.

'Mrs Carla Wilde, ladies and gentlemen. Supposedly a lady of society. The wife of a respectable Harley Street surgeon.'

Carla was shocked to hear her name mentioned so openly, as well as her status. Normally she was most discreet in protecting her identity, careful to use only her first name. Yet here he was announcing who she was to a roomful of people. She felt her face glow as she imagined the eyes of all those in the room upon her, and she struggled to concentrate on what the man was saying.

'Carla Wilde,' he went on, 'a young woman of twenty-three with everything she could possibly need. A husband, a large house, servants. There was nothing this lady could possibly want for. Yet I put it to you that, far from treating these gifts with the gratitude one might expect, Carla Wilde responded with infidelity, wantonness and the most sluttish behaviour imaginable. Which is why she is here today. She must answer those charges, or accept the punishment of this court.'

Carla listened with incredulity to his words, unable to fully take in their meaning. What on earth was going on? Was this some kind of joke on Phaedra's part? If so it wasn't a very funny one.

'The time has come for Mrs Wilde to face her accusers,' said the man. 'Please remove the blindfold.'

Carla heard someone mount the steps behind her, then felt fingers at the back of her neck fumbling with the knot. The blindfold fell away and she found herself blinking in the bright lights of the room. The pressure of the cloth against her eyes had blurred her vision and it was a few

26

seconds before she was able clearly to see about her. Then she gave a gasp of surprise.

She was standing on a platform in the centre of a large room. In front of her and on both sides people were sitting at tables. How many people she couldn't tell, but at least fifty, she estimated. All were dressed smartly, the men in dinner jackets with black bow ties, the women in long, elegant gowns. All were staring up at her as she stood, alone and bound, in their midst.

But it wasn't just the number of people that shocked her, or the elegance of their dress. It was who they were. Almost every face was familiar to her.

Down there was the bank manager. Across from him was the golf club secretary. On her right were the women with whom she played bridge. Over there were her nextdoor neighbours, and the couple from across the road, sitting with her hairdresser and her manicurist. Other faces seemed to spring out at her. Her husband's business partner and his wife, local dignitaries whom she had met at cocktail parties, the chairman of their local Conservative party. Even the gardener was there, sitting near the back of the room, his eyes fixed on her.

But it was the table immediately in front of Carla that held her attention. The man in the centre holding the gavel was unknown to her, but the poeple on either side were familiar enough. To his left sat Phaedra, her green eyes fixed on Carla's face.

On the other side, his face grim and expressionless, was her husband, Eric.

Chapter Four

For a few seconds Carla was quite speechless, staring open-mouthed at the people about her. She had known it was intended to put her on display. That had been obvious. But to have to face so many people that she knew so well. Somehow, acting as she had done previously in front of strangers had never seemed too bad. But these were people who knew her. Who socialized with her. Who knew where she lived. For some reason that made the whole thing seem doubly mortifying.

In a moment of panic she tried to free herself, pulling at the shackles on her feet and trying desperately to snap the chains on her cuffs, but it was useless and she was forced to stop for fear of allowing the cape to fall open and expose her nakedness beneath. Instead she simply hung her head, unable to meet the eyes of those below her.

'Carla Wilde,' said the man with the gavel, 'you have been called here before your peers to stand trial.'

'T-trial?'

'That is correct. The charges, please.'

Phaedra picked up a sheet of paper from the table in front of her and passed it to the man. He reached into his top pocket and produced a pair of glasses which he perched on the end of his nose. Then he began to read.

'Carla Wilde. You are accused of unfaithfulness to your husband. Further, you are accused of lewd and lascivious behaviour, of whoring, of displaying your body for the gratification of men, of placing yourself in the hands of pornographers, and of numerous perverse and wanton acts that have brought you, your neighbourhood and all associated with you into disrepute. How do you plead?'

Carla just stared at him dumbly, unable to believe her ears. She knew herself to be guilty of all the things he was accusing her of. But how had he known? The only other person who could possibly be privy to her behaviour was Phaedra. But why should Phaedra betray her? After all, it had been Phaedra who had been the instigator of most of the things that had happened. She looked across at the woman, but she was staring down at the table, apparently studying a sheet of paper.

Bang!

The man struck the table hard with his gavel, making Carla jump in surprise.

'Answer the question,' he barked. 'How do you plead?'

'I don't. You have no right to keep me here like this. Let me go.'

'May I remind you, young lady, that you came here of your own accord. Do you deny that?'

'No, but . . .'

'And that you voluntarily removed your clothes and allowed yourself to be cuffed. And that you walked into this room on your own two feet and made no complaint when the bonds were applied. Is that not true?'

'I didn't know it was going to be you.'

'Yet you knew the room to be full of people. And still you allowed yourself to be stripped almost naked and chained to that platform. Am I not right in saying that one of those chains is in a most intimate position?'

Carla did not reply.

Bang!

The gavel came down once more.

'If you continue to refuse to answer my questions I shall ensure that everyone in this room sees the position of that chain for themselves,' he said. 'Now, young lady. How do you plead?'

'I plead nothing,' said Carla. 'You have no right to ask me to. In fact you have no power over me at all. You're just a bunch of stupid people.'

The man's eyes narrowed, and for a second Carla thought he would strike the table again. Then his brow cleared and he sat back in his chair.

'If you refuse to co-operate it will be the worse for you, young lady,' he said. 'However, since there is much to do tonight, the court will take your refusal as a plea of not guilty.'

He picked up another sheaf of papers from the table and began to read aloud.

'Carla Wilde, you have many grave charges against you, and we shall be calling a number of witnesses for the prosecution. It will, however, be better for you if you recount what happened in your own words. The court will look kindly upon that. Remember that if you are found guilty you will be punished in the severest manner.'

'Punished? How?'

He put down the papers and stared into her eyes.

'There are institutions. Places of correction for young women, especially set up for fallen members of the gentry.

They exist in remote parts of Africa and Asia. Recalcitrant girls are sent there to learn obedience.'

'Obedience?'

'Certainly. Many a young debutante who stepped out of line has been trained at such places. The men who run them tend to favour the whip as their chief method of persuasion. That, followed by a year or two in a brothel or harem in one of the less enlightened parts of the Dark Continent usually does the trick. I'm sure one with your reputation would fare extremely well in such a place, where you would learn to use your body to honour only men of importance, or those approved of by your master.'

'But you can't!'

The man smiled grimly. 'I think you'll find we can,' he said quietly.

Carla stared around at the people in the room. They were all mad, surely? They couldn't possibly be serious. Yet the faces told her that they were deadly serious, and there was nothing she could do about it.

'Listen,' she said, an edge of desperation in her voice. 'If you don't stop this I'm going to scream the bloody place down.'

'It would do no good,' the man replied. 'Nobody would hear you. We're miles from anywhere. Besides it will be a simple act to gag you. And that would mean we would be deprived of hearing your side of the story.'

'I won't co-operate.'

'We have ways of persuading you. First we'll deprive you of that gown. Do you want to face this tribunal naked? Then of course, if you persist, there are all manner of ways we can inflict pain upon you. I know of very few young women who would relish having their bare behinds caned,

32

especially in public. I really think co-operation is your safest option, don't you?'

Carla glared at him, but said nothing.

'Now,' he said. 'Time to proceed. I will act as judge. Phaedra here will record proceedings. The jury will consist of the rest of those present, with the exception of your husband, at whose request these proceedings were instigated. Call the first witness!'

Almost as he spoke a pair of double doors swung open on the far side of the room and a man entered. He was dressed in a brown suit and wore a loud tie. He was about thirty, with lank hair and the beginnings of a beer belly. Carla stared at him, trying to think who he could be. His face was certainly familiar, but for the time being she couldn't remember from where.

The man strode out in front of the tables until he stood in front of the Judge and to one side of the platform where Carla was standing.

'Thank you for coming,' said the Judge. 'I understand you prefer to remain anonymous?'

'Yes, your Lordship.'

'Simply refer to me as Judge.'

'Yes, Judge.'

The man's voice was loud, his accent betraying his east London origins. He seemed to ring a bell with Carla, though she couldn't be certain why.

'You know the accused?'

'In a manner of speaking, yes.'

'And you, young lady. Do you know this man?'

Carla shook her head. 'I'm not sure . . .'

'Course you do, darling,' said the man. 'It wasn't that long ago.'

'How did the two of you meet?' asked the Judge.

'At a party.'

'Tell us about it.'

'It was a real high-class affair. All cocktails and tiny little things to eat brought around by sexy waitresses. It was thrown by the mayor. I wasn't actually invited, but my boss was and he couldn't make it, so he gave me his invite.'

'And you encountered the accused there?'

'Yeah. I thought the little darling might be lonely. Looked as if she might enjoy a bit of rough shagging with the likes of me. So I tried it on.'

'You tried it on?'

'Sure. Turned on the old charm, got her on the dance floor, had a bit of a grope. I thought she was going for it at first. Then she got cold feet.'

'Cold feet?'

'Yeah. Gave me the happily-married woman bit. Never been unfaithful, all that crap.'

'And you didn't believe her?'

'I thought maybe she was on the level at first. Then later she turns out to be a fucking lesbo. And a bit of a voyeur as well. Quite a hot little bitch when she had another girl to grope her.'

'That's not how it happened.'

Carla's exclamation seemed to take both the man and the Judge by surprise. They turned to look at the young captive, whose face was red as a beetroot.

'You recall the occasion?' asked the Judge.

'Yes,' muttered Carla quietly. 'It wasn't how he described it at all.'

'Then perhaps you'd better tell us precisely what

happened,' said the Judge. 'But be sure not to leave out any details.'

'Can't I just tell you in private?'

'Certainly not. This is a trial. The jury must hear all the evidence.'

Carla looked about at the expectant faces. It was clear that she would have to stick up for herself, or they would accept the story exactly as he had told it. She took a deep breath.

'Well,' she said. 'I remember the party now. It was in a large country hotel. I went along with my husband, but somehow we got separated . . .'

Chapter Five

The party wasn't really Carla's scene at all. She had gone along at her husband's insistence. The venue was a large and well-appointed hotel, a converted country house with dozens of rooms. They had been greeted at the door by the mayor and his wife, then had moved into the ballroom, where most of the guests were gathered.

It wasn't the usual crowd that Carla was accustomed to encountering at parties, though. Apart from a few local dignitaries, most of the guests were tradesmen from the town as well as other assorted hangers-on. Carla found herself in conversation with the man who ran the town's butcher's shop and his wife, whilst Eric excused himself and wandered off into the crowd.

Carla very quickly became bored with the company and moved on. She skirted the crowd for a while, picking up nibbles from tables about the room and nodding and smiling to people who greeted her, though avoiding being drawn into their conversations. She wandered into the room next door, desperately seeking some kind of diversion. On the far side of the room she could hear music playing and decided to investigte.

She went through a door and found herself in a small discotheque. The ceiling was studded with coloured lights that flashed on and off in a random manner whilst loud beat music was pumped from huge speakers on either side of the dance floor. Carla paused to watch as a group of young dancers cavorted about the floor, their bodies moving in rhythm to the music.

'Do you come here often?'

The words were spoken close to her ear, and Carla started, swinging round to confront the speaker. It was a man, about thirty years old, and he was smiling at her. For a moment she considered cutting him dead, then she felt the infectiousness of his smile, and found herself smiling back.

'That's a bit of a corny old chat-up line, isn't it?'

'I'm a bit of a corny old feller. Frank's the name. Frank Burrow.'

'Carla Wilde.'

'Hi, Carla. Enjoying the party?'

'Not particularly.'

'Me neither. This place isn't exactly swinging, is it?'

'Well, it's a bit better in here. At least this lot have got a bit of life in them.'

'You fancy joining them?'

Carla hesitated. It was a long time since she had last danced. Eric wasn't keen at all, claiming he was getting too old for such things, so she seldom had the opportunity. All of a sudden dancing with this friendly stranger seemed quite an appealing idea.

'All right,' she said.

He took her hand and led her onto the floor. At once the pair of them dropped into the rhythm of the beat. Carla was an expert dancer, her lithe young body twisting and turning amongst her fellow revellers. She was wearing an extremely short cocktail dress that was cut low at the neck, revealing a wide expanse of cleavage and she knew she looked great as she shimmied across the floor.

They danced to two or three numbers, their bodies weaving back and forth, occasionally brushing against one another as they lost themselves in the rhythm. At last they staggered from the floor, both giggling like a pair of children.

There were bar stools placed around the walls with shelves for drinks and Frank took her to a pair of these, pulling his up close to hers and sitting down.

'Fancy a drink?'

'Yes. Why not?'

Carla was feeling oddly euphoric after the dance and was beginning to enjoy the company of this rather forward man. She watched as he raised a finger and hailed one of the circulating waitresses.

The girl approached them. She was blonde, and extremely pretty. About nineteen, Carla estimated.

'What's your name?' he asked.

'What's it to you?' the girl replied.

'Just trying to be friendly. Anyhow, it's written on your badge. How's things, Judy?'

'Boring, if you must know.'

'Let's give you something to do then. We'd like a bottle of champagne, please Judy.'

'I'm not allowed to serve champagne. The mayor says it's strictly wine and beer only.'

'That's because the mayor is a cheapskate and a philistine.' He reached into his pocket and pulled out a fifty pound note, which he dropped onto her tray. 'See what you can do, Judy, there's a good girl.'

The girl picked up the note and inspected it. Then she shrugged her shoulders and headed off into the other room.

'Do you always get your own way?' asked Carla.

'Whenever I can.' He gave her a searching look, and suddenly she felt an odd feeling inside her. It had been a long time since a man had tried to seduce her. So long that she had almost forgotten what it was like. She was starting to remember now, though, and an odd thrill ran through her as she looked into his eyes.

The champagne arrived and he poured them both a glass. Carla sipped at hers. It wasn't the best, but it was palatable and she drank some more. Frank began telling her jokes, and the more she drank the funnier they seemed to her, so that soon she was giggling hysterically. He ordered a second bottle from Judy, and Carla began to feel quite light-headed.

'Let's go somewhere quieter,' he suggested when the bottle arrived. 'This music's getting a bit much.'

He took her hand and led her from the room into a passageway. At the end was a staircase, and he headed for it, pulling her along behind.

'Where are we going?' she asked. 'We can't go up there.'

'Why not? Come on.'

They ascended the staircase and found themselves in a corridor with doors on either side. Frank tried one of them and it opened. He pressed a light switch on the wall, and Carla saw that they were in a hotel room, with a double bed, private bathroom and a television in the corner.

'This looks comfy enough,' he said.

'Do you think we should?' she asked nervously. 'After all, these are supposed to be for guests.'

'Let's pretend we're guests, then,' he said. 'Sit down and stop worrying.'

He sat on the edge of the bed and patted the eiderdown

beside him. Carla hesitated. She wasn't at all sure about this. After all, to be alone with a man in a hotel room put her in a pretty compromising position.

'Come on,' he said encouragingly. 'Have some more bubbly.'

He held out the bottle and tipped it over her glass, filling it once more, then patted the bed again. Carla sat down rather gingerly.

They started to talk again. Frank had a very good line in patter, and before long Carla felt herself relaxing and laughing at his remarks once more. When he placed an arm about her shoulders she scarcely noticed it. Nor did she notice the way the drink was beginning to go to her head.

Suddenly he leant across and placed his lips over hers. At once she felt the pressure of his tongue. She resisted for a second, then allowed it inside. It intertwined with her own and she found herself quite breathless at the passion of his kiss.

He began to press her backwards onto the bed. Once again she tried to resist, but found she lacked the willpower. He took his lips from hers for a second as he deposited her glass on a side table, then he was lying half on top of her, his lips clamped to hers.

Carla's mind was a whirl. On the one hand she revelled in his treatment. It was ages since a man had kissed her in that way, and she was almost shocked by the way her body responded. Eric hardly ever made love to her these days, and when he did it was a short affair with little passion. Often she didn't even achieve orgasm. And now here was a man kissing her like a true lover, and when he slid his hand inside her bra she felt her nipples harden at once under his touch.

'Christ, you're gorgeous,' he muttered, his hands squeezing her firm breasts as he kissed her neck and the tops of her swelling mounds.

Carla gave a groan as he pulled the top of her dress down, exposing her breasts completely, and began sucking at the hard brown teats with relish. Her whole body was beginning to light up with desire now, and she writhed and gasped under his ministrations.

It was only when he began sliding his hand under her skirt that she suddenly came to her senses.

'No!'

She grabbed his wrist, trying to push him away as he forced his way towards her honeypot, his fingers on her panties now.

'Stop it. You mustn't.'

'Don't be silly, baby. You want it as much as I do. Ease up.'

'No!' She clamped her thighs together, preventing him from worming his way inside the skimpy garment. Still he pressed on, his mouth trying to close over hers once more.

'My husband . . .'

'To hell with your husband. It's me you're with now.'

But this time her mind was made up. With a heave she pushed him off her, staggering to her feet and trying to straighten her dress.

'What's the fucking problem?' he said, suddenly angry. 'I thought you wanted it.'

'Well, I don't. I'm going to find my husband.'

'Sod your husband. Stay here with me. He's probably getting his rocks off somewhere anyhow.'

'Don't say things like that. You don't even know him.'

'I know that any guy who lets a sexy little chick like you

out of his sight must either be queer or have something better on the go.'

'Shut up. You're talking rubbish.'

He grabbed her hand. 'Come on, Carla,' he insisted. 'I've really got the hots for you.'

She pulled away from him.

'No! I'm going to find my husband.'

'To hell with you then,' he said, his voice angry. 'Go and find him. As far as I'm concerned it's good riddance. Fucking prick-teaser.'

Carla made for the door, still trying to make herself decent. Once in the corridor she headed for the stairs and back toward the party.

When she reached the large room she had regained some of her composure, though she was still slightly shaky and her body was even now tingling with the remnants of her desire. She began to search for her husband, checking all the rooms, but could see him nowhere.

'Are you looking for Eric?'

The woman was tall and alluring, with dark hair and mysterious green eyes. She spoke with an accent that Carla could not place, her voice low and sexy.

'Who . . . who are you?'

'My name is Phaedra.'

'How did you know I was looking for Eric?'

'You're his wife, aren't you?'

'Yes but . . .'

'So naturally I assumed it was him you were seeking.'

'Is Eric a friend of yours?'

'I know a little about him.'

'Have you seen him?'

'Yes.'

'Where is he?'

'I expect he'll be down soon.'

'Down?'

'Just be patient.'

'He's gone upstairs?'

Phaedra cast a glance across at another staircase on the far side of the room, but made no answer.

'When did he go upstairs? Who with?'

'Don't worry. He won't be long.'

Carla stared hard at the woman. Then turned and almost ran toward the staircase. She took the stairs two at a time, arriving on a landing not unlike the one she had been on only minutes before. Then she heard a groan.

She paused, listening intently. She heard the sound again. It was a woman's voice, and it was a long, soft groan of pleasure.

Carla moved closer to the first door in the passageway and placed her ear against it. The groan came again, this time much clearer. Her heart thumping loudly Carla slowly turned the doorhandle.

She pushed the door open a crack and peered through. The light was on in the room, and the sound was coming from the direction of the bed. She pushed the door further open and put her head round.

Then her jaw dropped.

Stretched across the bed, her skirt around her waist, was a woman. She was in her early twenties, pretty with red hair. Between her legs was a man, his trousers discarded, his long, thick tool pumping in and out of her vagina whilst his hands mauled at her breasts, which had been pulled free of her dress.

The man was Eric.

There was no mistaking him, even from behind. She knew his body, his backside, and she recognized him at once.

For a moment she froze, unable to take in what she was seeing. There was her husband, in a hotel room, fucking some young woman whilst he imagined her, his wife, to be downstairs enjoying the party. It was outrageous!

Suddenly she realized that the woman was looking at her. She waited for her to scream and to cover herself, and for the inevitable row that would follow. But it didn't happen. Instead, to Carla's surprise, the woman simply smiled coolly and mouthed a kiss. Then she turned back to her lover, still groaning as he continued to thrust into her, clearly unaware they were being watched.

Carla wanted to say something. To shout. To scream at them. But she found herself struck dumb.

The woman smiled at her again, and she knew she had to get out. She shrank back, closing the door quietly, then collapsing against it, breathing hard. That bastard! After she'd been faithful for so long, suppressing her natural desires in the misguided notion that her fidelity would be rewarded! She thought of the prospective screw she'd just turned down, and a sudden anger filled her, accompanied by a desire for revenge.

She contemplated bursting back into the room and confronting them. Of causing a major row. But the thought of being laughed at by that woman, and of being faced with the fact that her husband preferred the redhead to herself, made her hesitate. Still she desired, more than anything else, to get her own back on her two-timing bastard of a husband. Then she thought of Frank again, and an idea came into her mind.

That was it! She'd get her revenge all right. She'd go back to Frank and fuck him like there was no tomorrow.

Her face grim, Carla set off down the stairs again. Phaedra was standing at the bottom.

'See what you wanted?'

Carla scowled at her.

'You knew, you bitch. Didn't you?'

'I warned you not to go up there.'

'Two can play at that game.' Carla pushed past her and headed for the other staircase.

'I don't think that's a very good idea either,' called Phaedra. But Carla wasn't listening.

She almost ran up the stairs, grabbing the handle of the door to the room and shoving it open.

She had already taken three steps into the room before the scene in front of her registered in her brain. There, totally naked, crouched on the bed, was Judy, the young waitress. Frank was naked too and Judy's head was buried in his lap, his stiff penis in her mouth. She was fellating him hard, emitting loud slurping sounds as she did so, her hair dancing about as her head bobbed up and down.

As Carla entered she sat up and turned to face her. She had a lovely, slim, willowy body, her breasts large and succulent. The dark triangle at the top of her legs betrayed the fact that she was not a natural blonde.

'What have you come back for?' asked Frank. Carla marvelled at the calmness of the pair, apparently unworried to have been caught *in flagrante*.

'I . . . I just came back,' said Carla lamely.

'You're too late, darling,' grinned Judy. 'I've got him now.' She indicated his cock, which was stiff as a ramrod and shiny with her saliva. 'And this is all mine.'

She lowered her head again, taking his tool between her lips and sucking hard, so that an expression of sheer pleasure spread across Frank's face.

'Stay and watch if you like,' he said. 'Find out what you're missing.'

'I . . .'

Carla was speechless. Yet she couldn't tear her eyes from Frank's long, hard cock, or from the enthusiastic way that Judy was sucking it, her breasts dancing up and down as she worked her head back and forth, her hands caressing Frank's heavy balls. Carla's own yearning returned with a vengeance as she watched and at once she felt a wetness seeping into her panties.

Suddenly Carla sensed a movement beside her and turned to see Phaedra standing next to her.

'That's the second time you've ignored my warning,' she said.

'What is this, showtime?' exclaimed Frank. 'Go ahead and watch if it excites you. Lie on your back, Judy. I want to taste your cunt.'

Eagerly the naked blonde threw herself back onto the bed, spreading her legs wide apart. Carla stared in fascination at her sex, the pink lips parted so that the wet interior was visible. Then Frank was on his knees, his tongue working its way up the inside of her thighs, leaving a silvery trail behind it.

All at once a hand slipped into the top of Carla's dress and closed about her breast. She turned in astonishment to see that Phaedra had wrapped an arm about her neck and was caressing her intimately. She tried to pull away, but the woman was insistent, her fingers seeking out Carla's nipple, rolling the hard, brown flesh between finger and thumb.

'No.'

For the second time that evening Carla found herself the object of seduction in that characterless room. But this time it was a woman's hands that were delving into the private parts of her anatomy. Somehow, though, a combination of the drink, the shock of finding her husband fucking another woman, and the sheer eroticism of the scene on the bed where Frank was now licking hungrily at Judy's slit, all served to break down her resistance, and when Phaedra's lips closed over her own she willingly opened her mouth and let the woman's tongue inside.

She felt Phaedra's hand go to the back of her dress and seek out the zipper. It came down in a single movement, and all at once she was standing in her underwear, her dress a pool of material at her feet.

The tiny black bra she wore came instantly undone under Phaedra's expert fingers. Then the woman's mouth dropped to her firm breasts, taking the long brown nipples between her teeth and nibbling gently at them.

'Ah!'

Carla gasped with surprise and pleasure as she felt Phaedra's tongue run back and forth over the rubbery flesh. Her eyes were fixed on Judy, who was moaning aloud, her hips thrusting up at Frank's face as he continued to excite her with his tongue. As she watched he raised his head from her crotch.

'Get up on all fours, Judy,' he said. 'I want to fuck you doggy-fashion.'

Once again the waitress did not hesitate, scrambling up onto her hands and knees and thrusting her backside as Frank positioned himself behind her, his rampant tool twitching as he guided it towards her love hole.

'Oh!'

Carla's whole body jumped as she felt Phaedra's hand slide down inside her knickers and find the centre of her desires. Her clitoris was already swollen, the wetness coating the lips of her sex as she pressed herself down against the woman's hand.

There was a cry from the bed, and Carla looked up to see that Frank had penetrated his partner and was starting to fuck her, his hips working back and forth whilst she moaned softly with desire.

All of a sudden Phaedra's lips left Carla's nipples and she dropped to her knees in front of the smaller girl. She reached for Carla's panties, pulling them down with a smooth movement. Carla emitted a noise of protest, but made no attempt to stop the woman as she slipped the flimsy garment over her ankles and off.

'Open your legs.'

'You mustn't.'

'Open them.' Phaedra grasped the inside of Carla's thighs and pressed them apart, forcing the girl to widen her stance. Then she closed in on Carla's sex.

'Ahhh!'

Carla cried out with pleasure as Phaedra's tongue found her slit and began snaking along its length, causing shudders of delight to run up and down the naked girl's body. The woman pressed her tongue deep into Carla's vagina, darting back and forth whilst her fingers rubbed over the swollen flesh of her love bud.

Carla had never been so turned on. In front of her Frank was fucking Judy for all he was worth, the girl's breasts swinging back and forth beneath her as he drove his cock hard into her. Carla knew that she too must make quite a sight, her back pressed against the wall, her crotch thrust forward against Phaedra's mouth as the woman continued the exquisite lapping with her tongue.

Frank's motions were becoming more urgent now, and Carla was unable to tear her eyes from the copulating couple as she felt her own orgasm build within her. For her part, Judy's face was a picture, her eyes tight shut, her lower lip clenched between her teeth, faint whimpers escaping from her as she revelled in the treatment Frank was giving her.

'Ah! Ah! Ah!'

Frank was first to come, his cries loud as he pumped his spunk into Judy. The young waitress followed almost immediately, her own shouts of pleasure almost drowning out her partner's.

Frank continued to thrust into Judy, his motions beginning to lose their urgency now and Carla watched as he savoured the moment of ecstasy. Then he withdrew, his cock shining with Judy's juices.

Judy flopped forward onto her stomach, her legs still spread wide, her cunt lips twitching rhythmically.

It was the sight of the sperm that oozed from the girl's vagina that finally sent Carla over the top. She threw her head back and emitted a strangled moan as her orgasm overcame her, her hips thrusting down against Phaedra's mouth, trying to extract every ounce of pleasure from the woman's fingers and tongue as wave after wave of pleasure flowed over her.

When Phaedra finally sat back, her chin wet with a mixture of saliva and love juice, Carla found herself entirely drained. She staggered over and prostrated herself on the bed beside Judy, her chest heaving.

Phaedra rose to her feet and gazed down at the young girl.

'I think it's time we woke that slumbering nympho inside you, young lady,' she said.

Then she turned and went out the door, closing it behind her.

Chapter Six

'And did anything further take place between you and this man?' the Judge asked.

'Nothing took place at all, let alone anything further.'

'But you already told us he had been fondling your breasts.'

'Yes, but I stopped him. Listen, I wasn't the guilty one at the mayor's party. The guilty ones are sitting on either side of you. My husband and Phaedra.'

'They are not on trial here. You are. It is you who must answer.'

'But what about that floozy Eric was in bed with?'

'We only have your word for that. What was the woman's name?'

Carla dropped her eyes. 'I don't know.'

'Who was she? Where was she from? Have you seen her since?'

Carla shook her head. 'I don't know. What does it matter? I saw them. He was screwing her there on the bed.'

'Yet you only saw him from behind. How can you be sure?'

'He's my husband, for Christ's sake. I know what he bloody well looks like. Why won't you believe me, you stupid old sod?'

Bang!

The Judge brough his gavel crashing down.

'You will refer to me with respect,' he roared. 'I have already warned you of the consequences of not co-operating with this court.'

Carla opened her mouth to speak again, then thought better of it and closed it once more. She glared at the Judge.

But he had turned his attention to the man standing in front of him. The man that Carla now recognized as Frank.

'Was that a true and accurate assessment of what happened that night?' he asked.

'More or less, Judge. But I can't vouch for the bit when she says she found her husband. I was out pulling that waitress at the time.'

'Quite,' said the Judge. 'But otherwise the story was true?'

'Yeah. True enough.'

'In that case I must thank you for attending. Naturally what you saw and heard here is confidential.'

'Sure. Don't worry about me. I'm only sorry the little bitch didn't see sense and let me fuck her in the first place. She's quite a sexy piece. Sluts like that Judy are two a penny.'

'Thank you again,' said the Judge, rather snootily. 'You may go now.'

'Right. Goodbye, darling. I hope you get what's coming to you.'

And with that he turned on his heel and headed for the exit.

'Now,' said the Judge once the door had been closed, 'have you anything to say before I call the next witness?'

'You mean there are more?'

'Of course. We intend to get to the bottom of this thing once and for all.'

'Couldn't I sit down? I don't like everyone watching me.'

'Certainly not. The defendant's place is up there, in full view.'

'You really believe in that stuff, don't you?'

'Stuff?'

'That this is a courtroom and I'm on trial. You've all been watching too much *LA Law* if you ask me.'

Bang!

Down came the gavel again.

'Your lack of respect is doing your case no good at all, young lady,' fumed the Judge. 'Call the next witness!'

All eyes turned towards the doors as they swung open and a man walked in. He was older than Frank, in his early forties probably, and he wore a dark business suit and tie. He made his way around to the front table. As he came closer, Carla scrutinized his face carefully. Once again she was certain that his features were familiar. The trouble was, she thought, there had been so many men over the past few months that their faces just became a blur. She concentrated hard, but was, for the moment, unable to place this one.

'Thank you for attending,' said the Judge. 'I understand that you too wish to retain your anonymity?'

'Yes please, Judge.'

The man's accent betrayed him as coming from the north of England, probably Lancashire. He looked nervous as he surveyed the ranks of faces staring at him.

'Don't worry,' the Judge reassured him. 'You're among friends here. Now, do you recognize the defendant?'

'The girl on the platform?'

'Yes.'

The man squinted at her. 'Yes,' he said at last. 'That's the woman.'

'And when did you first encounter this woman?'

'I'm not sure. Nine months ago? A year, possibly?'

'I suggest that it was in June of last year.'

'That sounds about right.'

'What were you doing down here? I understand you live some distance away.'

'Up north, yes.' The man pronounced the words 'Oop north'.

'Well then?'

'I was down here on business. I'm in the rag trade myself. You know, wholesale clothing. Well, the job brings me to London quite often. I think I was down at a trade fair that week.'

'And you were staying in a hotel?'

'The Royal, yes.' The man sniffed. 'Some title, the Royal. I can't exactly see the Queen or the Duke staying there.'

'And as with so many men in a similar situation to your own, you found yourself feeling lonely in the evenings.'

'A man has his desires, Judge. And you understand I was a long way from home.'

'So what did you do?'

'I went out and picked up a whore.'

'Any particular whore?'

'That one, standing on the platform. She *is* a whore, isn't she?'

'Some may consider that an apt description.'

'Wait a minute,' said Carla angrily. 'Who are you calling a whore?'

'Quiet!' barked the Judge. 'That is one of the matters we are here to establish. Now, sir. Tell us what happened.'

'Well, I went out in my car. I generally know the area to go. She was standing at the kerbside, flaunting herself like they do. I hadn't seen her before, but she looked the type, so I stopped and asked her if she was on the game.'

'And she was?'

'Couldn't get into the car fast enough.'

'So what did you do?'

'Took her back to the hotel. Bought her a drink in the bar. Normally they like that. Makes 'em think you're interested in their company as well as their cunts. This one didn't seem bothered, though. She was really in a hurry to get upstairs and get on the job.'

'And did you?'

'Yeah. I was a bit pissed off at first. Thought she just wanted a quick jump then get out there for another mug. But she was really hot. Gave me the full works, then stayed and did it again. I've never met such a randy tart.'

'She was willing, then?'

'Christ, yes. Best I've ever had. Reminded me of the Chinese sluts in Hong Kong. I looked out for her next time I was down, but I never saw her again. Until now, that is.'

'Listen,' broke in Carla. 'He's telling it all wrong. It wasn't like that at all. He's exaggerating just like the last one.'

'Then perhaps you'd like to give us your version?'

'Must I?'

'No. But if you don't we would only have this gentleman's word to go on.'

Carla hesitated, scanning the faces of those watching. She spotted two members of her bridge circle, sitting side by side, their prim faces creased in disapproval. Suddenly she was angry again.

'It was her,' she shouted, nodding in Phaedra's direction. 'She set it all up. She's behind all of this. If it wasn't for her nothing would have happened.'

'Explain yourself,' said the Judge.

Carla hesitated. Then began.

'It all started after some crummy fashion show I'd been persuaded to attend . . .'

Chapter Seven

When she was first married, the fashion shows had been one of the highlights of Carla's life. She would thoroughly enjoy occupying a seat close to the catwalk and watching the models sashay past in the most outrageous clothes. Sometimes she would see something she liked and it would be a thrill to be able to purchase it afterwards. For a long time she made it a habit to go to the launches of the major spring collections, and revelled in the opportunity to mix with the rich and the famous.

The attraction soon began to pall, though, as she realized what an incestuous trade the fashion world was and how little real talent was on display. That June evening, the clothes had been particularly bad, dull, baggy and shapeless, so that they were quite wasted on the bodies of the lovely young women wearing them. Carla liked tight clothes that showed off her slim figure. On this occasion she had worn a white silk blouse with no bra underneath so that her nipples were beautifully outlined as they pressed against the fabric, and a small, black miniskirt that barely covered the tops of the black hold-up stockings encasing her legs.

She had stayed for about fifteen minutes in the hope of seeing something she liked, then had walked out. Carla was irritated at the poor nature of the show. She had hoped it would be an enjoyable way to pass the evening. Eric was away at a conference and she knew the house would be empty when she returned. Another evening in front of the television seemed to loom before her. The show was being held in a large, modern hotel and, reluctant to return home straight away, she decided to seek out the bar. A gin and tonic might at least make things seem brighter, she reasoned.

It was a large, busy cocktail lounge and she found herself a seat at the bar, where she ordered a drink. It came in a long glass with ice cubes and a slice of lemon, and after a few sips Carla was feeling considerably better. She glanced about her at the clientele. They were mainly couples or groups of businessmen. She felt slightly awkward sitting there alone.

'Hello, Carla.'

The voice in her ear made her jump. She swung round, to be confronted by a tall, dark figure who smiled down at her.

'You!'

Carla hadn't set eyes on Phaedra since the incident at the mayor's party nearly two months before, but the events of the evening had never been far from her mind. Ever since that night she had found herself lying awake night after night, wondering at the way she had behaved. She couldn't rid her mind of the image of herself, standing and watching two complete strangers fuck whilst she herself was being tongued by another woman. The whole thing was quite unbelievable. She had tried to convince herself that it must have been the drink, and had vowed never to touch champagne again. Yet still, in those dark waking hours, she would find herself extraordinarily turned on by the memory, and often her fingers would stray down to her crotch to feel the wetness there.

She had never confronted Eric about what she had seen. Somehow, after her own escapade, she found herself unable to discuss the party with him at all. Instead she behaved as if nothing had happened, and their lives had resumed their old pattern, though, if anything, she felt his indifference to her in bed had increased.

And now here was Phaedra once again, large as life. Carla felt her cheeks go crimson as she confronted the woman with whom she had behaved so extraordinarily, though Phaedra displayed no such discomfort.

'Didn't you like the dresses?'

'The dresses?'

'At the fashion show. I saw you walk out.'

'Oh, that. No, I thought they were awful.'

'Certainly not your kind of thing at all.'

Phaedra ran her gaze up and down Carla's body, taking in the inadequacy of her skirt to hide her thighs, and the way her breasts were outlined by the silk of her blouse. The woman's eyes had a strangely penetrating quality, as if they were able to see the bare flesh inside the garments. All of a sudden Carla felt as if she was naked once more, and the colour in her cheeks deepened.

'Wh-what did you think of the show?' she asked, trying to keep her voice level.

'I agree with you. Shapeless rags.'

Carla suddenly found herself giggling.

'I bet that's not what the fashion pages say tomorrow.'

Phaedra smiled back. 'Naturally not. The journalists want to keep their free perks. Do you mind if I join you?'

'Well, I . . .'

'Good. Waiter! Two more large G and Ts.'

'Please don't. I was just having the one.'

'Eric waiting for you, is he?'

'No. He's . . .' Suddenly Carla found herself reluctant to let Phaedra know she was alone for the evening. But it was too late.

'Gone to that medical conference up north, I expect.'

At that moment the drinks arrived. Carla's glass was still half full, but Phaedra simply tipped the contents of the fresh glass into it and topped it up with tonic.

'Now,' she said, 'for a cosy chat.'

She placed a hand on Carla's knee and at once the girl drew away. Phaedra looked into her face.

'Are you still embarrassed about what happened at that party?'

Carla lowered her eyes. 'I've never done anything like that before. Especially not . . .'

'With a woman? What's so wrong about that?'

'I'm not sure. It just is, that's all.'

'Carla, have you ever had sex with another man since marrying Eric?'

'No.'

'And Eric satisfies your sexual needs, does he?'

Carla didn't reply.

'I see.'

'You don't see anything,' said Carla defensively.

'Okay, take it easy. It's not my place to ask a question like that. But seriously, a sensual thing like you with that gorgeous body . . . You really ought to enjoy it whilst you have the chance.'

'I enjoy life fine.'

'But you're a girl who ought to be getting her share of

sex,' said Phaedra. 'I could tell from the way you acted at the party that there's a real firebrand inside you. After all, look at the sexy way you dress.'

Carla took a gulp of her drink. It was very strong indeed, but tasted good. She drank some more.

'What makes you the expert on sex then, Phaedra?'

'I'm not an expert. Just an enthusiast. And I hate to see a natural like you wasting away.'

'I'm not wasting away.'

'You're not exactly having a ball. When did Eric last give you an orgasm?'

'Orgasm's aren't everything.'

'So it's been a while, then?'

Carla glared at her. 'You're getting personal again,' she said.

'I just think you're letting some opportunities slip away, that's all.'

'What do you suggest, then?'

'Try something adventurous. Something new.'

'Like what?'

'Sell yourself.'

'What, you mean advertize?'

'In a way. But more literally. What I'm suggesting is whoring.'

Carla stared at her, shocked.

'How dare you . . .'

'There you go, getting all worked up again,' replied Phaedra with a grin. 'What's so terrible about a little evening diversion? Look around at the single guys in this bar. They're all businessmen down here on their own. They'd pay good money to get inside your pants. And what have you got to lose? Just an evening of uncomplicated fucking with a hundred quid pocket money thrown in.'

Carla took another swig of gin.

'You're mad.'

'Waiter! Two more gins! No, Carla, not mad. Just adventurous. I mean, just imagine it, stretched out in a luxurious hotel room with a randy bloke fucking you for all he's worth. Giving you as many orgasms as you can manage. Then in the morning it's goodbye and thank you, and both of you go away satisfied.'

'It's outrageous.'

'But the thought doesn't half turn you on, doesn't it?'

Once again Carla did not reply. But she knew the colour of her cheeks betrayed her true feelings. Phaedra was right. The idea was a sexy one and the thought was already causing a warmth and a wetness between her legs. She reached for the fresh glass that the waiter put down before her and began pouring in the tonic.

'Let's talk about something else.'

They stayed at the bar for some time longer, talking together. By the time Carla glanced at her watch it was quite late.

'I really should be getting back,' she said.

'How did you come?'

'By car.'

'But you can't drive tonight. You've had four gins.'

'Have I really? I thought I was feeling a little tipsy.'

'We'll walk,' said Phaedra decisively. It's only a couple of miles, and it'll help you sober up. You can come back for the car tomorrow.'

'Walk? I'd almost forgotten what walking was like. I haven't walked anywhere for ages.'

'Come on then.'

'But what about you? Where do you live?'

'I know a route that goes close to my place. It's only another half mile from there to yours. Come on, I'll show you.'

She rose to her feet, and Carla did the same. For a second she felt quite dizzy, but she steadied herself. Then she set off after the already retreating Phaedra. They stepped out of the hotel together. It was a warm summer night, and the sky was still quite light.

'Right,' said Phaedra. 'Best foot forward.'

And she linked her arm with Carla's as they headed off down the road.

Chapter Eight

Carla was surprised at how pleasant the walk was, though she wished she'd worn more comfortable shoes. The high heels she had worn were not exactly designed for walking long distances. The closeness of her companion felt good too, and she leaned against the taller woman's body, enjoying the scent of her as they strolled along. She thought of that night in the hotel room, and the sensation of the woman's tongue licking at her so intimately, and once again she felt the stirrings of arousal within her.

They walked in silence, following a twisting course that left Carla somewhat confused. When Phaedra drew to a halt at a junction, Carla had little idea where they were.

'This is where I leave you, sweetie,' said the older woman.

Carla was at once relieved and disappointed. She had been certain Phaedra would want to lure her back to her abode and continue what she had begun those weeks before, and Carla was not certain she would have been able to resist. Now, it seemed, the choice had been taken from her, and she was not sure whether to be pleased or sad.

'How do I get home from here?' she asked, suddenly remembering that she didn't have a clue where she was.

'Straight down to the end, then turn left. It's a back way onto your estate.'

'Well, good night then.'

Carla turned to leave, but suddenly her hand was grasped and the woman twisted her round to face her. Then she placed an arm round the girl's shoulder and brought her face close to her own.

The kiss was long and passionate, the pair licking at each other's tongues, their bodies pressed together. Phaedra placed a hand over Carla's breast, massaging it through the thin material of her blouse and making the nipple harden at once. When they finally broke apart Carla found herself panting hard.

Phaedra looked down into the younger girl's eyes.

'You see?' she said. 'So much passion in such a gorgeous young body. You must let it out, Carla. You mustn't deny yourself, or the men who want to enjoy you. Go out and fuck, Carla. You owe it to yourself.'

And with that she turned and walked away.

For a few moments Carla simply stood and watched her go, feeling slightly dazed after the passion of the kiss, her shoulders still rising and falling as she struggled to get her thoughts under control. She looked down at herself. Perhaps Phaedra was right. Perhaps she was suppressing her feelings. Once again she thought about Frank and Judy and the scene in the hotel room, and the heat inside her began to increase still further.

She set off in the direction Phaedra had indicated. She would go home and strip off and masturbate on the rug by the fire. Perhaps she would use something, like a wine bottle, maybe. All at once a picture formed in her mind of herself lying spreadeagled and naked whilst Phaedra brought her off with a bottle and a new shudder of lust ran through her body.

She scarcely noticed the car, or that it was slowing down beside her. In fact she didn't become fully aware of it until she heard the man's voice call to her through the open passenger window.

'You working, love?'

'I beg your pardon?'

'Fancy getting in?'

'I don't under—'

Then all at once she did understand. He was a kerb-crawler, and he thought she was on the game.

She shook her head. 'No. You've got it wrong,' she stammered.

The man shrugged. 'Sorry to bother you.'

Then the car was accelerating away.

Carla watched it go, her mind in a whirl. About two hundred yards away it stopped again, beside a girl who was leaning against a tree. A short conversation ensued through the car's window, then the girl climbed in and it sped away once more.

It was only then that Carla realized that the road must be a pick-up area for whores. For a second she was shocked. She had no idea that such a place existed so close to her home. She had always thought of it as a respectable area. And yet, as she looked up and down the tree-lined road, with houses set discreetly back behind hedges, she could clearly discern three other figures standing by the roadside. Then another realization dawned. This was Phaedra's doing. She must have known what went on along this road, and she had deliberately lured Carla there so that she could find out.

She thought of what Phaedra had said to her about whoring, and imagined what would happen to the girl she had just seen picked up. Would they do it in the car? Or beside the road? She imagined herself stretched out on the grass whilst the man rammed his cock into her and a sudden spasm of desire ran through her.

Then she heard the second car begin to slow, and suddenly her heart was in her mouth. This was part of Phaedra's plan too. The woman knew how turned on she was, and had deliberately tempted her into straying by bringing her here in the hope that she would submit to her desires. The car was almost alongside her now and she felt herself tremble as she listened for his call.

'Want a ride?'

She glanced sideways. He wasn't bad looking, in his early forties, she estimated. His car was smart too, almost new.

'Hey. You getting in or not?'

Carla knew she should run. Get off this street and back home. What the man was suggesting was out of the question. Treating her as if she were a common whore. She was a respectable woman, wasn't she? The wife of a surgeon living in an expensive house. There was no question of her climbing into a car with a stranger.

'All right.'

With a shock Carla realized that it had been her own voice that had said the words, and her own hand that was reaching for the doorhandle.

It was as if she was dreaming or watching a movie, quite detached from the beautiful young girl in the mini skirt who was climbing into the car beside the man. She watched the girl pull the door and it clicked shut. Then the car pulled away from the kerb.

'What's your name?'

'Carla.'

'You're really gorgeous, Carla. How come I haven't seen you around here before?'

'I'm new. Where are we going?'

'My hotel. That okay?'

'Fine.'

Carla sat and stared out the window of the car as it made its way through the streets. She still couldn't believe she was here. She stole a glance sideways at the man. He was just an ordinary looking businessman, of the sort she met at parties every day. And yet he was going to fuck her. She was going to have intercourse with a man whose name she didn't even know.

They pulled into the hotel car park. She recognized the Royal as somewhere she had been with her husband occasionally to functions of one sort or another. She wondered if anyone would recognize her. Probably not, she thought.

They climbed out of the car and he took her hand.

'Fancy a drink?'

'Okay.'

The bar was small and almost empty. He ordered a scotch for himself and a gin for Carla. She sipped at it nervously, her eyes darting about, suddenly certain that someone she knew would enter at any moment. When he offered her a second drink she declined.

'Let's go up, shall we?' he said.

Carla nodded, unable to bring herself to speak.

The hotel room was large and anonymous. The furniture was modern, the bed wide. The man closed the door behind her, then went to the fridge and pulled out a bottle of white wine. He opened it and poured them both a glass, handing one to her. They stood opposite one another sipping their drinks. Then he took her glass from her and placed it on the table.

He moved close. He was a good eight inches taller than her, and he had to incline his head downwards as he pulled her face up towards his own.

It was the second intimate kiss Carla had experienced that evening. But this time it was a man's strong arms that held her as his tongue delved into her mouth. She raised her arms and placed them round his neck, pulling him downwards, suddenly extraordinarily aroused by his closeness, the smell of him, the taste of him.

His hand slipped down to her blouse and he began undoing the buttons. The two of them remained locked together whilst he did this, their tongues circling each other inside her mouth.

'Ah!'

Carla gave a little sigh as he pulled her blouse open and his hand closed over her bare breast. At once the nipples puckered to hard points under his caresses. He took each between finger and thumb, rubbing them and sending electric pulses down to her now red-hot crotch.

He took his mouth from hers and held her at arms' length, his eyes roving over her delectable breasts, admiring their plump firmness. He slipped the blouse from her shoulders and tossed it aside.

Carla lowered her eyes, her cheeks glowing as he studied her. She was more aroused now than she had ever been. When he reached for the zipper on her skirt, her heart was hammering so hard against her chest she felt sure he must hear it.

He pulled the skirt down over her hips and let it drop to

the floor. Carla stepped out of it and kicked it aside. Now she wore only her hold-up stockings and a skimpy pair of panties, cut so low that some of her dark nether curls were visible over the top of the waistband. He ran his hand slowly down her stomach and over the silky briefs, then down to her crotch.

'Mmmm,' she breathed as his fingers traced the length of her slit. She knew the gusset must be wet, and that he would be able to feel that wetness, but still she pressed her crotch hard against his hand, gasping with pleasure as he rubbed her.

'Take them off,' he murmured.

Carla let her hands drop to the waistband of the panties. Then she hesitated, aware that they were all that still preserved her modesty, and that their removal signalled her final surrender to the lustful feelings that Phaedra had kindled inside her. She stared into his eyes, and slowly slid them down, over her thighs and off. She dropped them onto the floor beside her skirt, then straightened and stood, her hands hanging by her sides, her legs slightly parted whilst his eyes took in her naked body.

'Christ you're something,' he said as his eyes travelled from the full pertness of her young breasts down to the perfectly flat belly, then lower to the small dark crop of pubic hair and the pink wet sex lips that showed beneath it. He reached out his hand for her crotch, this time finding not the damp satin of her knickers but the soft fleshiness of her cunt lips and the solid little nut of her clitoris.

'Aaah!'

Carla was quite unable to suppress the cry as she felt her sex penetrated by his hard, rough fingers. The tension that had been building in her since she had left Phaedra was suddenly released with the touch and she almost orgasmed then and there, pressing her pubis forward and down against his palm in a shameless betrayal of her desires.

'Suck me.'

It was an order and he was the boss. He was paying the bill for the evening. A new thrill coursed through Carla's body as she realized that she was entirely in his hands, and would do whatever he said. Somehow his taking control seemed to exonerate her from blame in her mind. She thought momentarily of her husband, and of what he would say if he could see her now, selling her naked body to a stranger in a hotel room. Then she cast the thought from her mind and dropped to her knees.

Her fingers went to his belt and she unfastened it quickly. Then she disposed of the clip at his waist and eagerly tugged down his zipper. She reached inside and her hand closed about something thick and hard, encased by the thin nylon briefs. She tugged at them, pulling them and his trousers down his legs. As she did so, his cock sprang to erectness. It was big. Bigger than Eric's. It was uncircumcised, the end of his foreskin parting to reveal a tip shiny with his own lubrication. His balls were large too, the scrotum pulled tight by his erection.

His penis was level with her face, the heavy end twitching occasionally, making it bob up and down. Carla was fascinated by its elasticity. She held her finger above it and watched as it repeatedly sprang up, brushing the outstretched digit, leaving a wet sheen on her fingertip which she licked off sensuously.

'Suck me, damit.' She looked up and saw the frustration in his face.

She took his cock in her fist, thrilled by its heat and

hardness. She ran her fingers up and down the shaft a few times, working his foreskin back and forth. Then she leaned closer to it and opened her mouth.

He smelled and tasted of arousal, a scent that sent a pulse of wetness coursing through Carla's vagina as she began to suck him. He gave a groan of pleasure as she ran the tip of her tongue back and forth over his glans whilst sucking hungrily at his shaft. As she sucked she reached down for his balls, stroking them gently, feeling the coarse hairs against her palm.

Carla the wife was no expert at blow jobs. It was a service her husband never required of her. But now Carla the whore was taking on the job with relish, slurping greedily at his long, stiff manhood, her erect nipples brushing against his thighs as she worked her head up and down.

As she fellated him he removed his shirt and tie. He had a broad, strong chest with a thick covering of black hair. She reached up her hands and ran them through it, finding his nipples and stroking them gently. And all the time he was grunting with pleasure, his hips thrusting against her face in rhythm with her own movements.

Suddenly he took hold of her hair and pulled her head back. She looked up at him questioningly, her chin wet with saliva.

'I want to fuck you, Carla,' he said, quietly. 'Kneel down facing the bed.'

Carla scrambled to obey him, turning to the bed and kneeling in front of it.

'Lean forward and put your arse in the air.'

She did as she was told, raising her backside and spreading her legs apart, affording him a perfect view of her open crotch. It felt deliciously wicked to be flaunting herself like this, and all of a sudden she was aching to be fucked, the muscles in her sex convulsing in anticipation of what was to come. She pressed her body down against the surface of the bed, the rough material of the bedspread chafing against her nipples in the most exquisite way.

Something long and hard suddenly brushed against her backside and she turned to see the man, now quite naked, kneel down behind her. He had his cock in his hand, and he was guiding it towards its destination.

'Ah!'

Once again, the sensation of something touching her sex brought a gasp from the aroused young woman. Only this time it was not a couple of fingers that sought admission to her most private place, but a stiff, erect cock, nuzzling down between her soft, fleshy lips, then beginning to press.

He pushed gently at first, but Carla's vagina was tight, and she knew that gentle pressure would not be enough. She thrust her firm behind back at him, signalling that he must use more force. He responded by pressing harder, bringing fresh cries from his young partner as he tried to violate her portals. Then, all at once, he was inside, sliding his cock into her, using small jabs to embed himself deeper and deeper until, at last, she felt the coarseness of his pubic hair against her backside.

He started to fuck her, his hips moving slowly back and forth as he pumped his stiff organ into her hot, wet hole. Each stroke invoked a gasp of pleasure from his wanton young partner, the muscles of her sex tightening involuntarily about his weapon as Carla's body responded to him.

Carla was in seventh heaven. Never in her life had she felt so turned on. Somehow the sheer audacity of her position, bent naked over a bed in a hotel bedroom whilst a man she didn't even know performed the most intimate act possible with her, was spurring her on to new heights of arousal.

She came suddenly and unexpectedly, unable to contain her passions any longer, her cries ringing out as her body shook with lust. He held firmly onto her thighs as she bucked and heaved beneath him, wave after wave of pleasure flowing through her.

All at once he withdrew, turning her cries of pleasure to ones of dismay as she found herself suddenly without his cock inside her. He dragged her up from the bed and turned her to face him.

'Here's an odd thing,' he said, staring into her crimson face. 'I never had a whore come first with me before.'

'I'm sorry,' she muttered, cursing her body for its responsiveness. 'I just couldn't help it.'

He grinned. 'At least I know now that you're not faking it. You want some more?'

'Please.'

He pushed her backwards so that she was lying across the bed. Then he grabbed her legs and pulled her towards him until her backside was over the edge.

'Spread your legs,' he ordered.

Carla obeyed at once, planting her feet wide apart on the carpet and granting him an unrestricted view of her still twitching sex.

This time he slid in easily, filling her deliciously with his hefty rod. There was a new urgency in his screwing now, his backside pumping back and forth with vigour, each thrust causing Carla's lovely breasts to shake in a delightful way. In no time the girl was shouting out anew as her passions began to build once more.

He fucked her long and hard, his hips crashing against

her own as she revelled in the sensation of his cock inside her. Then, suddenly, he slowed, and she saw the muscles in his face tighten.

All at once he was coming, spurting hot semen into her open vagina, his rod twitching violently as he filled her with his seed. Carla screamed, and then she too was overcome by her climax, her second orgasm even more delicious than her first, the sensation of his sperm gushing into her sex doubling the pleasure he was giving her.

The two of them writhed and gasped, their bodies locked together on the bed as they rode out their passion together. It was fully two minutes before they finally came to rest, panting in each other's arms.

'That was good,' he gasped. 'You're the best I've ever had.'

She smiled up at him. 'You're not so bad yourself,' she said. 'Can we do it again later?'

Chapter Nine

'And you left after that?' asked the Judge.

'Not at once,' replied Carla.

'What, you stayed?'

'Yes.'

'You had sex again?'

'Yes.'

'How many times?'

'Twice.'

A murmur went up from the crowd as Carla made this confession, and she looked down at the sea of accusing faces, trying to maintain a defiant expression in the face of their disapproval.

'Twice?'

'We showered together. By the time we had finished he was hard again. He took me on the floor of the bathroom.'

'And you had an orgasm?'

'Yes.'

'Then what?'

'Then we went to bed. We woke at about five in the morning and he fucked me again.'

'And you came again?'

'Yes. He was good. I enjoyed it.'

'Do you always come when your husband, as you so elegantly put it, fucks you?'

'No.'

'Yet you came with this stranger three times?'

'Four actually.' Carla was beginning to become impatient with his questions. 'So what? So my husband can be a lousy fuck. When was the last time you made your wife come, Judge?'

The Judge reddened. 'Be quiet,' he barked. 'You are here to answer questions, not to ask them.'

'So you don't know,' said Carla. 'She probably faked it anyhow.'

Bang!

The gavel came down hard on the table once again.

'Speak out of turn again and you will be punished,' fumed the Judge.

Carla sniffed. She felt rather pleased with the exchange. It was the first time she had felt on top since she had entered the room.

'Now,' went on the Judge, turning to the man, who had stood silently throughout. 'Can you corroborate this woman's story?'

'That's how it happened, Judge,' he said. 'I thought all my birthdays had come at once.'

'And you paid for the sex?'

'Fifty pounds. I thought she'd want more. After all, most whores will just give you a quick fuck for fifty. This one stayed all night, and seemed to really enjoy it.'

'And that didn't make you suspicious?'

'I did wonder if I hadn't stumbled on amateur night, but what the hell? She was absolutely dying for it, and I wasn't about to complain. I reckon she had as much fun as I did.'

The Judge turned back to Carla. 'So you accepted money for the sex?'

'Yes.'

'That makes you a whore then, doesn't it?'

'If you say so.'

'No. What do you say?'

'It's not a very nice word.'

'Yet you admit that you gave this man sex and took money for it?'

'Yes.'

'So you're a whore?'

'All right, I'm a whore. What's in a name anyhow? Do you want to be my pimp?'

'I warned you about asking me questions. You're in a rather precarious position, young lady.'

'Fuck off.'

The Judge's face darkened and it suddenly occurred to Carla that she might have gone too far. Her suspicions were confirmed when the Judge rose to his feet.

'You are in contempt of this court,' he said, his voice like thunder.

'If you mean I'm contemptuous of you, you're right,' replied Carla, though there was a quaver in her voice as she sensed the Judge's anger.

'You were warned about such behaviour,' he went on. 'Until now you have been allowed the sanction of a cloak to preserve your modesty before these people. That privilege is now withdrawn. Strip her!'

Carla heard footsteps on the step behind her and she looked around fearfully. One of the maids was ascending to the platform.

'No!' she said. 'You can't. Not in front of all these people.'

'You should have thought of that beforehand,' said the Judge. 'Strip her.'

Carla tugged at her bonds, but her struggles were quite futile. The girl was behind her now, her hands reaching round her collar and fumbling with the cloak.

It came undone easily and fell away from Carla's body. A gasp went up from those watching as her naked body was revealed to them. Carla blushed scarlet as she looked down at her plump, jutting breasts and thought of the sight her shaven slit must make, positioned as she was above the onlookers, her legs spread apart. Worse still, she knew they could see the chain that ran down the centre of her sex, and that it must by now be shiny with wetness from the way it was chafing against her clitoris.

The maid descended the steps once more, leaving Carla alone to face her accusers naked.

'Now,' said the Judge, 'we will continue. And I hope that from here on your behaviour will improve.'

This time Carla did not reply.

The Judge turned to the man, who seemed unable to tear his gaze from Carla's bare breasts.

'Thank you for your evidence,' he said. 'It was most enlightening, and seems to have confirmed at least one of the charges against this young woman.'

'That's okay,' replied the man. 'It was an experience I wouldn't have missed. Best shag I've had in ages.'

Carla watched him as he left the room. So that was what she was, a good shag. The best in fact. She supposed she should feel ashamed, but the fact was, the experience had been a good one. Simply telling the story had aroused her tremendously. Her only fear was that her arousal would show. At least with the cloak it hadn't been immediately apparent. Now, though, she knew that the stiffness of her nipples and the convulsions of her sex muscles would be apparent to all. She wondered how much longer her ordeal would continue. Surely they couldn't know much more? Then her heart sank as the Judge spoke again.

'Call the next witnesses.'

This time there were two of them, and Carla recognized them at once. They were big men, with broad chests and ham fists, both dressed in jeans and open-necked shirts, their brawny arms decorated with tattoos. The shorter of the men was about thirty-five, balding, his broken nose revealing that he had once been a boxer. His companion was taller, with long, lank hair and thin lips. The two of them grinned broadly at the sight of the naked, trussed girl on the platform.

They made their way round to the front, beside the stage. Carla gazed down at the ground, unable to meet their eyes as they leered at her. Then the Judge spoke.

'Thank you for coming, gentlemen.'

'That's okay,' said the older man. 'Long as we gets paid.'

'Have no fear on that score. Ladies and gentlemen, this is Lenny and his taller friend is Sam. Would you mind telling us what you do, gentlemen?'

'Well, I guess we're kind of managers,' said Lenny.

'Yeah,' put in Sam. 'People managers.'

'And the sort of people you manage?'

'Young ladies, mainly. Escorts, models, that kind of thing.'

'Ladies of the street?'

'If you want.'

'So to use the colloquial term, you're both pimps?'

'That's not a very nice way of putting it. But some people call us that, yeah.'

'And you've met this young lady once before?'

The men ran their eyes over Carla's body.

'Yeah,' said Sam.

'When?'

'Last summer. Bitch was trying to work our patch.'

'To work your patch?'

'Sellin' herself. On our bit of ground. Without thinking of the business it was costing our girls.'

'She was streetwalking in an area that is worked by the women you control?'

'That's right. Bloody liberty.'

'And how long had she been working?'

'Just started that night. According to some of the girls she'd had it with about five punters already.'

'That's not true,' said Carla indignantly.

'You'll get your say,' said the Judge. 'Now, gentlemen. Did you actually see her with all these men?'

'Nah. But if the girls said that's what happened, I believe them.'

'I see. So you found her selling her body in your area. What did you do?'

'Took her on one side and gave her a bloody good rogering.'

'You raped her?'

'Nothing like that. She was begging for it. Never saw such a randy slut. Even wanted it in her arse. Couldn't get enough of us.'

'It wasn't like that,' shouted Carla.

'You threw yourself at us, you randy tart.'

'No!'

'Well,' broke in the Judge, 'it seems that you disagree on some points. Perhaps you'd like to tell us your side once again, Mrs Wilde.'

'I don't want to.'

'Nobody's going to force you. At the moment the record states that you walked the streets picking up men, had sex with at least five of them, then threw yourself at these two gentlemen, begging them to give you sexual satisfaction, including sodomizing you. Do you want that to remain the sole record of what happened?'

'No. It didn't happen like that.'

'Well then?'

'It was nothing special. A Wednesday night, I think. Eric was away on business as usual. I was alone at home. I watched this video and, well, I was feeling bored. I just went out to see whether anyone would stop for me. I didn't really intend to do anything.'

'Nevertheless, something happened.'

'Yes.'

'What?'

'Well, for a start, someone did stop . . .'

Chapter Ten

It was a warm evening, muggy almost. A night for summer dresses and strolls through the park with one's lover. If one's lover wasn't hundreds of miles away, that was, reflected Carla bitterly. And as for summer dresses, her current attire wasn't exactly what was being worn at Hendon this year. In fact her clothes were decidedly skimpy. On top she was wearing a bright red blouse, tied just below the breasts so that her midriff was bare. Her skirt was long and black, but split all the way up to her waist at the side, so that to even the most casual observer it was clear she was wearing no panties. On her feet were a pair of high, slim stiletto heels, also scarlet. There could be no doubt that Carla was dressed for seduction, and she felt herself blushing as she climbed out of the car in the quiet, deserted car park and gazed guiltily about her.

A car suddenly descended one of the ramps and swept past her, the couple inside staring at her as they passed. At that moment Carla almost lost her nerve and climbed back behind the wheel of her Mercedes sports car. What on earth was she doing here? she asked herself. The whole thing was crazy. The sensible thing would be to go home and bring herself off with a dildo or something.

But she had come so far it seemed defeatist to turn back.

Anyway, she told herself, she hadn't actually done anything wrong yet. She could just turn the whole thing into a quiet stroll if she wanted to. Having reached this point, she should at least go down to the street and assess the lie of the land.

She locked the car door, then stared at the key. She didn't even have a pocket to put it in. So much for being prepared! She would have to hide it somewhere. Checking to ensure that nobody was watching she crouched down and placed it on top of one of her rear tyres. Then, her mouth dry, she headed for the exit.

Ever since the incident with the motorist in his hotel room, Carla's thoughts had been preoccupied by what she had done that night. She just didn't seem to be able to rid it from her mind. She had tried to play it down, telling herself it had been a one-off, an aberration that would never recur. But then the memory of those glorious orgasms would come back to her and she would feel her fingers creeping down to her slit once more.

It was the video that had finally triggered her escapade this evening. It had arrived through the letterbox that day. There was no stamp or postmark on the parcel. Just an anonymous brown jiffy bag that was lying on her doormat when she came home that night.

She had prepared herself a light meal, slid the cassette into the slot on her VCR, and settled down in front of the television. There was a momentary flash of fuzz on the screen, then it lit up, and the action started.

The girl in the film was young, with a shapely body and large breasts. Carla had watched in fascination as she strolled down the road, flashing her legs at the passing cars. When, inevitably, one stopped for her, the hunk at the wheel was young and blue eyed. The ensuing action was explicit, no camera angles missed as he stripped and fucked her, first in the back seat of his car and later up a lovers' lane, where he had stretched her out on the grass and taken her *al fresco*.

Carla had found the whole thing extraordinarily erotic. It was her first experience of a blue movie, and she had continually rewound the tape to allow her to watch again as the man's thick tool plunged into the girl's vagina under the camera's watchful eye. By the time she had watched it four times she was feeling very horny indeed.

It was then that the idea had come to her. She had done it before, why not again? Why not sell her body to a man? After all, who would know? The house was empty, the servants having gone off duty, and nobody would call. It was a perfect opportunity. The more she thought about it, the more turned on she became.

She went into the bedroom and sought out the tartiest clothes she could find, eschewing the use of underwear. Then she made up her face, overdoing it just enough to give the effect she wanted. At last she stood, admiring herself in the mirror. The whole thing was just right. She looked stunningly beautiful, yet cheap at the same time.

She'd made her way down to the garage. She had decided that the road from which she had been picked up previously was too close to home. There was a danger of being seen by someone she knew if she went there. Instead she intended to drive across town to a far seedier area, whose strip clubs and sex shops attracted the tarts, and thus the punters. She had driven through the area before at night and had seen the women plying their trade, though she had never imagined that one day she might find herself joining them.

And now here she was, her heart beating hard as she stepped out of the side door of the car park onto the street. The feeling inside her had changed to one of apprehension now, her stomach a tight knot. Yet, at the same time she felt incredibly excited, and when she held up her hand she could see it was trembling.

It wasn't the prettiest part of town. The street was dirty and strewn with litter. On each side, bright neon lights announced go-go dancers, topless waitresses and strip shows. And at various places down the street, in the orange glow of the street lamps, she could discern the figures of young and not-so-young women, plying their trade.

She took up a position beneath one of the lamp posts, feeling suddenly very conspicuous. She leaned back against the lamp, thrusting one leg forward, her skirt falling aside so that it was bare all the way to her thigh. Then she waited, watching as the cars passed by.

Soon one car in particular caught her attention. It was a blue family saloon, probably a company car, she thought. It circled the block three times, each time crawling past her, the driver stretching his head round to get a good look at her. On the third occasion she waved.

The car drew to a halt a short distance up the road. At first she thought it had stopped for another girl, and an unexpected feeling of jealousy overtook her. Then she saw the car's reversing lights come on and it moved back until it was alongside her. The man leaned across the passenger seat and rolled down the window.

'How much?'

'For what?' Her voice sounded oddly croaky.

'Blow job. How much?'

Carla was momentarily flustered. She hadn't thought much about price. The money wasn't important, after all.

'Twenty pounds,' she said impulsively.

'Get in.'

The man pushed the door of the car open and Carla climbed inside. The interior was cluttered, with papers and sweet wrappers strewn about the floor, confirming her suspicion that the man must be some kind of sales rep.

He said nothing, simply engaging gear and pulling away from the kerb. It was altogether very different from the smart car or the courteous manner of her previous "client".

She studied the man. He was in his early thirties, slightly overweight, his hair receding. He wore a creased grey suit, his tie loose and his top button undone. Scarcely the hunk from her video, she thought.

He pulled off the street and drove up a side road. Then he turned through an archway. With a shock of recognition, Carla realized they were back in the car park where she had left her Mercedes. In fact he pulled the car up almost next to her shiny motor.

He pulled on the handbrake and killed the motor. Then he turned to her.

'Here?' she asked.

'What did you expect, the Ritz? Show me your tits.'

Carla's immediate reaction was to tell him to fuck off, but she restrained the impulse. After all, he was the customer. Instead she reached up and began undoing the knot beneath her breasts.

She unfastened the buttons and let the blouse fall open. He gave a low whistle as her firm, round breasts came into view, the dark nipples standing hard and proud. He reached out and ran a hand over them, bringing a low sigh from Carla as his fingers drifted over her teats.

'Better get on with it,' he said. 'I don't want to hang around here.'

Carla looked at him quizzically, and he nodded his head in the direction of his crotch. All at once, she realized that the next move was hers. She hesitated for a second, then, taking a deep breath, she leaned towards him and her hand dropped to his lap. His trousers were bulging, and a tremor of excitement coursed through her as she felt the hardness beneath the coarse material. Her fingers shook slightly as she undid his waistband and slipped down his zip. Then she reached into his pants.

His cock was not long, but it was thick, the circumcised helmet bulging and rubbery. He was only semi-erect, but as she ran her fingers over his flesh she felt the stiffness increasing almost at once.

She ran her hand up and down his shaft, watching in fascination as it hardened until it was standing stiffly erect, jutting from his fly. Then she moved her head down into his lap.

She took his glans into her mouth. His cock had a musky aroma to it and a slightly bitter taste. She sucked at him, and he gave a groan. She ran her tongue over the end, seeking out the little hole and licking at it. Then she began to move.

Carla wormed her hand into his pants as she bobbed her head up and down, feeling for his balls. His scrotum had contracted about the base of his penis, and she was able to cup it in her hand. With her other hand she masturbated him, working it up and down the lower part of his shaft whilst she continued to suck hard at the end. He was moaning aloud now, mouthing obscenities as he thrust his hips up against her face, forcing his rod even deeper into her mouth.

The lights of a passing car suddenly illuminated the walls and roof of the car park and she heard the sound of the engine as it moved swiftly past. She thought of the couple who had stared at her earlier, and wondered if the occupants of the car that had just passed had been able to see what she was doing. Certainly anyone walking by would get a perfect view of the bare breasted young beauty fellating her partner so enthusiastically, and the thought sent a new surge of wetness to her already sopping vagina.

His groans were becoming louder now, his cock twitching violently inside her mouth, his muscles tensing. Carla responded by sucking him even harder, her hand flying up and down his shaft as she sensed his orgasm approaching.

He came suddenly, his groans turning to hoarse cries as he filled her mouth with his hot, sticky semen. She kept her lips clamped over his knob as she gulped down the fluid, spurt after spurt escaping from the tip, so that she began to doubt whether she could swallow it all.

His cock went on pulsing for some time, each pulse unleashing yet another gob of spunk. She could sense that his passion was ebbing now, though, as the jets became smaller. At last he relaxed, sinking back into his seat, a final moan escaping his lips.

Carla sat up and gazed down at his organ. The end had a ring of cheap red lipstick about it and it glistened with her saliva.

'How was that?' she asked.

'Good, baby, good,' he murmured. 'One of the best I've had. You really acted as if you were enjoying it.'

Carla smiled. 'I was.'

He ran a hand over her soft breasts. 'Such lovely tits, too,' he murmured.

Carla waited until he had finished caressing her, then began to fasten her top once more.

'Time I was going,' she said, reaching for the door handle.

'Aren't you forgetting something?'

She turned to him, momentarily puzzled. What could he want? Surely he didn't expect her to button him up again? Then she saw the banknote in his hand.

'Oh yes,' she said, feeling rather stupid. She took the money from him and gave him a kiss on the cheek. Then she climbed out and slammed the door behind her. At once the car's engine roared into life and he drove off, leaving her standing alone.

She looked across at her own car. Should she call it a day? After all she had achieved her purpose after a fashion. But she still had a burning in her cunt. She badly wanted to be fucked. The blow job had been adventurous, but it had come nowhere near satisfying her own carnal desires. She looked down at the twenty pounds in her hand. Her earnings for the night.

'You can do better than that, Carla Wilde,' she told herself.

Then, pausing only to slip the banknote under the keys of her car, she set off towards the exit once more.

Chapter Eleven

When Carla had stepped back onto the street she was feeling a good deal calmer than she had the first time. The aftertaste of the man's spunk was still in her mouth and she knew she had performed well. Suddenly she felt able to take on anything that came along.

She walked slowly up the street, her eyes and ears alert for passing cars. Ahead she saw a woman leaning on a lamp post. Her lamp post in fact. She smiled to herself even as the thought entered her mind. Her lamp post indeed! One blow job, and she already thought she owned part of the street.

She walked past the girl. She was slightly older than Carla, probably in her mid-twenties. She wore a bright red silk dress which hugged her skin closely. Glancing at it, Carla was sure that, like herself, she wore no underwear. The girl watched Carla closely as she passed, her eyes piercing. The look unnerved Carla, making her feel more than a little uncomfortable.

As she moved on up the street, Carla heard the click of high heels following her. She knew it had to be the girl, and she began to feel somewhat uneasy at the thought of being followed, albeit by another woman. She was approaching the next lamp post now, and she noticed that this too had a rather sexy looking woman leaning against it. This one was black, with a stunning figure encased in one of the shortest dresses Carla had ever seen, the tops of her fishnet stockings clearly visible below the hem. She too eyed the approaching girl with a venomous expression, and Carla's trepidation increased as the black girl suddenly left her place and began walking towards her.

She tried to step aside, but found her way blocked by the girl. She turned to make a retreat, but the other one was close behind.

'What do you want?' she asked, trying to keep the tremor out of her voice.

'You're new around here, aren't you darling?' said the black girl.

'Sort of.'

'And I suppose you know the rules,' said the other.

'I didn't know there were rules.'

'That's what we thought,' said the black girl. 'I reckon we'd better explain a few things, eh Mandy?'

'I guess so, Cassandra,' came the reply.

The two moved closer to Carla, so that her nostrils were filled by their cheap scent.

'Listen, ladies,' she said, trying to put on a bold front. 'There's no need for trouble.'

'Trouble?' The black girl, whom Carla now knew to be called Cassandra, smiled. 'We don't want no trouble. Just to introduce you to the guys who make the rules.'

'What guys?'

'Lenny and Sam, of course.'

'Lenny and Sam?'

'Sure. They look after us girls, and in return we give them a share of our earnings.'

'You mean you have pimps?'

Cassandra moved forward so that her face was only inches from Carla's.

'Pimps is a dirty word,' she said. 'These guys protect us.'

'Yeah,' put in Mandy. 'And you're going to need protecting by them too. That's why they want to meet you.'

'I-I don't think so.'

'Sure you do,' said Cassandra. 'That is, if you know what's good for you.'

'Listen, girls,' said Carla, backing away, 'you've got me wrong. I was just passing by. I'm not . . .'

'Not what?'

'Well . . . I don't usually hang around here.'

'What about the guy in the Mondeo?'

'Mondeo?'

'The guy who just picked you up. Don't tell me you were just seeing an old friend.'

Carla didn't reply.

All of a sudden she found both arms being grabbed by the two women. Then they were frogmarching her off down the road. She tried to struggle free, but their grip was firm, their fingers digging into her flesh.

'Let me go,' she cried.

But they weren't having any of it, and the pair were much stronger than the petite Carla.

They took her past two more whores, who grinned and nodded to her antagonists, then turned off the main street and up a darkened alley.

For a moment, Carla was afraid they might be about to beat her up. Then she discerned a single yellow street lamp at the top of the alley, beneath which she could just make out two figures.

As they came closer, Carla was able to make out the scene more clearly. It was a cul-de-sac full of dustbins. The figures she had seen were both men, one short and heavily built, the other thinner with long dark hair.

'Hi Lenny, hi Sam,' said Mandy. 'Look what we found.'

The shorter of the two men, whom Mandy had referred to as Sam, stepped forward. The two girls held Carla fast whilst he cast his eyes over her.

'Hmm. Very nice,' he said. 'What's your name, darling?'

Carla simply glared at him, but said nothing. The two women tightened their grip on her arms.

'Come on dear,' said Cassandra. 'Tell Sam your name.'

'It's Carla.'

'Well, Carla,' said Sam. 'Don't you know this is our patch you're working?'

'I wasn't doing anything.'

'Bitch has been taking our trade,' said Mandy. 'Must have had five or six tricks.'

'Only one!' exclaimed Carla. Then closed her mouth as she realized the admission she had made.

'So, you admit turning a trick with the guy in the Mondeo?'

Carla remained silent.

'Come on, sweetie,' said Cassandra. 'I know that guy. He's a regular. A quick blow job in the car park, then he's on his way.'

'So how much did he pay?' asked Sam.

Carla lowered her eyes. 'Twenty pounds,' she muttered.

'Now we're getting somewhere,' said Sam. 'Where's the money?'

'I haven't got it.'

Sam moved closer. 'Listen, babe,' he said. 'Don't play games. Just hand over the money. Before I get the girls here to search you.'

Carla eyed him with apprehension. The whole thing was getting rather out of hand, and she was beginning to regret that she had ever had the idea. What had began as an erotic adventure was rapidly turning into a situation over which she had no control. She daren't tell him where the cash was hidden. That would lead him straight to her car. Once he saw that, he could find out who she was. Worse still, he may want to steal it.

'I . . . I threw it away,' she said.

'Don't give me that. Now I'll ask you once more. Where is it.'

'I haven't got it.'

'Okay girls, search her. And make sure you don't miss anything.'

A grin spread across Mandy's features. 'Grab her, Cassandra,' she said. 'Whilst I take a look.'

All at once, Carla found her elbows gripped from behind by the black girl. She tried to struggle, but the prostitute was too strong for her. She watched with apprehension as Mandy moved round in front of her.

What happened next took her completely by surprise. One minute Mandy was running her hands over the material of her blouse, as if feeling for concealed notes, the next she had taken hold of Carla's collar and was tugging hard at it.

Rip!

The garment split apart, buttons flying in all directions. Carla gave a cry of surprise and dismay as her blouse was reduced to a rag in a single move. Then Mandy dragged down on it and the shoulders gave, so that the whole thing came away in two halves. She tossed them aside and turned to face Carla, grinning triumphantly.

'It wasn't in her top,' she said, unnecessarily.

Carla stood, unable to believe what was happening, the creamy white of her firm young breasts exposed to the eyes of the two men. She struggled to free her hands so that she could cover her long, brown nipples, but Cassandra held her fast.

'Now try the skirt,' said Sam.

'No!'

'Tell us where the money is.'

'I haven't got it. Believe me.'

Sam gave a nod to Mandy.

Rip!

Once again the tearing of material and the clatter of buttons filled the air as Carla's skirt went the way of her blouse, ripped to shreds and then flung down into the gutter.

Carla was completely naked now, her shapely young body totally exposed to the whores and their pimps. Her face glowed scarlet as she watched Sam's eyes feast on her flat belly and pubic thatch, and the prominent lips of her sex beneath.

'Let me go,' she shouted, trying to maintain her dignity, despite the loss of her modesty.

'So,' said Sam. 'There's only one place left where she could be hiding the cash. Have a look, Mandy.'

At first Carla was unable to understand what he meant. Then she watched in dawning realization as Mandy dropped down on one knee in front of her.

'No!'

But once again her cries were ignored as the woman forced her thighs apart, then reached for her sex.

'Ah!'

A shudder ran through Carla's body as the woman slipped a finger into her vagina. She delved deep inside, bringing gasps from the naked girl as she felt herself explored so intimately. Suddenly she felt the muscles of her sex tighten about the prostitute's fingers and a gush of wetness invaded her sex.

Mandy looked up at her in surprise. Carla had her eyes shut, her mouth open slightly as she fought to contain the arousal that was beginning to well up inside her.

'Nothing in here,' she announced, continuing to twist her finger about in a manner that was, to Carla, quite delicious. 'But I think this is turning the bitch on.'

For the first time the tall man with the long black hair straightened up and strolled over to them.

'Fuckin' amateur hour,' he said, grinning.

'You reckon?' asked Sam.

'Sure. Hubby's probably away on business so she thought she'd come out and try a bit of rough. Look at the labels on those clothes. That skirt probably cost a couple of hundred quid.'

'That right, darling?' asked Sam.

Carla opened her eyes, finding it too difficult to concentrate as Mandy continued to slide a finger in and out of her vagina.

'Course it's right,' said Lenny. What is it, love, the old man can't get it up any more? Or did you just fancy a change from the silk sheets? That's enough, Mandy, let's hear what she's got to say.'

Mandy slipped her finger out, bringing a soft moan from

the naked girl. She straightened, holding her finger up in front of Carla's face. It was glistening with moisture.

'That right?' she asked. 'You just doing this for fun?'

Carla did not reply, but her silence spoke volumes.

'So you really did throw the twenty away,' said Sam. 'Now that's a real pity, don't you think, Lenny?'

'It sure is, Sam. It means we're going to have to get our cut some other way.'

'Cut?'

'Yeah. We get a percentage of all the money taken on this street. Isn't that right, girls?'

The two whores nodded their agreement.

'But I told you. I haven't got anything. Surely you can see that.'

Sam grinned again. 'I can see quite a lot,' he said. 'But Lenny and I gotta get paid. After all, we'd lose our respect if these girls thought we were letting amateurs work our patch.

'Seems to me, this little slut's only got one thing to offer,' said Mandy, running her hand over Carla's breast.

Carla stared at her. 'You can't,' she said.

'What you gonna do, call a policeman?' asked Sam. 'You'd have a bit of explaining to do if you did. I'm sure hubby would be very interested. Now, you gonna do this willingly, or have we gotta use some persuasion?'

Carla looked at the two men, then down at her own body. Her nipples were hard as bullets, and she could feel the twitches as the muscles of her sex convulsed, threatening at any moment to force a drop of wetness onto her thigh. All at once she realized that she was extremely turned on. Her situation, naked and helpless in this scruffy alley at the mercy of the two men, became suddenly incredibly erotic to her. She was going to get fucked, whether she liked it or not. It was a similar feeling to the one she had felt with the man in the hotel room. She was no longer in control. For the next few minutes she belonged to these two pimps. And she recognized with a shock that she was ready to give herself to them.

The men must have sensed her surrender, as a slow smile of satisfaction spread across Sam's face. He reached out and cupped Carla's breast, causing her already hard nipples to stiffen even further.

'She'll come quietly,' he murmured to the others. 'Look at her. She really wants it.'

Carla couldn't deny it. Now that her resistance had gone, she felt her whole body trembling with desire, and she knew it showed. When Sam's hand dropped to her crotch and his fingers slid down her slit she gave an audible gasp, her hips pressing forward against his touch.

'Fancy a sandwich, Lenny?' said Sam.

'Yeah. Why not?'

Carla was confused by the exchange. A sandwich? What could they be talking about? They were going to fuck her, weren't they?

Cassandra continued to hold Carla's hands behind her back as Sam frigged her. There was no need now, though. All Carla's concentration was fixed on the hard, coarse fingers that were arousing her so wonderfully. She watched with almost detached interest as Mandy closed in behind the man and reached down to his crotch.

The whore slipped down the man's zipper in a single movement, releasing his rampant tool. Carla licked her lips as she gazed down at the meaty truncheon that rose stiffly from his groin.

Mandy began gently to masturbate the pimp, wrapping her fist about his shaft and working his foreskin back and forth. Now it was his turn to groan as his cock and balls were expertly manipulated by her.

'You ready, Sam?' asked Mandy.

He nodded.

Sam removed his fingers from Carla's crotch and moved across to where the dustbins were standing three deep against the wall at the back of the alley. He leaned back against one of the bins, his groin thrust forward, his thick cock still standing proudly from his fly whilst Mandy continued to caress him.

Carla felt a shove at her back, and she realized with a gulp that the time had come. She stepped forward towards the man. She still wore her high heels, which sounded loudly on the road as she walked. The air felt cool suddenly against her naked flesh, and she realized that a sweat of anticipation had seeped from her pores, forming a sheen all over her body.

To Carla, everything seemed quite unreal. Here she was, Carla Wilde, wife of a distinguished member of society, who moved in the highest circles, and she was stark naked up the end of an alley with two whores and their pimps, and about to be fucked by a man she didn't even know. It was the same feeling she had had when she had been picked up the first time in the street near her home: as if she was detached, a mere spectator to a drama that was being played out before her.

Cassandra stopped her just in front of where Sam was half reclined over the bin. She let go of Carla's arms, taking hold of her thighs from behind and forcing them apart. Then she was pushing her forward again, whilst Mandy was pulling her from the front, her hand still grasping Sam's tool.

Between them the two women raised the trembling young girl up until she was just above Sam's twitching shaft, then pressed her downwards.

'Ah!'

Carla cried aloud as Sam's cock slid into her. It felt massive, forcing the walls of her sex apart as it drove even deeper inside her.

The two women continued to force her down until Sam was all the way in. Then they shoved her forward so that her breasts were pressed hard against his shirt.

Carla could hold back no longer, and she began to move her hips, pumping them back and forth as she took her pleasure on his rampant cock. But, to her surprise, Cassandra stopped her, taking hold of the cheeks of her backside and forcing them apart. Then came a sensation that sent a shock through Carla's body.

Something was brushing against her anus. Something thick and stiff, that throbbed with life, and at that very moment it began to press hard against her flesh.

Carla craned her neck round, unwilling at first to accept what was happening to her. Behind her, Cassandra had Lenny's cock in one hand, whilst the fingers of the other were stretching apart the small star of her anus. Even as she watched, Carla felt it push harder and harder against her nether entrance.

'No!'

She started to struggle, but Sam had his arms about her holding her fast. Carla gritted her teeth as the pressure on her backside became almost unbearable. Then she gave a cry of surprise and pain as Lenny's cock slipped into her rectum.

'Oh!'

Carla couldn't believe the sensation as Lenny's thick, hard weapon slid relentlessly into her backside. No man had ever taken her there. Her anus had been completely virgin. But no longer, and she gave a groan as she felt Lenny's pubic hair pressing against her backside, confirming that he was all the way inside her.

'Now move,' muttered Sam in her ear. 'Fuck the pair of us. Get those hips pumping.'

Tentatively Carla began to move her hips. As she did so she felt the two cocks move inside her, one slipping out as the other rammed deeper inside. She pressed her hips down again, and the opposite happened.

Suddenly, Carla's body was alive with arousal. All at once the two rampant cocks that filled her so intimately became the most important thing in her life as the realization that she was satisfying two men at once hit her. Two men! She could scarcely believe her own wantonness as she gasped and moaned between the pair.

As Carla's arousal increased, so did that of the two she was satisfying, their cocks seeming to become harder and thicker with each stroke. So filled was she by the two penises that Carla began to feel that they might meet inside her, uniting the two men with the same intimacy that she felt with them.

The men's groans increased in volume suddenly, and Carla peered round to see that Cassandra had positioned herself behind them and had taken a pair of balls in each hand. As the naked girl worked her backside back and forth, so the whore caressed the men's testicles, clearly redoubling their pleasure as they enjoyed their 'sandwich' to the full.

The dustbins clattered as the threesome's urgency increased. Carla felt as if she was being physically battered as the two men began driving into her harder and harder, no longer content simply with her own efforts. She was crying aloud now with every stroke. It was as if her entire being was concentrated in her arse and cunt, the exquisite feeling of the double penetration sending her almost insane with pleasure, her backside pumping back and forth as she struggled to maintain a rhythm with the two men.

Then, as if responding to a single signal, the two men suddenly stiffened, and she knew they were about to come.

When they let go, they did it simultaneously, twin jets of hot spunk suddenly filling Carla's young body. She gave a gasp as she felt the hot, sticky fluid invade her rectum and vagina at the same time. For a second she was still, the muscles of her sphincter and sex contracting violently about the thick, meaty rods inside her. Then she too was coming, her screams piercing the night air as the most extraordinary orgasm of her life overtook her.

For the next few minutes, Carla's mind was total confusion as she thrashed back and forth between the two men. Somewhere, someone was shouting aloud, but she couldn't be sure which of her two ravishers it was. Then she realized with a shock that it was her own voice she could hear, and that the obscenities she was listening to were coming from her own lips. The pair went on fucking her, spurt after spurt of semen pumping deep within her, until at last she sensed they were slowing down. Still they went on, however, until they had no more seed to deposit. Then, as they had climaxed, the two relaxed as one, pinning her between their panting bodies.

Lenny moved first, sliding his cock from her backside as he rose to his feet. Then Carla felt her arms grasped and she too was pulled to a standing position, gasping as Sam's penis slid out of her. She stood and watched, her chest rising and falling, as the two men tucked themselves back into their trousers. She looked round for her own clothes, but could see no sign of them. She realized that, even if she found them, they wouldn't be of much use to her. Mandy had seen to that. For the first time she began to wonder how she would get back to her car.

The two whores continued to hold her arms as Sam approached her, his cock safely back in his pants. Carla felt a mess, her body still shiny with sweat, her hair dishevelled, the spunk already beginning to leak from her vagina and anus as she faced her ravisher.

He took hold of her breast, squeezing it roughly.

'Right, Miss Amateur Hour,' he said. 'Next time you try to work this street, make sure you know who gets the money. Otherwise, go and sell that cunt of yours elsewhere. You get me?'

Carla nodded silently.

'Now clear off.'

'But . . .'

'But what?'

'But I'm naked.'

'Better be careful how you go, then. There's some funny types around here. Now fuck off.'

'I can't.'

Mandy tightened her grip on Carla's arm, her fingers digging painfully into her flesh.

'Better get going, darling,' she said. 'If you know what's good for you.'

The two whores shoved Carla toward the exit to the alley. She hesitated, then Sam took a step towards her and she turned and ran.

When she reached the road, Carla paused for a moment,

gazing fearfully round the corner. She estimated it was about three hundred yards to the entrance to the car park. Along the street she could see the figures of the whores. She took a deep breath, then started to run.

Almost at once the catcalls began to sound as the whores spotted the naked girl dashing down the street. To Carla's consternation, men began to emerge from the shop doorways to see what the commotion was. The sight of the young beauty dashing down the pavement, her breasts bouncing delightfully with every step, brought new shouts. In front of her someone stepped into the street to try to cut her off, but Carla managed to dodge him. Then more appeared, reaching out for her as she ducked and weaved. She was almost in a blind panic now, as she heard more footsteps approaching from behind.

Then, with a shock, she realized she had run past the entryway that led into the car park. She gave a cry of dismay and stopped. As she turned round the figures pursuing her came to a halt.

There were four of them, all young men, dressed in jeans and vests, their hair closely cropped, their arms adorned with tattoos. Carla shrank back as they closed in on her.

'What have we here?' said one of them. 'Aren't you cold like that, darling?'

'Let me pass,' said Carla, trying to keep her voice steady.

'Try and pass,' said another of the men.

'Yeah, come on, darling,' said the third, beckoning with a finger. 'You try to get past us.'

Carla stood rooted to the spot, cursing herself for ever having come down this awful street. Now she was really in trouble. The fucking she had received from the pimps had been one thing, and if she admitted it to herself it had been one of the most erotic experiences of her life. But these four were a different prospect.

The first skinhead took a step towards her, and for the first time she realized he held a knife in his hand. She took a pace backwards, but there seemed nowhere to go.

Suddenly there was a screech of brakes beside her and she saw from the corner of her eye a large car draw up. At once the rear door opened and a woman's hand reached out and grasped her wrist, pulling her inside. At the same moment the four men realized what was happening and they surged forward.

But it was too late. Carla almost fell onto the smooth leather of the car's seat. Then the door slammed and they were accelerating away.

Carla turned to look at the figure beside her, who was still grasping her wrist. Then she gave a gasp.

It was Phaedra.

Chapter Twelve

The Judge looked down at Sam and Lenny over the top of his glasses.

'Does her story tally with yours?' he asked.

'I suppose so,' said Sam. 'But Mandy did tell us she'd had at least four johns before she gave the guy in the car a blow job.'

'She was lying,' said Carla. 'He was the only one.'

'Even if we accept that,' said the Judge. 'It still makes your behaviour completely despicable. Allowing two strangers to screw you in an alley. And one of them sodomized you. That is not the behaviour expected of a woman of your class.'

'Wait a minute. You heard my story. Damn it, they practically raped me.'

'The operative word being *practically*. From what we've heard this evening, you were not exactly reluctant.'

'What choice did I have?'

'You could have screamed.'

'And find myself gagged as well as stripped and pinned down?'

'As I understand it, you had an orgasm. Is that not true?'

Carla dropped her eyes. 'Yes.'

'So the idea of two men at once having intercourse and sodomizing you was something you found arousing?

'I couldn't help it.'

'You could have helped it by not being in the street in the first place. However, there is another factor that makes me believe that you enjoyed the experience more than you have admitted.'

Carla looked up at him, her expression puzzled.

'I was observing your behaviour whilst you were telling the story. Particularly during the more shameful episodes. And I know these two gentlemen were doing the same. Isn't that so, gentlemen?'

'Yeah,' said Sam.

'Not half,' said Lenny.

'And what did you observe?' asked the Judge.

'Bitch was frigging herself. On the chain. You could see her hips moving. She was wanking.'

Carla's face went suddenly scarlet at the words. It was true. The sensation of the chain that cut so intimately into her was extraordinary, and as she had told her story, the hard little bud of her clitoris had grown wetter and more sensitive. She had thought her movements barely visible as she had allowed the rough links of the chain to rub back and forth over it. Now she realized with deep embarrassment that they had known all along what she was doing. Not for the first time she cursed the responsiveness of her body as she tried to steady herself.

The Judge grimaced. 'So,' he said. 'Even in this grave situation you are incapable of controlling your lust.'

'It's hardly fair, is it?' complained Carla. 'You make me strip off in front of all these people, you put that damned chain between my legs, then you make me tell you some of the most erotic things that have ever happened to me. I bet half the blokes in the audience will dash out for a wank once this is over. Including you, Judge.'

Bang!

'Silence! You have been warned often enough about these outbursts. One more and I shall have you whipped. Maybe that will beat some sense into you.'

Carla stared at him. She couldn't believe the threat. Yet he had threatened to strip her and she hadn't believed that either. Now here she was, naked before the whole gathering. She decided it would be imprudent to reply.

'Now, gentlemen,' said the Judge, turning to Sam and Lenny. 'If you have nothing else to say, then you can be dismissed. Thank you for your time.'

'That's okay, Judge,' said Lenny, cheerfully. 'It was worth it to get another look at that gorgeous body.'

'Yeah,' said Sam, turning to Carla. 'If you get kicked out by this lot, come and work for us. We'll see to it that that tight little cunt of yours gets filled at least four times a night. You won't need to frig yourself then.'

And with that the two men winked at one another and headed for the door.

'Now, young lady,' said the Judge, once the room was quiet once more. 'We move on to the next phase of your descent into lascivious degradation. The agency.'

Carla hardly had the capacity to be surprised any more. It seemed that these people knew everything there was to know about her. As if they were privy to the innermost depths of her mind. So she said nothing as the Judge went on.

'The Elite Agency, I believe it was called. Escorts for discerning visitors. Company for those in a strange city. Isn't that what they offered?'

'The idea was to provide company for businessmen,' said Carla quietly.

'Company? Is that what you call it? Wouldn't prostitution be a better word?'

'We were escorts,' said Carla firmly.

'So flaunting your body on a street corner for sex is prostitution, but offering yourself to men by advertising in magazines is something different?'

'We were there for company. The ads said nothing about sex.'

'Nevertheless, you had sex with your clients?'

Carla remained silent for a moment, then nodded.

'And tell me, Mrs Wilde, how many customers did the agency supply you with?'

'I'm not sure.'

'Ten? Twenty? Fifty?'

'In all about twenty, I guess.'

'About twenty. And of those twenty, how many did you not have intercourse with?'

'They didn't all fuck me. Some wanted my mouth. Or other places.'

'Let me rephrase the question. Of the twenty, how many did you not give an orgasm of some kind to?'

'You know the answer. I had sex with all of them one way or another.'

'So the ads to which you referred earlier were misleading?'

'The point was, it wasn't compulsory to screw with them. It wasn't like whoring.'

'Yet you chose to in every case?'

Once again Carla didn't reply.

'Naturally it would not be possible to have all these

people in the courtroom to testify,' the Judge went on. 'Besides, I feel twenty is a somewhat conservative estimate on your part. However we do have a letter here from one of your customers that seems to sum up the sort of behaviour that went on during your so-called escorting sorties.'

Carla looked with some unease at the letter the Judge was unfolding. The paper was thick and expensive-looking, and even from where she stood she could see it was written in a bold, flowing hand.

'I shan't read the whole letter,' said the Judge. 'But there are some passages here that tell us all we need to know.'

He began to read in a loud voice.

'"The young woman, who told me her name was Carla, was one of the most willing and obliging that I have ever come across. She was good and enthusiastic company during our meal, and it was at her suggestion that we went up to my hotel room afterwards. There she immediately began making advances to me and soon instigated one of the most enjoyable sex sessions I have ever experienced. As if this wasn't enough, she also seduced the waiter who brought our room service. All in all she proved the most lascivious young woman it has ever been my pleasure to encounter."'

Carla frowned. 'Anyone could have written that,' she said. 'It doesn't prove anything.'

'Do you want to know the identity of the writer?' asked the Judge.

'I suppose so.'

'It is signed A. Kristen.'

'Oh . . .' Carla's voice was subdued as the Judge made the announcement.

'Does that name mean anything to you?'

'Yes.'

'You mean out of all those names you actually remember this one?'

'That one was different.'

'I'm sure he was. In fact the letter goes on to be quite explicit about what passed between you. And it tends to point to you as the instigator of most of what went on. Shall I read more?'

'No.'

'In that case, perhaps you'd care to give us your own account?'

Carla looked down at the sea of expectant eyes. She wasn't sure how much longer she could go on with these reminiscences. The trouble was that even the memory of them was extremely arousing to her, and she knew this was obvious to all those watching. She gazed down at her breasts. Her nipples were as hard as ever, like two brown buds that stood proud from her breasts. But it was her sex that was affected the most. It felt as if it was burning, and she knew her swollen clitoris was visible to all. It wouldn't be so bad but for the chain that continued to chafe against that most sensitive spot. The urge to move her hips was almost overwhelming and she knew that at any second the love juices that were welling up inside her were in danger of leaking out onto her thigh.

'Well, Mrs Wilde? Are you prepared to describe what happened in your own words?'

Carla sighed.

'It was on a Friday night,' she began. 'I had told Eric I was staying at a friend's house . . .'

Chapter Thirteen

As usual, the escort agency had been Phaedra's idea, another seed planted in the fertile plot that was Carla's mind. She had made the suggestion on the night she had rescued Carla from the street where she had been cornered by the youths.

At first, as she had stumbled into the vehicle, Carla had been in no state to take anything in, her body still shaking from her encounter with the skinheads. She had sat in dazed silence as the long, dark car pulled away from the curb, leaving the young men shaking their fists after it. They had driven without speaking for some time, Carla staring blankly at the street lights as they flashed by. Then she had felt a hand on her thigh.

'What were you doing there?' asked Phaedra.

Carla did not reply.

Phaedra's hand moved up the inside of her thigh. She tried to close her legs, but the woman was too strong, forcing her fingers into Carla's sex. She delved deep inside, making the girl gasp with the intimacy of the touch. Then she pulled the fingers out and sniffed them.

'Spunk,' she observed. 'And I'll wager it's not your husband's. Turn and kneel on the seat.'

Carla made a noise of protest, but Phaedra was firm, so

she did as she was told, kneeling up on the seat so that she was facing out the rear windscreen of the vehicle.

Once again a gasp escaped her lips as she felt Phaedra force the cheeks of her buttocks apart and insert a digit into her still sore anus, pushing it deep inside before withdrawing it.

'They buggered you as well,' she observed. Was it both at the same time?'

Carla nodded.

'So what do you think of whoring?'

Carla turned and sat down beside her again.

'It's too dangerous,' she said flatly.

'It is if you approach it like that. That's one of the most dangerous parts of town. You're as likely to get a knife in you as a cock. Those skinheads wouldn't have let you go without gang-banging you, you know that.'

'It was your suggestion that I sell my body.'

'And you enjoyed it, didn't you?'

Carla frowned. 'Some of it.'

'The sex?'

'Yes. And the sense of adventure. You were right about that. But that place was just a little too adventurous.'

'So you need a different approach.'

Carla shook her head. 'Listen, Phaedra,' she said. 'This thing has gone far enough. Before I met you I was faithful to my husband. Since then, all kinds of things have happened I'd never have dreamed of. I mean, look at me now, stark naked in the back of your car.'

Phaedra ran a hand over Carla's breasts. 'Yes,' she said. 'But isn't life much more exciting?'

'You call narrowly escaping being raped by a gang of yobs exciting?'

'It beats watching the telly.'

'Speaking of that,' said Carla, gazing at Phaedra suspiciously. 'Did you have anything to do with a video dropping through my letterbox this afternoon?'

'What would I be doing with a video?'

'Never mind. Just take me back to my car, would you?'

'Of course. But you really should consider an escort agency, you know.'

'An escort agency?'

'They advertize in magazines. Especially the freebies you get when you stay in a big hotel. Gentlemen's companions, they call them. A much better class of whore, and none of the hanging about on street corners.'

'You're crazy, Phaedra.'

'No darling,' Phaedra was still stroking Carla's breasts. 'Just sensitive to your needs.'

The car came to a halt, and Carla realized with surprise that they were in the car park, alongside her Mercedes. She reached for the doorhandle, pushing the door open.

'Think about it, Carla,' said Phaedra.

'Get lost, Phaedra,' she replied.

She slammed the door, and the car immediately accelerated away down the ramp. She watched it disappear, her mind still whirling. Then, all of a sudden, she remembered her nudity, and the feeling of panic almost enveloped her again. The key! Where had she left it? For a moment she was quite unable to remember. Then it came back to her and she hurried round the vehicle, dropping to her knees and fumbling under the wheel arch. She gave a sigh of relief as her fingers closed about it.

There was something else there, resting on the wheel. A crisp, new banknote. Despite her hurry to get into the car, she paused for a moment, staring at the twenty pounds and remembering the sensation of having the man's cock between her lips and the taste of his semen in her mouth. There was no doubt that it had been a thrilling encounter, and her fingers dropped to her crotch, feeling the wetness that still lingered there.

Then she shook her head, remembering where she was, and climbed hastily into the car, glad of its protection. She gunned the motor and in no time was heading out of the car park and down the road.

It wasn't until she was half-way home that it occurred to her to wonder how Phaedra's driver had known where her car was parked.

It was three days later that the envelope arrived on her mat. Like the video it had no stamp or address on it. It simply came through the letterbox whilst she was out shopping. When she opened it there was no letter, just a business card bearing the name 'Elite Escort Agency' along with an address and telephone number. Her first instinct was to throw it in the bin, but even as she flipped the lid open she paused, fingering the card. Then, on an impulse, she dropped it into her handbag.

Weeks passed. The summer grew hotter, the days emptier. She had almost given up the bridge parties, bored by the interminable gossip that accompanied them. She spent her days lying beside the pool reading bad novels or watching even worse television. Eric seemed more distant than ever from her now, spending more and more nights away from home so that she became convinced that he was having an affair. When he came home she could smell the woman on his clothes, and occasionally she would answer the telephone only to find that the caller had hung up immediately. The strange thing was that she didn't really care. Sex with her husband was now all but non-existent and she felt litle desire to remedy the situation.

This did not mean that her own sex drive was in any way diminished, though. On the contrary, she seemed more horny than ever, and many was the night she would lie in bed frigging herself and thinking of the double fucking she had received in that dark alley.

Then, one evening when boredom had finally driven her to decide to go out for a drink on her own, she was rummaging in her handbag for her mascara when the agency card fell out.

She picked it up and read it over again. The 'Elite Escort Agency'. A better class of whore, Phaedra had called them. She read and re-read the address, then flung the card down and headed for the living room to fix herself a whisky, determined to forget the idea.

Ten minutes later she was back, picking up the card and reaching for the phone.

When the woman's voice came on the other end she almost lost her nerve.

'Elite Escorts. Can I help you?'

'I . . .' Carla's throat was dry.

'Yes?'

'It . . . It was nothing . . .'

'Are you looking for an escort, or a job?'

'Er . . . I think maybe I misdialled.'

'Have you done this kind of work before?'

'No.'

'That's all right. The girls are always nervous when they call the first time. You're married, aren't you?'

'I . . . I'm not sure.'

'Faxing us a photo won't hurt, surely? Just include a cover sheet with your name and number. There's no obligation, you know.'

'All right.'

'Send it now. Then I'll call back.'

There was a click and the instrument went dead. Carla stood gazing at it for a few moments, then replaced the receiver and went up to her room.

The photos had been a whim. She had gone to a glamour photographer, paid a fee and posed for him in a skimpy bikini. She had intended to give them to Eric as a present, but somehow had never done so. Now she leafed through them and selected a print showing her standing, her hands on her hips, looking back at the camera, her body twisted round so that her breasts showed in a stark silhouette. She went downstairs to the fax machine and dialled in the number on the card.

Then minutes later the phone rang, its trill making her jump. She let it ring three times, then picked it up.

'Carla Wilde.'

'Carla. That's a pretty name to go with a pretty girl. How recent is this shot, Carla?'

'About six months.'

'You certainly look gorgeous, despite the mess that the fax makes of the picture. Are you free tonight, Carla?'

Carla took a deep breath. 'Yes.'

'Do you know the Hotel Miradel? There's a gentleman called Soames there who'd love to have some company tonight.'

'What do I do?'

'Just go to the lobby, use the hotel phone and ring room five-one-five. Shall I tell him to expect you?'

A pause.

'Yes.'

Carla's first experience with the agency was better than she could have expected. Soames turned out to be a personable man in his early thirties and Carla found herself immediately attracted to him. By the time the cab was halfway to the restaurant he already had her knickers off and two fingers rammed deep inside her, and before they had finished the first course they had risen from their table and slipped into the gents where he had fucked her bent forward over the seat in one of the cubicles. After the meal they had hurried back to his hotel where they had spent a night of unbridled passion, screwing in every way they knew. It was after five in the morning when Carla, tired and dishevelled, slipped from his room clutching a handful of bank notes.

After that she started working for the agency on a regular basis. Whenever she had the opportunity she would ring the number. The same woman always answered, and always sounded pleased to hear from her. Before long she would be on her way to one hotel or another, where a man would be waiting to wine, dine and ultimately fuck her.

For Carla it was a wonderful time, able to indulge her lascivious desires without any real fear of discovery or danger. The men were invariably courteous and charming hosts, and once in their bedrooms showed few inhibitions in revealing their own secret fantasies. Carla was screwed on the bed, on the floor, in the bath, in the open air and, on one memorable occasion, in the back of a black cab.

But few of her encounters were more memorable than

with the customer called Kristen, whose letter the Judge had begun to read out.

It was a midweek evening, and Eric had called unexpectedly to say he would not be home. Carla had reacted at once, dialling the agency number and waiting anxiously for the woman to reply.

'Elite Escorts.'

'It's Carla.'

'Hi, Carla. Not much happening tonight, I'm afraid.'

'Oh.' Carla's voice betrayed her disappointment.

'Just a quiet week, I guess. I've got nothing for you, I'm afraid.'

'Nothing at all?'

'No. There's only the one who always asks for Connie, and she's sick tonight.'

'The one who asks for Connie?'

'Yes. A regular. Always gets the concierge at the hotel to call us. Never rings in person.'

'Couldn't I take Connie's place?'

'I'm not sure. This customer insists on Connie. I'm not certain what goes on. Connie never says. Only that the pay is good.'

'I'll do it. Can't you call and say I'll do it?' Carla was almost pleading.

'Say, you sound pretty desperate. Money a bit tight this month?'

'Yes. That's it.' Carla reddened at the lie, looking about her at the possessions of an extremely rich man. It certainly wasn't money she needed. It was sex. Raw, crude sex. A cock in her cunt that released her from her pent up desires and filled her with spunk. Carla wanted to be fucked, and fucked hard.

'I'll see what I can do. Don't go away.'

Carla spent an anxious ten minutes sitting by the phone sipping at a glass of neat whisky. When it rang she snatched it up at once.

'Carla speaking.'

'The Derbyshire Hotel. Wear a short, red dress and wait at the bar. Okay?'

'Okay,' said Carla. 'And thanks.'

Chapter Fourteen

Carla felt a familiar sensation of fear tinged with excitement as she walked up the steps of the Derbyshire hotel. A man in a grey coat and top hat opened the door for her, his eyes travelling down her young body as she flashed a smile at him. The lobby was large and brightly lit, bustling with people, mainly tourists. Carla slipped into the ladies' to check her appearance.

She stood before the full-length mirror, admiring herself. She looked very good indeed. The dress she wore was extremely short, made of bright red satin and buttoned down the front. When she moved she had to be careful not to show the inch of bare thigh above her black hold-up stockings. She wore no bra, her firm breasts pressed against the top of the dress, a generous expanse of cleavage on display. On her feet she had a pair of elegant high heels, also red. Altogether she looked very sexy indeed.

She emerged from the cloakroom and made her way to the bar. It was an elegant room, discreetly lit, most of the customers sitting at tables. Carla hoisted herself onto a bar stool, taking care to tuck her dress under her bottom when she sat down. She ordered a scotch, then settled down to wait for her companion.

Five minutes passed. She sipped at her drink, watching

the door. Occasionally a man would enter and she would watch him expectantly. But each one would give her no more than an admiring glance before joining someone else.

'Good evening.'

The voice took Carla by surprise. She swung round to see a woman standing beside her. She was expensively dressed in a one-piece silk dress that hugged the voluptuous contours of her body, her curvy hips and jutting bustline filling the garment beautifully. Her hair was long and blonde, held back from her eyes by a simple band. Her face was beautiful, with long eyelashes, a perfectly shaped nose and full lips.

Carla stared at the newcomer, wondering what she might want.

'Hello,' she said lamely.

'You all by yourself?'

'I'm meeting someone. A gentleman.'

'What's his name? I know a lot of the gentlemen around here.'

'I doubt if you'd know this one. He's called Mr Kristen.'

'Mr Kristen, eh? And what does he look like?'

'I don't know. We haven't met before.'

'I see. Blind date, is it?'

Carla shifted uncomfortably, slightly unnerved by the woman's interrogation.

'It's business, actually.'

'And what sort of business are you in?'

'I'm . . . Listen, what's it to you?'

'Quite a lot actually.' The woman held out a hand. 'Allow me to introduce myself. I'm Annabelle Kristen.'

Carla stared open-mouthed at the woman.

'You're . . .'

'Your date. Right. You got a problem with that?'

'But you're . . .'

'A woman. Do you always need people to finish your sentences, Carla?'

'It's just a bit of a surprise, that's all.'

'If you want to pull out, now's the time.'

Carla thought for a moment, then shook her head.

'No. That's okay.'

After all, she mused, the alternative was a night at home on her own. Besides, she was intrigued by Annabelle Kristen, and wanted to know more.

'Right,' said Annabelle, taking the stool next to hers. 'What's that you're drinking?'

Annabelle ordered two more drinks and the two women began to chat. Carla soon warmed to her companion, who was both witty and interesting. Soon she had Carla giggling hysterically at her anecdotes, most of which concerned her experiences with men. Some of the stories puzzled her, however, and when there was a lull in the conversation, she ventured a question.

'Listen, Annabelle. If you've had all these experiences with guys, then how come . . . Well, how come I'm here?'

Annabelle laughed. 'My, you are the conventional one, Carla,' she said. 'You've got to live life to the full.'

'I've had that advice before. It's just you're so gorgeous looking. Too pretty to be a lesbian. I reckon you could have any man in this room if you wanted.'

'That's what's so boring about it. Forbidden fruits are much more interesting. Anyhow, who says I'm a lesbian? There are other ways to have fun with a girl?'

'Like what?'

'That depends. Connie is always quite amenable to my whims. Do you think you would be?'

'I . . . I don't know. What kind of whims?'

Annabelle suddenly lowered her voice and leaned forward towards Carla.

'Listen, Carla. I need you to trust me. Do you?'

'Yes.'

'And do you agree to do whatever I say during this evening?'

'Up to a point.'

'No. Not up to a point. Anything I say. It's all about trust.'

'But I hardly know you. How do I know you're worthy of my trust.'

'That's all part of the game. That's what makes it exciting.'

'What if I say no?'

'That's your prerogative. I just don't think you're the kind of girl who'll turn down a challenge.'

'And I have to do anything you ask?'

'Anything.'

Carla stared at Annabelle. There was something about the woman that excited her greatly. Something mysterious and deeply sensual. Something arousing.

'All right.'

'Promise?'

'I promise.'

'Take off your knickers.'

'I beg your pardon?'

'You heard me.'

Carla looked into Annabelle's eyes, then down at the skimpy minidress that barely covered her thighs.

'You mean in the ladies'?'

'No. Right here. Take them off and put them on the bar.'

'But I . . .'

'I thought we had an agreement, Carla. Don't tell me you've changed your mind already.'

Carla stared at her for a moment, then shook her head.

'Of course not.'

She looked about her. All the other patrons were deep in conversation with one another. The barman was standing at the far end, polishing glasses. Nobody seemed to be paying any attention to the two beautiful women who sat at the bar.

Carla pulled up her skirt and hooked her thumbs into the waistband of the panties. Then she lifted her backside from the stool and pulled them down, raising her knees in order to slip them over her shoes. For a few moments Annabelle had an unrestricted view of her pubic bush. Then she pulled the skirt back down over her thighs. She met Annabelle's eyes.

'All right?' she asked.

'Put them on the bar. Right there, where the barman can see them.'

Carla did as she was told, placing the small, lacy panties onto the surface in front of her.

'That's better,' said Annabelle. 'Let's have another drink.'

Carla sat, trying to keep her expression calm as the barman came across. The panties were lying right by her glass, so that the man's hand touched them as he picked it up. She wondered if he could feel the warmth of her body on them. If he could, he didn't betray the fact on his face.

'How does that feel?' asked Annabelle.

'It feels funny,' replied Carla. 'Sort of cool. I wish I'd worn a longer skirt.'

'I don't. Undo your bottom button.'

'But that will expose my crotch.'

'That's right. You still don't trust me, do you?'

Carla made no reply, simply dropping her hands into her lap and undoing the button. As she did so the tight dress parted, baring the tops of her thighs and the dark mat of her pubic bush.

'How do you feel now?'

'Exposed. If anyone comes to the bar, they'll see me.'

'Turn and sit with your back to the bar.'

'But . . .' Carla began to protest, but the look in Annabelle's eye silenced her. She took a sip at her drink, then slowly, reluctantly, she rose to her feet and seated herself so that she was facing into the room.

'Part your knees. Just a little.'

Carla allowed her knees to part about nine inches. She glanced down at herself. Anyone looking in her direction would have been able to see stocking tops, thighs, pubic mound and above all the lips of her sex. Her face glowed red, but she remained just where she was.

'Tell me how you feel now.'

'I don't know. Embarrassed. But something else too.'

'Anybody glancing over here can see your cunt. Look, that guy in the corner. See how he's staring. He's telling his mates now. They're all looking at you. Does that make you feel horny, having those guys getting an eyeful of your snatch?'

'Yes. Yes, you're right. It's really turning me on.'

'You're not just telling me what I want to hear? Like a faked orgasm?'

'No honestly, Annabelle. It's a real turn-on. I'm getting wet already.'

'Let me feel.'

'Go ahead.'

'What, with those guys watching?'

'Why not?'

Now it was Annabelle's turn to be surprised.

'Hey, you're really something else, Carla. Even Connie never went that far.'

'Maybe Connie was faking. Feel my cunt, Annabelle.'

The woman moved closer and placed a hand on Carla's leg. She slid it slowly upwards to the top of her stockings, and over the smooth bare flesh of her thigh. Then she touched Carla's clitoris, making the younger girl shudder. She ran a finger down her slit and slipped it inside.

'Ah!'

Carla gave a gasp as Annabelle rotated her digit inside her vagina, sending pulses of pleasure through her body. She looked across at the men, who were staring in undisguised interest at her crotch, watching as her companion fingered her.

'See how wet I am?' she asked.

'You're fantastic, Carla,' replied Annabelle.

She slipped her finger out of the excited girl and held it up. It was shiny with wetness. Carla again glanced across at the men. Then, taking Annabelle's hand in her own, she pulled it to her mouth and began to suck it, savouring the taste of her own juices as she stared into their eyes.

Annabelle slid her finger from Carla's mouth and took hold of the younger girl's chin. Pulling her face up to her own. She closed her lips over Carla's, kissing her passionately. Carla responded eagerly, pressing her lips up against Annabelle's and pushing her tongue into the woman's mouth. When they finally broke away, Carla was panting with excitement.

'Let's go eat,' said Annabelle.

Carla made no attempt to button the front of her dress as they rose to leave. She knew that every step she took revealed her crotch, but she didn't care. If that was what Annabelle wanted, then it was fine with her. She gave a wink to the men who had been watching as she passed, aware of their continued interest. Behind her, on the bar, her knickers remained.

In the cab, Annabelle undid the two buttons at the top of Carla's dress, sliding her hand inside and caressing her breast. The girl moaned with pleasure, her nipples hardening at once under the soft touch of her companion.

Carla's flesh was tingling with pleasure as they entered the restaurant, her breasts and crotch barely covered by the half-unbuttoned dress. Throughout the meal the waiters vied for her attention, leaning over her as they served her, their eyes fixed on her firm young breasts.

'You really like showing off your body, don't you?' said Annabelle.

'It's you that's showing it off,' replied Carla. 'I'm just doing as I'm told.'

A hand squeezed her knee beneath the table. 'Yeah, but you're enjoying it, aren't you?'

They finished the meal and took a cab back to Annabelle's hotel. All the way they were necking in the back of the vehicle and somehow more of Carla's buttons became undone as Annabelle's hands roved over her body.

Walking through the hotel lobby, Carla was aware of all eyes on her as she flashed her pubic mound with every step. By the time they reached the lift all conversation in the lobby had ceased.

Even before the lift doors slid closed, Annabelle had the

rest of the dress undone, slipping it from her shoulders and letting it drop to the floor. Carla was naked now, apart from her stockings and shoes, and she responded enthusiastically as Annabelle placed her lips over her own and slid a hand down her belly, feeling for her love bud.

The lift stopped and Carla glanced over Annabelle's shoulder at the floor indicator. It wasn't their floor! The doors slid open and a man stepped inside. He was in his early twenties, with dark hair. Because Carla was pressed into one corner behind Annabelle she realised he had barely noticed her as he climbed in, but now he saw her nudity and his jaw dropped.

Annabelle saw his surprise and, grinning impishly, suddenly stood aside, giving him an unrestricted view of Carla's body. Carla stood quietly and obediently, making no attempt to cover herself, even when Annabelle pulled her forward, moving in behind her and slipping two fingers into her crotch before the astonished man's eyes. They remained like that as the lift ascended, Carla leaning back against her companion, her legs spread, her hips bearing down on Annabelle's fingers in a lewd dance of lust, moaning quietly as the woman's other hand caressed her breast.

The lift stopped once again and the doors slid open. Annabelle removed her fingers from the panting girl's vagina and gave her a shove.

'This is our floor,' she said.

Carla stepped out into the corridor, Annabelle scooping up her discarded dress as she followed. Carla turned, blowing a kiss to the young man as the doors of the lift closed. Then she took Annabelle's hand and allowed herself to be led to the room.

As she stepped inside, Carla reflected on the number of hotel rooms she had been in over the previous weeks. There was a certain smell about them that she had come to recognize, and she found an almost Pavlovian response overwhelming her now. To Carla, hotel rooms were places for fucking in, and the scent of the room immediately triggered a shudder of lust in her.

As soon as the door was closed, Annabelle pushed her back onto the bed.

'You're a proper little exhibitionist and no mistake,' she said, gazing down at Carla's outstretched body. 'Connie would never have gone that far. Did you see the way that guy's crotch was bulging? I thought his pants would give way.'

Carla smiled. 'What now, Annabelle?'

'I think I'll get room service to bring up some drinks.'

'Drinks?' pouted Carla. 'I thought we were going to have some fun. I'm incredibly horny, Annabelle.'

'That's why I'm calling room service,' said Annabelle, picking up the telephone. 'You're going to answer the door.'

'What, like this?'

Annabelle nodded. 'You want to, don't you?'

'I . . . I'm not sure.'

The woman felt for her crotch once more. 'I think you are,' she said.

By the time the knock sounded at the door, Carla was once again gasping with lust, her lovely young body alive with passion from the intimate caresses of her companion. Now, at the sound of the knock, a new thrill ran through her body.

'Right,' said Annabelle softly. 'You going to answer that?'

Carla rose uncertainly to her feet as Annabelle sank into an armchair beside the window. There was a full-length mirror on the wall of the room, and Carla paused to inspect herself.

She looked gorgeous, the stockings merely serving to enhance the fact that she was stark naked. Her breasts stood out, firm and lovely, the nipples protruding deliciously. Down below, her sex lips were swollen by the attentions of Annabelle and her clitoris was like a little bullet, clearly visible between the pink folds of her sex lips.

With her heart hammering in her chest, Carla placed a hand on the doorknob and turned it.

'Room ser—'

The waiter stood, staring in amazement at the beautiful young girl standing in front of him, totally naked, her legs slightly apart, her hand on her hip.

'Come in,' said Carla quietly. 'I've been expecting you.'

On the outside, Carla maintained an air of quiet calm, eyeing the man up and down. Inside, though, her stomach was churning, her sex wet with her juices as she flaunted her body at the waiter.

The man seemed stunned, his feet rooted to the spot, his eyes fixed on Carla's breasts as she stood aside to let him in. Carla took this opportunity to scrutinize him. He was young, younger than her. About eighteen, she guessed, with a slightly innocent air about him. He had short hair and a pleasant face and his tall body, though it made him appear slightly gawky, was also quite muscular.

'Come in,' she urged again.

He stepped into the room. He was holding a tray but, from the way his hands shook, Carla feared he was about to drop it so she took it from him and placed it on a side table.

'Aren't you going to serve my friend her drink?' she asked.

The waiter nodded dumbly, picking up one of the drinks from the tray and taking it across to where Annabelle was sitting. She took it from him, smiling sweetly.

'And mine?'

He picked up the second glass and handed it to Carla.

'Mmm. It's lovely and cool,' she murmured, running the ice-cold glass across her breasts and leaving a smear of condensation. 'Look at the way it's making my nipples stand out.'

'W-will there be anything else?'

'There might be. That's up to you.'

'I beg your pardon?'

Carla moved closer to him so that her breasts were brushing against his shirt. She dropped a hand to his trousers and cupped it around his crotch. His cock was hard as iron, straining against his fly.

'My, but you're excited,' she murmured. 'I think you need a bit of relief.'

'No. I have to go back downstairs.'

But Carla had already dropped to her knees in front of him and was unfastening his fly, oblivious to his protests.

His cock sprang from his pants, standing to attention, the shaft angling upwards like a flagpole. Carla gave a little gasp as she felt how hard he was, her fingers lightly tracing the length of his shaft. He was a good size, and she licked her lips as she examined him, pulling back the foreskin to uncover the thick, purple glans. She couldn't resist tasting it, and her lips closed over the end.

'Ahhh.'

He let out a groan as the wanton young girl began to suck

his knob, ramming it deep inside her mouth, her tongue licking around his shaft as she did so. He tasted of sweat and arousal, and Carla slurped greedily at him, loving the sensation as his weapon twitched violently with every move she made.

She withdrew him from her mouth and gazed up at him.

'What's your name?'

'Alan, Miss.'

'Well, Alan. How do you fancy a fuck?'

'I . . . I have to get back . . .'

But already Carla was dragging him toward the bed by his cock, laying back on the duvet and spreading her legs wide.

'Do you like what you see, Alan?' she asked.

He nodded, his mouth open.

'Take me, then. I'm yours. Ram that lovely great cock of yours into me, Alan.'

He hesitated for a moment longer, then fell on her, his hands mauling at her breasts as he tried to get his erection inside her.

'Take it easy,' she chided. 'There's no hurry. Here, let me guide you in.'

She took hold of his shaft and positioned the end at the entrance to her vagina.

'Now push gently, Alan,' she said. 'Slide it into me. Ah!'

For Carla the sensation was totally delicious as she felt herself penetrated by his hot, hard organ. He rammed it all the way home, with no finesse. Carla didn't mind, though. She liked the idea of having an inexperienced lover to coach and she contracted the muscles of her vagina, smiling at the groan of pleasure this gave.

'Do you have a girlfriend, Alan?' she asked.

'Yes. Sort of.'

'Does she do this to you?' She asked, pressing her hips up against his.

'No.'

'Enjoy me, Alan,' she coaxed. 'Savour me. Fuck me like I was your first. Make me come.'

He began pumping his hips back and forth, his backside rising and falling as he slid his tool in and out of Carla's hot wet cunt. She moaned with pleasure at the sensation, her own hips gyrating in rhythm with his, her breasts shaking back and forth with every stroke.

She glanced across at Annabelle. The woman was sitting forward in her chair, watching intently as the young waiter fucked her escort. Carla winked at her and she smiled back, her eyes fixed on Carla's crotch.

Carla knew instinctively that Alan would not last long. He was too aroused, as the jerkiness of his movements testified. She wondered if it was the first time for him. She hoped it was. To have taken his virginity seemed to her a wonderful thing, a privilege almost, and she thrust up at him with renewed vigour at the thought.

He came with a gasp, his hips ramming hard against her as he filled her vagina with hot, sticky semen. Carla screamed aloud, allowing her own climax to engulf her as the delicious sensation of being filled with spunk overcame her. She wrapped her arms about him, hugging him close to her as their hips continued to crash together, each stroke bringing a new spurt from the end of his throbbing knob.

At last, though, his movements began to slow, and she sensed that he had shot his load. She brought him down gently, moving her hips in a circular motion, groaning quietly as her own excitement ebbed. Soon they were both still, stretched out across the bed, their breath rasping in their throats.

Next moment Carla felt Alan being pulled aside, his cock slipping from her as Annabelle moved him over and knelt down between Carla's thighs. Then the woman began to lap at Carla's cunt, sucking the semen from it and swallowing it down. Carla raised her head to watch as the woman slurped up the viscous white fluid that leaked from deep inside her. Alan watched too, his mouth agape as Annabelle buried her head between the younger girl's thighs and devoured his seed whilst Carla moaned and writhed with pleasure.

'Ah! Ah! Ah!'

Carla's cries rang about the room as a second orgasm racked her body, Annabelle's persistent lapping bringing her to a climax even more exquisite than the one that Alan's cock had triggered.

When Annabelle rose to her feet her lips and chin were smeared with spunk and cunt juices. She turned to Alan, a smile on her face.

'You taste good,' she said. 'Especially mixed with my friend here. She's a wanton little thing, isn't she?'

He nodded dumbly.

'You can go now,' said Annabelle, beginning to unfasten her dress. 'My friend and I have an appointment with a particularly large dildo.'

She pushed the young waiter through the door, closing it firmly behind him. Then she turned slowly, dropping her dress to the floor and approaching the naked lovely who lay waiting for her on the bed.

Chapter Fifteen

When Carla came to the end of the story there was complete silence in the room, all eyes fixed on her naked body. She stood for a moment, waiting for someone to speak, but no-one did. Then she dropped her gaze and realized with a shock what was holding their attention. Almost unconsciously she was moving her hips back and forth, rubbing them over the rough surface of the chain that split her sex lips so blatantly. She tried to stop, biting her lip and closing her eyes, but still her hips ground down against the metal.

'What are you doing?'

The Judge's voice seemed to come from miles away, as if from another world, so lost was Carla in her own pleasure. She didn't know how long she had been masturbating, possibly during most of the telling of the story. What she did know was that the sensation of the chain against her clitoris was giving her a blessed relief from the sexual tension that had been building inside her ever since she had been brought into this room.

'I said, what are you doing?'

Carla opened her eyes to stare blankly at the Judge. Her motions were more violent now as she thrust her pubis down, her hips moving back and forth as if she were being fucked by an invisible lover. She moaned softly to herself, her body alive with desire, her breasts shaking up and down, the nipples puckered into thick brown teats.

'Stop at once or I shall have you punished.'

But it was too late. With shudders and groans Carla was coming, her thrusts turning to jabs as she extracted her pleasure from the hard metal that pressed so deliciously into her crotch. She threw back her head, her mouth wide open, her backside pumping back and forth as the orgasm shook her shapely young frame, oblivious to the lewd exhibition she was making of herself, intent only on her own fulfilment.

It was fully two minutes before she was finally still, her breasts rising and falling as she panted for breath. When at last her motions stopped she let her head fall forward, her face reddening as she contemplated her own disgraceful behaviour before all these people. She looked down at the chain, which was glistening with wetness, drops of her juice dripping from it onto the floor beneath. Then she raised her eyes to look at the Judge.

'You will receive ten strokes of the cane for that behaviour.'

A gasp went up from those watching, but Carla said nothing. She was incapable of being shocked at that moment. All she could think of was the fact that she had just brought herself off, naked and chained, before a roomful of people, and that she had loved every second of it. Not for the first time she wondered if there were any bounds to her promiscuity. Then she realized that the Judge was talking again.

'The court will prepare to administer your punishment,' he said. 'Meanwhile we will hear from the next witness.'

Once again silence descended as the doors were opened. This time it was a woman who was admitted. She was about thirty-five, slim and beautiful with long blonde hair. Her skin was tanned a deep brown and she walked with a swagger, the heels on her shoes making a clacking sound as she sashayed up towards the top table.

Carla knew her at once, and knew too that the story she would have to tell would be yet more damning evidence against her. She felt her face glowing anew as the young woman cast her eyes over her naked body, taking in the sheen of wetness about her puffy sex lips and the prominence of her still hard nipples. She gave a little smile of recognition, then turned to look at the Judge.

'Good evening,' he said. 'May we know your name?'

'Lindy,' she replied. She spoke in a soft voice, her accent betraying her upper class origins.

'Thank you. And do you know why you're here, Lindy?'

'You wanted me to tell you about Carla.'

'And do you recognize Carla?'

'Of course. She's up there, flashing her body as usual. And by the look of her she's just been fucked. Mind you I think she always looks like that, probably because she usually just has been.'

'What do you mean by that?'

'She's a slut. That cunt of hers has had more cocks in it than most people have had hot dinners. She's never happy unless she's stretched out on her back with her legs open. Or in half a dozen other positions.'

'You're not exactly an angel yourself,' spat Carla.

'That's rich,' replied Lindy. 'Look at you. Most men probably don't know what you look like with clothes on.'

'Most men probably wouldn't want to see you with your clothes off.'

'Slut!'

'Bitch!'

Bang!

The Judge's gavel descended with some force, bringing a sudden end to the exchange.

'That's enough!' he barked. 'We are not here for a slanging match. Now, Lindy, I believe you have a tale to tell us. How did you meet this young woman?'

'At my father's house. He had a penchant for little floozies like her. It's a weakness of his that has developed since my mother left him.'

'So she came to your home?'

'That's right. Not the manor of course, to our holiday home on Kofru.'

'Kofru?'

'It's a small Greek island. Daddy owns most of it. He had a villa built there and that's where he goes to relax.'

'And where he took Mrs Wilde?'

'Oh, she's a Mrs, is she?' sniffed the girl. 'I pity the poor husband. He must be very tolerant.'

'Nevertheless, he took her there.'

'He didn't take her precisely. She turned up, like they always do.'

'They?'

'His little playthings. She wasn't the first. But at least the others took some time off occasionally. This one just went at it like a rabbit. And unlike the others it wasn't just a job for her. She really loved it, you could tell. She's got the hots for anything in trousers, that one, and a few in skirts as well.'

'Tell us what happened.'

'It began as it went on. She turned up totally starkers at the front door, stripped off again during the party that evening and went on to fuck everyone in sight. Then next day she was at it again, posing for dirty pictures, then

letting all and sundry get into her . . .' She broke off and
giggled.

'What is it?'

'I was going to say get into her knickers, but I don't think
she's got any. She's a total slut.'

'That's not fair,' said Carla indignantly. 'I was only doing
what I was asked to do. You certainly played your part in
what went on.'

'That's a lie. You just gave yourself to those men.'

The Judge brought his gavel down again.

'This is getting us nowhere,' he said. 'Now, Mrs Wilde.
You have heard the accusations. Do you wish to give your
side of the story?'

'What's the point? Nobody's going to believe my word
against hers.'

'Even so, this is your opportunity to tell it as you saw it.'

Carla stared out at the sea of faces upturned towards her.
She gave a little shrug. After all, she had nothing to lose.
She might as well tell the truth.

'It all began with a call from the agency,' she said. 'Only
this time the job was a bit different . . .'

Chapter Sixteen

The call had come one afternoon, whilst Carla was alone in the house. It had taken her by surprise. It was most unusual for the agency to ring her, since her availability for the work was so irregular. When she heard the soft tones of the woman at the other end, her heart leapt.

'Carla? Is that you?'

'Yes.'

'Is it safe to talk?'

'Yes. I'm on my own.'

'We've had a rather unusual request, and I think you'd be eminently suitable.'

'What is it?'

'There's a man. A millionaire. He's absolutely loaded, mansion in the country, own yacht, Greek island. Just the kind of guy any girl would be after.'

'The money's not important.'

'I know. I long ago realized you do this for pleasure. I get very good reports about you from my clients. But that's why you're perfect for this job. I need someone to whom the money doesn't matter. Who won't screw things up by overdoing her act. From what I hear, Carla, with you it's not an act.'

Carla found herself blushing. 'Go on,' she said.

'Our man, who'll remain nameless for now, is entertaining some very important people on his island over a weekend.'

'A weekend? You know I can't manage that.'

'Why not? You only need to invent an old school friend who's invited you down to the country for a couple of days. Surely your husband won't object.'

'A whole weekend?' Carla's pulse quickened as the idea sunk in. A whole weekend. On a Greek island with a group of men. The idea was a thrilling one.

'How would I get there?'

'He'd fly you down first class. Then a boat would pick you up and ferry you across.'

'When?'

'Two weeks' time. Say you'll do it, Carla. You won't regret it.'

Carla hesitated for a moment longer. Then her mind was made up.

'All right,' she said. 'I'll do it.'

And so it was that she found herself gazing from the window of the small passenger aeroplane as it turned in towards the runway in the Mediterranean sunshine. The woman had been right, Eric had swallowed the story about the old school friend with hardly a murmur. In fact, Carla suspected that it gave him an opportunity to pursue his own extra-marital needs. And now the whole weekend stretched before her, and her flesh tingled as she imagined what was to come.

The aircraft made a smooth touchdown and was soon taxiing towards the apron. Then the engines died and Carla rose from her seat.

At the foot of the first-class gangplank was a long dark

stretch limousine, a chauffeur with a peaked cap standing beside it. As Carla reached the bottom of the steps, a young woman stepped forward.

'Excuse please. You are Carla?'

She was tall and pretty, with a willowly figure clad in tight jeans and a short blouse that left her midriff bare. She had long dark hair and spoke with a Greek accent.

'That's me,' replied Carla.

'Please. The car.'

The girl indicated the shiny vehicle, and as she did so the driver opened the rear door, holding out his hand to take her bag from her.

Carla stepped into the spacious interior and the girl climbed in beside her. The driver closed the door with a click. Inside, the air conditioned car was cool and fresh after the harsh glare of the Mediterranean sun, and Carla settled back into the soft seat as the driver let in the clutch and they purred away.

'What about Customs?' she asked.

'Mr Gambati has seen to it,' the girl replied.

They drove down a narrow road through dry olive groves, neither woman speaking as the car sped along. Before long they rounded a corner and there, stretched out before them, was the sparkling blue of the sea. The car came to a halt beside a jetty and the chauffeur climbed out, once again holding the door open for the two of them.

The boat was a smart cabin cruiser with two powerful outboards at the back. At the wheel was a surly looking Greek, who watched them board without speaking. The chauffeur placed Carla's bag on the deck, then gave a little salute and withdrew. The motors grumbled into life, and a boy appeared on the shore. He ran to unfasten the moorings and throw the ropes on board. Then the man gunned the motor and they were off, roaring across the water, a long, white wake stretching out behind them.

Carla stood beside the helmsman, revelling in the way the wind blew her hair back as they sped along. Before long the jetty was no more than a pinpoint behind them as they sped out to sea.

'There it is.'

They had been going for about half an hour when the girl gave the shout, pointing at a patch of green that had risen above the horizon on the port bow. As they came closer, Carla began to make out the details of the island. It was about three miles across, a hill dominating the centre. Near the foot of the hill, something glowed white in the sunshine. Carla picked up a pair of binoculars that lay on a table beside her and placed them to her eyes. At once the white object revealed itself as a large, modern looking house.

The girl said a few words to the helmsman, who nodded silently, touching the wheel so that they veered towards the left. They were much closer now, less than a mile away, and the building was starting to disappear behind the trees. Ahead Carla saw a small beach, its golden sands quite deserted. At the same moment the man cut the throttle and they were gliding silently through the water.

They came to a stop about a hundred yards offshore and the man threw an anchor over the bow. It dragged for a moment, then seemed to catch, and the boat's momentum carried it gently round until it came to a stop facing away from the beach. As it did so the girl undid her blouse, throwing it down onto the deck. Her jeans quickly followed and soon she stood clad in the briefest of bikinis.

'Come. We swim,' she said to Carla.

'But I haven't got my costume.'

'That's okay. Who's to see you except this guy? He won't care.'

Carla looked over the side. There was no doubt about it, the sea looked very inviting. It was a lovely azure blue colour, so clear that she could see all the way to the sandy bottom. She glanced at the helmsman, who was fiddling with the engines.

'Okay,' she said.

She unzipped her dress and pulled it down her hips and off. Underneath she wore matching white bra and panties. She reached behind and unhooked the bra, releasing her breasts, which stood our firmly with no sign of sagging. She took a final furtive glance at the helmsman. He had stopped tinkering and was sitting back against the bulkhead watching her. For a second she hesitated. Then she slipped her fingers into the waistband of the panties and pulled them off, dropping them onto the deck.

She stood for a second, her hands on her hips, her face upturned towards the golden warmth of the sun, posing for him. Giving him a good look at her charms. Then she leapt agilely up onto the boat's rail and launched herself into a dive, her body cutting cleanly into the water with barely a splash.

The water was clear and warm, enveloping her like a great green shroud as she swam down. She turned and gazed upwards. Even despite the blur caused by the pressure of water on her eyes she could clearly see the outline of the boat above her. At that moment a lithe figure splashed into the water and began swimming down to where she was. She watched as the lovely young girl approached, waiting until she had nearly reached her, then kicking for the surface, breaking into the open air her lungs straining for air.

The girl came up next to her. 'You stayed under a long time,' she said. 'I was starting to worry.'

Carla smiled. 'I was swimming champ at school,' she explained. 'Never lost the knack. Come on, I'll race you to the beach.'

The two girls headed off at great speed. When they reached the sand Carla ran up the beach with her companion in hot pursuit. There followed a hilarious game of tag at the water's edge, each of the girls shrieking and laughing as they chased one another back and forth. Eventually Carla collapsed against a tree at the water's edge, gasping for breath. The girl joined her, the pair of them dripping wet.

For a while they said nothing, content merely to regain their breath. Then the girl turned to face Carla.

'You are here for the weekend?'

'Yes.'

'You are a whore, I think?'

Carla stared at her for a moment, then laughed.

'There are some that would put it that way, I guess.'

'You would not?'

'I'd prefer to call myself a paid companion.'

'Yet these men who are your companions, they fuck you?'

'Yes.'

The girl reached out a hand, cupping Carla's breast and caressing it lightly.

'You are very beautiful.'

'Thank you. So are you.'

'May I kiss you?'

'If you like.'

The girl moved closer and, stretching her neck forward, planted a kiss on Carla's lips. She hesitated for a moment, staring into the English girl's eyes. Then she kissed her again.

The third time she didn't remove her lips. Instead they parted and Carla felt her little tongue forcing its way into her mouth. The girl tasted wonderful and she pulled her close, feeling the cold wetness of her bikini top as it pressed against her own bare breasts.

They continued to kiss, their mouths locked together, Carla pressed back against the rough bark of the tree by the Greek girl. Then she felt a small, delicate hand run down her back, over her hips and delve down between her thighs. She moved back a little to allow the girl access, shivering slightly as the fingers ran over her pubic mound and down to the centre of her desires.

'Mmmm.'

Carla's gasp was muffled by the kiss, but there was no mistaking the shudder of pleasure that ran through her as the girl's fingers penetrated her vagina, sliding inside her, delving deep into the heat of her sex.

The girl began to frig her, her fingers moving with a steady rhythm. Carla slumped back against the tree, widening her stance and pressing her pubis hard against the slim, delicate digits that were bringing her such delicious pleasure.

The girl broke their kiss, standing back from Carla, her fingers still embedded inside her. She watched as the naked girl writhed under her touch, her breath coming in short gasps, her hips pumping back and forth. Carla stared at her, then across at the boat, where the man was standing in the bow, a pair of powerful looking binoculars trained on them. The thought of the man seeing her thus aroused served only as a fresh stimulus to the wanton young girl, and she moaned aloud, her backside pounding against the tree as her hips thrust back and forth.

Suddenly there was a roar of powerful engines from the centre of the bay. Carla looked up sharply, just in time to see the boat surge forward, leaning hard over as it turned away from them and headed out to sea.

'Hey!' Carla's pleasure was momentarily forgotten as she stepped forward, allowing the fingers to slip from inside her. 'Hey, where's he going?'

'Back. He'd delivered his cargo.'

'But my bag's on board. And all my clothes.'

'Don't worry. They're safe with him.'

'But I'm stark naked.'

'That is how Mr Gambati wanted you delivered.'

'You mean I've got to go up to the house like this?'

'What is the problem? You are a whore, aren't you?'

'Escort,' said Carla petulantly.

'Escort, whore, what's the difference? You fuck for money. Or is it for money?'

'What do you mean?'

'You like sex, I think. Just now, you were going to come?'

Carla flushed. 'Yes.'

The girl laughed. 'I think Mr Gambati will like you very much. Now you must go. They are expecting you.'

'Couldn't we finish what we were doing?'

'What I was doing.'

'All right then, what you were doing.'

'You want me to make you come?'

'Yes.'

The girl laughed again and shook her head.

'You will come plenty of times at Mr Gambati's,' she said. 'Besides, he will prefer if you arrive feeling horny. Now you must go.'

'Aren't you coming?'

'No. My house is on the other side of the island.'

'But I don't know the way.'

'It's easy. Just follow the path. You can see the house from miles away.'

'What if I meet someone?'

'Everyone on the island works for Mr Gambati. You will not be stopped.'

Carla grabbed the girl's hand. 'And will I see you again?'

'It is possible. Would you like to.'

'Yes.'

'You like me to use my fingers on you again? Maybe my mouth?'

Carla pulled the girl closer. 'Yes, please.'

The girl broke away, laughing. 'Maybe, little English girl. But now you must go to the house and get fucked. And I must go home. Goodbye.'

'Wait! You haven't even told me your name,' called Carla. But it was too late. Already the girl was running off down the beach. A moment later she rounded a promontory and was lost to sight.

Carla glanced about her at the deserted beach, then down at her naked body. Her nipples were still erect after the treatment she had received from the girl and she could feel her sex lips twitching slightly as her arousal ebbed from her.

It seemed there was nowhere else to go but to seek out the mysterious Mr Gambati.

With a sigh she turned away from the sea and headed up the path, wondering what fate awaited her at the house.

Chapter Seventeen

The sun was sinking in the sky as Carla made her way down the dusty path towards the white house on the hill. It still retained its warmth, though, and felt good on her bare breasts and belly. She walked quickly, glancing from left to right as she did so, convinced that she might meet someone at any moment. She felt extremely vulnerable, a feeling that was hardly surprising in the circumstances. After all she was alone in a foreign place, totally naked and with absolutely no belongings whatsoever. It was the loneliest position she had ever been in, and she trembled slightly as she contemplated her situation.

At the same time, though, there was an unmistakably erotic aspect to her position. They had engineered it so that she would arrive at her client's house completely in his power, and unambiguously available to him. She ran her hands down her body, feeling the silky smoothness of her skin, the soft pliability of her breasts and the heat and wetness between her thighs. She thought of the girl on the beach, who had called her a whore and then touched her up so deliciously. She contemplated the girl's description of her. In a way she was just that, a whore who sold her body to men for money. She wondered what her friends on the coffee and bridge party circuits would think if they could see her now, brazenly striding down this path with all her charms on display?

In the distance she could see the house. About half a mile away, she estimated. It wouldn't take her long to get there. She was setting a fast pace and the ground was thankfully soft under her bare feet.

Suddenly there was a loud rustling noise behind her, accompanied by the sound of hooves on the ground. She swung round to see a horseman emerging from the trees just a few yards away. The rider was a young man, his skin a dark brown. He wore jeans and a T-shirt, a sort of cowboy hat perched on his head. When he saw the girl his eyebrows rose and he reined his horse round in her direction.

For a second Carla almost panicked and ran, but even as the thought crossed her mind she realized the futility of it. On his horse he could ride her down easily. Better to stand where she was and brazen it out. She watched him approach, her hands by her sides.

'Hello,' he said brightly. 'You English?'

'How did you know?' Carla managed to keep her voice steady.

He laughed, revealing a row of perfect white teeth.

'Your skin is so pale. The marks of your bikini hardly show. Or maybe you never wear a bikini?'

She reddened. 'I lost my suitcase.'

'No matter. I like you like that.'

'What do you want?'

'To ask where you are going. We do not get many beautiful Englishwomen on this island, especially naked ones.'

'I'm going to the big house.'

'Mr Gambati's?'

'Yes. I'm his guest.'

'What a strange way to visit. Come, I'll give you a ride.'

'It's all right. I can walk.'

'Better to ride. Come up here.'

He sat back on his saddle and patted the space in front of him.

'I'm all right, honest.'

'Ride.'

He spurred his horse forward and took hold of her arm. Carla resisted for a moment, then relaxed.

'All right,' she said. 'Help me on.'

He removed his foot from the stirrup and she put hers in its place. Then, with a little help from him, she hoisted herself aboard, swinging her leg over in front of him, aware that she was affording him a perfect view of her sex as she did so.

She settled into the saddle as he wrapped one arm about her waist. Then he dug his heels into the horse's flanks and they moved off.

The horse moved with an easy gait. The feel of the strong animal between her legs felt good to Carla, a feeling enhanced by the way the pommel on the front of the saddle was in contact with her clitoris, so that every movement sent a delicious sensation though her.

The man said nothing as they rode, but all of a sudden Carla felt his hand begin to move from her waist up toward her rib cage. She placed her hand over his, trying to stop him, but he paid no attention, his hand creeping higher and higher until it was brushing the underside of her breast. Then he moved it higher still, closing his palm over her succulent orb.

'Stop it,' she said quietly. Someone might see.'

'There's nobody around,' he replied. 'You have lovely breasts, so smooth and soft, and your nipples so hard. Don't you like me feeling them?'

'You mustn't' she said lamely. But she did like it. She liked it very much, as she did the constant rub of leather against her love bud. Why was it, she wondered, that her body was so sensitive, that the slightest touch could make her juices flow like they did? Being naked didn't help. Having a man see her with her breasts, crotch and backside bared was strangely thrilling, especially in so exposed a spot. He squeezed her breast, making her sigh and lean back against him. She could feel the hardness of his cock pressing into her back, and she longed to take it in her hands.

'Couldn't we stop for a while?' she asked him.

'Why should we stop?'

'I thought maybe I could relieve some of the tension in you.'

'Tension?'

'Your cock is hard.'

'I think you have tension too.'

'I do.'

He laughed again. 'You like what my horse and my hands do to you?

'Yes.'

He squeezed again. 'To stop would be very nice. To fuck maybe. But you are Mr Gambati's guest. He would not be pleased if I took you without his permission.'

'I don't belong to Mr Gambati.'

'On this island everything belongs to Mr Gambati, including little naked Englishwomen. Maybe later he will allow me to have you. For now, we ride.'

The words sounded odd to Carla. So she belonged to Mr Gambati here, and her favours were his to bestow. It was an outrageous concept, yet one she found extremely erotic. It was as if she was some kind of harem girl reporting to her new master, who would then use her as he saw fit. And despite her desire to give herself to this personable young man, she was forbidden to do so. Gambati and Gambati alone would decide who could enjoy the pleasures of her body. She gave a little sigh of pleasure at the prospect and let her head rest on the man's shoulder, revelling in his caresses.

The house was reached up a long, winding drive. On either side were well cultivated lawns and flower beds. Beside one of these an ancient gardener stood, watching with some interest as they passed. The rider seemed oblivious to the watcher though, continuing to intimately caress his passenger whilst, for her part, Carla was too turned on to care who saw her.

Outside the front door the horse halted. Carla turned and kissed the man on the mouth.

'Thank you,' she said. 'I hope we meet again.'

'I too,' he said.

Carla raised herself up on her stirrups, her face reddening as she saw the imprint her sex had made on the saddle, a perfect outline of her open slit that glistened in the sunshine. She swung her leg over the horse's neck, then slid to the ground. As soon as she was off, the man reined the horse around and, without another word, cantered off down the drive. Carla stood watching him until he disappeared from view, then turned back to the house.

Her heart was beating fast as she approached the door. She glanced up at the edifice before her. It was a large house, built in the local style, but with added balconies and terraces. There was a bell-push beside the door and, taking a deep breath, she pressed it.

She waited for some time, then there was a movement behind the door and the sound of a key being turned. The door swung open and a woman confronted her. She was tall and stern-faced, clad in a black uniform, her hair tied up above her head. She wore a pair of horn-rimmed spectacles and she stared down her nose at Carla in obvious distaste.

'Yes?'

'I'm here to see Mr Gambati.' Once again Carla found her voice breaking slightly under the woman's gaze.

'From the agency, I suppose?' the woman spoke with clipped tones. She was clearly British, and had the demeanour of an old-fashioned servant.

'Yes.'

'Follow me.'

The woman turned and set off down a long corridor. Carla followed. Behind her she heard the door close with a bang.

The house was designed for the hot climate of the island, with white walls and bare stone floors, the furniture standing on thick Persian rugs. The ornamentation was modern, large oil canvases were dotted about the walls and pieces of strangely-shaped sculpture rested on ledges and in niches in the walls. Carla glanced into the rooms as they passed. All about were servants making preparations for what was obviously to be a large party. The servants paused to stare at the naked girl as she went by, exchanging glances with one another and making Carla blush.

The woman took her up a flight of stairs, then another, then down yet another corridor to a door at the end.

'This is your room,' she said, pushing open the door. 'You are to bathe and be ready to come with me to meet the master in fifteen minutes. Do not be late.'

'Are there any clothes in here?' Carla asked hopefully.

'The master will instruct you what you are to wear. Remember you are not a guest. You are being paid to attend.'

With that the woman turned and left, closing the door behind her and leaving Carla alone.

She glanced about the room. It was bare apart from a bed and a small table beside it. On the bed was a duvet cover and nothing else.

On the far side was another door, and Carla ventured across, pushing it open. Behind was a bathroom, with shower, sink and toilet. Beside the shower was a towel rack, on which hung expensive-looking towels. Carla examined them and noted that they were tethered to the wall by thick silk cords. Clearly every effort was being made to stop her hiding her nudity.

She turned on the tap in the shower and a stream of warm water cascaded down onto her. She picked up a bar of soap from the rack beside her and began lathering her skin, washing the salt of the sea from her body. Once she was satisfied she shampooed her hair, then stepped from the shower and dried herself carefully. There was a hairdrier affixed to the wall and she used this to dry her locks, combing them out as she did so. When this was done she crossed to a full-length mirror on the wall and examined herself critically.

There was a small pair of scissors beside the sink and she used them to trim her pubic hair, shaping it into a neat triangle and cutting it short about her sex lips. As she did so she smiled wryly to herself. That was one part of her anatomy that she had never had to worry about in public before.

As she walked back into the bedroom the door opened. No knock, she reflected, but there again all the normal rules were changed here. After all, what was there to worry about? Not whether she was decent, certainly.

The woman ran her eye over Carla, sending a shiver down the young girl's spine as her cold eyes took in every inch of her body. Then she turned.

'Come,' she said, heading off down the corridor.

Carla followed obediently, padding along behind the tall, angular figure. They descended to the first floor, and stopped outside an imposing pair of doors. The woman knocked.

'Enter.'

The woman opened the door and indicated for Carla to go through, then closed it behind her. She found herself in a large office, with an imposing-looking desk at one end, behind which sat a man.

'Come closer.' He had a booming voice with a note of authority in it that she knew at once demanded full obedience. She walked across the room until she was standing just in front of the desk.

'You must be Carla.'

Even sitting down she could see he was a big man. About fifty, she estimated, but still with a full head of hair. His eyes were dark and piercing and he ran them over her body.

'Yes, Mr Gambati.'

'And what do you think of my little place?'

'It's very . . . impressive.'

'And how have they been treating you?'

'Apart from taking my clothes away?'

He laughed. 'A little whim of mine, I'm afraid. I like the thought of having you in my power, and being naked increases that power, as I'm sure you'll concur. How do you feel about being controlled?'

'You're paying the bill, Mr Gambati.'

'And that's it? Just the money?'

She hesitated. 'No.'

'Being like that makes you horny?'

'Yes.'

'So Maria and Alex were right. Good.'

'Maria and Alex?'

'Your guides since you arrived here. They're brother and sister, you know. Maria is a very efficient secretary and Alex is an excellent horseman.'

'So Alex was expecting me?'

'Of course. I wanted him to test whether you were as lascivious as the agency said you were. You didn't disappoint. Apparently your cunt leaked all over his saddle.'

Carla blushed. 'I didn't know I was being tested,' she said.

'Of course not. If you had known Alex was anything other than a peasant you might have reacted differently. Especially if you had known he was working for me. As it was you behaved exactly as I'd hoped. Even asked him to screw you, so I hear.'

'I didn't exactly ask in so many words.'

'I know what you said.'

He rose from the desk and walked round to where she was standing. She had been right about his size. He towered over her, taller by more than a foot.

He placed a hand over her breast, smiling as the nipple

hardened at once. 'Who are you, Carla?' he asked. 'And what are you doing here?'

'I'm an escort. And you sent for me.'

He laughed aloud. 'I guess that's all the answer I'm entitled to,' he said. 'Now do you know what you're here for?'

'To help entertain you and your guests.'

'In any way I say.'

'In any way you say.'

'Good. Tonight we have a big party. Lots of important people are being shipped in. You are to make yourself available to them.'

'Yes, Mr Gambati.'

'One other thing. My daughter Lindy is here this weekend. She doesn't approve of my propensity for young women like yourself, and she may well take an interest in you that might not be too friendly. However, she is my daughter, and she's the apple of my eye, so you are to do whatever she asks of you. Do you understand?'

'Yes, Mr Gambati.'

'Right. Now, for tonight's party I have found a dress for you to wear. You will find it in your room when you return.'

Carla gave a little sigh of relief. Her enforced nudity was highly arousing to her, but at the same time extremely embarrassing. The thought of being able to cover herself at last was a welcome one.

'Trouble is,' went on Gambati, 'the dress is one of Lindy's and she may not take too kindly to your wearing it. May even demand it back.'

Carla eyed him. There was no doubt that he could easily have bought her a dress for the evening, or asked her to bring her own. Indeed there was such a dress in the bag she had been forced to abandon on the boat. There was clearly some kind of ulterior motive in making her wear his daughter's dress, and she wasn't at all sure that the decision had been made in her own interest.

'Now,' said Gambati. 'Do you fully understand your role for this evening?'

'Yes, Mr Gambati.'

'Good. Now bend forward over my desk, please.'

'Pardon?'

'Bend over the desk. I intend to fuck you, young lady.'

The words had come so out of the blue that Carla was struck dumb for a second. Then she pulled herself together. After all, it was her body that Gambati was paying for. She stepped forward until the bevelled edge of the desk was pressed against her bare pubis. Then she leaned forward, spreading her legs and pressing her bottom backwards as she did so, aware that this gave him perfect access to her sex. The wood felt cold and hard against her bare flesh as she pressed her breasts down onto its surface.

She felt him run his fingers down the crack of her backside, giving a start when he traced the outline of her nether lips.

'Still wet, I see,' he said. 'Good.'

Carla heard the sound of a zip as she pressed her cheek against the wood. The whole thing was rather clinical, she thought. She would gladly have sucked him if he had asked, but, since he was calling the shots, she was happy to comply with his methods.

'Oh!'

She gave a little cry as something thick and hot nuzzled up against her sex. Then fingers began to prise open her love hole. She pushed back her behind once again, encouraging him to penetrate her, and as she did so he pressed hard, his thick glans driving insistently against the mouth of her vagina.

Suddenly, he was inside, sliding his cock into her as far as it would go, moving forwards with short jabbing thrusts until she felt his stomach pressing against the soft globes of her backside.

He began to screw her, thrusting his hips hard against her so that her body banged against the edge of the desk. Carla clung tightly to the wood as he slammed into her. She had never been taken with such force, all the weight of his large body thumping against her small frame, almost taking her breath away.

Despite the violence of her lover, Carla was instantly aroused. The nudity, the fingering she had received from Maria on the beach and the exquisite pleasure of the horse ride had all combined in raising the sexual tension within her. Now, the sensation of a man's cock rutting deep inside her was precisely what she needed and she felt her own orgasm beginning to well up inside her.

The assault went on unabated, each stroke forcing her clitoris down against the hard edge of the wood and sending shocks of pleasure coursing through her body. She was sweating now, her breasts slapping down on the desktop and leaving circular marks of perspiration behind on the polished surface.

Carla was in her element, doing what she enjoyed most, stretched out naked with a thick cock inside her. She began to moan, the sounds coming out as rhythmic grunts as the man pounded against her backside, each stroke driving the breath from her lungs. Her cunt was on fire now, the muscles caressing the heavy weapon that filled her, as if it was trying to suck the sperm from his balls.

Then she felt his muscles go tense and heard a sharp intake of breath. She pressed back harder against him, urging him on, dying for the sensation of his orgasm, and for her own which she knew would follow almost at once.

All at once she gave a shout of pleasure as she felt him come, his cock filling her up with his spunk. She responded with a glorious orgasm of her own, hoarse grunts escaping from her throat once more as he pounded the breath out of her.

She stayed where she was, prostrate over the desk, until the last of his seed had spurted from his twitching cock. Only then did he withdraw and allow her to straighten up. She was panting hard, a rivulet of sweat running down her neck, between her heaving breasts and over her belly, disappearing into the dark thatch of her pubic hair. She threw back her hair and stood watching as he fastened his trousers.

He pressed a bell-push on the wall, and almost at once the door opened and the woman servant came in. Carla wondered at what she must think of her, her body shiny with sweat, her hair a mess, a tell-tale trickle of semen running down her thigh, but the woman betrayed no emotion, simply indicating the door.

'Come along,' she said.

And Carla padded out after her, pausing only to glance back at Gambati, who was settled behind his desk once more, working away as if nothing had happened.

Chapter Eighteen

The party began at eight o'clock sharp that evening. Long before that, though, Carla had been taken downstairs and given a guided tour by the housekeeper. It was clearly going to be a big event. There was a large terrace set out for dancing, with a five-piece band tuning up. The dining room contained rows of tables laden with delicious-looking food. One room was set up as a bar, with dozens of busy barmen and waiters putting the finishing touches to the decor. A further room had cushions and mattresses strewn about the floor, the lighting extremely dim. Carla was instructed to be close to the front door when the guests began arriving to greet them and ensure they were comfortable.

She stood in the cloakroom, making a final check of her appearance. The dress was lovely, in sheer black silk that clung to her contours. It was held up by a single velet ribbon tied in a bow about her neck and fastened to the bust in front, the low cut of the garment revealing her cleavage beautifully. The skirt was slit up to her thigh on one side so that, as she walked, the full length of her slender leg was revealed. They had given her nothing to wear beneath it, a fact that did not surprise her.

The guests began arriving promptly, ferried up from wherever their boats were being landed in a variety of vehicles. Carla didn't know how many cars, trucks and vans there were on the island, but she guessed that most of them had been commandeered for the evening. Some people even came in by helicopter, their searchlights cutting through the night as they droned over the house.

It was certainly a grand gathering. Men in black tie or outrageous Italian suits, whilst the women wore some of the most stunning gowns Carla had ever seen. All had an air of affluence about them, and Carla recognized some faces as high ranking government officials and members of the aristocracy.

Despite the high power of the gathering, Carla took to her duties with ease, greeting the new arrivals and showing them about the house, then going back for more. For the first hour she was run off her feet, flitting to and from the entrance hall, often having to avoid the gropes of the male guests as they brushed her breasts and backside with their hands in apparently accidental encounters.

At last, though, the flow of arrivals dwindled to a trickle and Carla was able to begin mixing with the guests in the bar and on the terrace. Wherever she went she got admiring looks, and a number of men asked her to dance, sweeping her across the floor, their hands roaming over her body. She wondered if they knew what she was there for, and that her instructions were to please them in any way they wished. She suspected not for, apart from some fairly heavy petting and a man who managed to slide his hand into the slit of her skirt and caress her bottom, no real advance was made to her.

Time passed and Carla began really to enjoy herself. She had a few drinks, but was careful to moderate her intake. The dancers were becoming less inhibited now, and as the band upped the tempo there was much hilarity on the floor. The bar too was filled with noise and laughter. At one point she looked into the darkened room where the mattresses had been laid out. The air in there was heavy with strange scents, the occupants stretched out on the floor, some in tight embraces. Across the far side of the room Carla saw a couple who appeared to be screwing, though it was impossible to be certain in the gloom.

Dinner was announced and the guests descended on the food, clearing the tables in what seemed only minutes. Carla collected a plateful and wandered out onto the terrace. Outside the band had slowed its tempo and people sat around at tables or on the ground, enjoying their food. Carla found a place on a wall that overlooked a large swimming pool and was joined there by a handsome young man who introduced himself as Nick and who soon had her giggling at his jokes.

It was just as Carla was finishing her meal and considering moving on that things suddenly changed. Nick had offered her a strawberry from his plate and she was eating it out of his fingers when she became aware of a figure watching them.

'Nick?'

'Oh, hi Lindy. Where have you been?'

'Where have you been, more likely. I've been looking everywhere for you. I thought we were going to smoke some stuff.'

'Soon enough. Have you had anything to eat? The food's great, isn't it, Carla?'

'Who the hell's Carla?'

'This is Carla. We've just been chatting, haven't we?'

Carla nodded, eyeing the girl with some trepidation. Lindy, she remembered, was the name of Gambati's daughter. The girl was extremely beautiful, with long golden hair and a figure that would have made a supermodel envious. Her eyes were deepest green and they were fixed directly on Carla.

'Carla, eh,' she said slowly. 'And who invited you, Carla?'

'Mr Gambati.'

'And who are you with?'

'Nobody.'

'Nobody?'

'I'm kind of a hostess. Here to help entertain the guests.'

'Oh I see. You're one of Daddy's whores.'

'Steady on Lindy,' said Nick. 'She's a nice girl.'

'Is that so? How did Daddy find you, Carla?'

'Through an agency,' said Carla quietly.

'What kind of agency?'

'An escort agency.'

'You see? She's a high-class tart. And has Daddy fucked you yet, Carla?'

'Why don't you ask him?' asked Carla, suddenly annoyed by the woman's attitude.

'Don't get smart with me, darling. It's you I'm asking. Now tell me, has he had his cock in you?'

Carla dropped her gaze. 'Yes.'

'From behind across his desk, I'll wager. That's how he likes his young girls. Am I right?'

'Yes.'

'There you are, Nick. Do you need any more proof?'

Carla glanced about her nervously. All around them conversations had stopped as people listened to what was being said. Now the trio was the centre of attention and across the floor she could see that Gambati himself was one of those taking an interest in the conversation.

'I . . . I'd better go and make sure the guests inside are

happy,' she said, and turned to leave. But before she could, a hand grasped her arm.

'Wait a minute!' said Lindy. 'Come here, you.'

Reluctantly Carla turned back to face Lindy.

'Where did you get that dress?'

'Carla's heart sank. 'Mr Gambati lent it to me.'

'Really? And did he tell you where it came from?'

'He said it belonged to his daughter.'

'Damned right it does. What the hell are you doing wearing it? Didn't you bring your own?'

'I did, but the man on the boat drove off with my bag.'

'Even so, you could have worn what you came in.'

'I didn't come in anything.'

'You must have been wearing something.'

'No. Maria asked me to go for a swim, and I didn't have a costume. So I went in nude. Then the man took the boat away.'

Carla looked about at the party guests once more. There was complete silence now as all strained to hear what was being said. Many of the women were shaking their heads with disgust, whilst most of the men looked on eagerly.

'So you turned up at my father's house absolutely starkers?'

'Yes.'

'Then you had the cheek to just borrow my dress.'

'I'm sorry. I would have asked had I known who you were.'

'That's all a bit late though, isn't it?'

'I suppose so.'

'You'd better give it back, then, hadn't you?'

'All right. I'll bring it to your room when the party's over.'

'Not when the party's over. Now.'

Carla stared at her. 'But I have to stay at the party. To entertain the guests.'

'Of course you do, but not in that dress. Take it off. Now!'

Carla stared about her, panic rising inside her. The girl must know she wore nothing underneath. The tightness of the silk against the curves of her body betrayed that. Yet she clearly intended that Carla remove the dress here and now, in the middle of the party. She gazed pleadingly at Gambati, but he was saying nothing, simply watching the scene unfold.

'I can't,' she said.

'Of course you can. You only have to undo the knot behind your neck. Here, I'll help you.'

So saying, Lindy moved closer to Carla and placed her hands behind the girl's neck. Carla knew now that she was beaten, and that Lindy would have her way whatever she said. She knew too that there was no point in resisting. Gambati had given her her orders and had warned her of Lindy's probable reaction. All she could do now was stand and wait whilst Lindy busied herself with the knot at the back of her neck.

The fastening came undone at once, and Lindy pulled the ties forward, allowing them to drop. At once the bodice of the dress fell, and a whisper went around the party guests as Carla's breasts were revealed to them, pale and plump in the terrace lights. Carla's eyes dropped, her face red as she saw how hard her nipples were. Then she looked up at Lindy again.

'All the way off,' said the young woman.

This time Carla did not wait for Lindy to intervene. She dropped her hands to the sides of the dress and gave them a tug. All that was holding the dress in place was the curve of her hips, and a single pull was enough to make the material slide down her body and fall in a heap at her ankles. Carla was totally nude now, apart from her shoes and she stood, her eyes cast down, as the crowd took in her beautiful young body.

'Give me the dress.'

Carla stepped from the garment, then stooped down and picked it up, handing it to the triumphant Lindy, who took it from her.

'That's better,' she said. 'You can spend the rest of the evening like that. Being naked is much more convenient for fucking anyhow, and I'm sure there's a few guys here will be keen to fuck you now they know you're available. Have fun, darling.'

She ran a hand down over Carla's breast, squeezing it softly. Then she turned and walked off into the crowd, leaving the naked Carla gazing after her.

The music started once more, and the guests resumed their conversations. Carla was left on her own, feeling very conspicuous amongst all the finely dressed guests. She contemplated returning to her room, but feared that would offend Gambati, who was now conversing with his guests once more, apparently unworried by her nakedness.

What the hell had she got herself into, she wondered? She could so easily be at home now, watching television or reading, like all the normal housewives who lived in her street. Instead here she was, in a strange and alien place, among people she did not know, and completely naked. The whole situation was exactly like a recurrent dream that she often had, where she found herself naked in a roomful of normally clothed people.

Except that this was no dream.

'That Lindy can be a bitch, can't she?'

Carla turned to see a young man standing beside her holding two champange flutes. He held one out to her.

'Here, you look as if you could use this.'

'Thanks.' She took the glass from him. 'I'm not sure what to do.'

'Just enjoy the party. Don't worry, you see all kinds of things at Gambati's parties. Nobody's going to be too offended. Not when it's a gorgeous body like yours anyhow.'

Carla smiled bleakly. 'Thanks.'

'Come on,' he said, taking the glass from her again. 'Let's dance.'

'I can't. Not like this.'

'Why not?' He took her arm. Let's go.'

He led her onto the dance floor. The band was playing a slow number and he wrapped his arms about her, pulling her to him. It felt strange to feel her naked flesh pressed against his dinner suit, but he held her close, one arm about her shoulders whilst the other dropped down to her backside, squeezing the soft flesh of her bottom. They began to dance, their two bodies dropping at once into the rhythm of the music.

Carla found herself feeling much better enfolded in his arms. He had a firm grip on her, and she buried her face in his neck, enjoying the feel and smell of him, and the way his hand strayed up and down her back, stroking her bare flesh in a wonderfully sensuous manner. When he slid it up her flank and under her arm she moved back slightly to give him the access to her breast that she knew he wanted. He closed his palm over her soft orb, caressing it gently as she pressed herself against him once more.

He guided her across to the far side of the dance floor, where he pushed her back against the wall. The stone felt rough and cool against her bare behind but she didn't care, simply offering her face up to his and allowing him to kiss her, probing his tongue into her mouth whilst he continued his intimate massage.

They had stopped dancing now, their bodies entwined together in a passionate embrace. Carla could feel the swelling in his trousers as it pressed against her and she responded by pushing her own crotch against his leg.

He had been holding her at the waist whilst she wrapped her arms about his neck, but now she felt that hand slip lower and round towards the front of her body. She gave a little shudder as she felt his fingers brush through her pubic mat, then an even more violent tremor shook her as his fingers found her clitoris.

She opened her legs, pressing her pubis forward onto his hand, moaning with pleasure as one of his fingers penetrated her. She opened her eyes and looked over his shoulder. Some of the dancers had stopped and were watching, as were many of the people at the tables. She knew that, despite the fact that his body was partially shielding hers from their view, they must know what he was doing. She knew too that the movements of her hips were betraying her own arousal as she thrilled to the intimacy of his touch.

She broke the kiss.

'Let's go somewhere else,' she murmured in his ear.

'Where?'

'Somewhere a little more private?'

'We could go in the Retirement Room.'

'What's that?'

'The room where all the druggies are getting out of their heads.'

'But there are people in there.'

'Its pretty dark. And besides, most of them will be too stoned to notice.'

'All right.'

He took her hand and led her across the dance floor. As they approached, the other couples parted to let them through, casting knowing glances at one another. Carla kept her head down, not wishing to catch anyone's eye and allow them to see the arousal and excitement in her own.

Back inside the lights were bright and she felt more conspicuous than ever, wandering naked amongst all the grandly dressed people. Lindy was there with a group of young men and they passed lewd comments at her escort as they passed, winking and making gestures with their hands. Carla was glad to get into the relative darkness and anonymity of the Retirement Room.

Inside the atmosphere was quite different. The band on the terrace could no longer be heard, and the room was filled with strange and drifting melodies that came from large speakers in every corner of the room. There was little conversation and the air was heavy with the smell of smoke. All about people were lounging on the floor, chatting together or just gazing into space. The arrival of the naked girl seemed to arouse little surprise and Carla stepped carefully over the prone bodies to a spot by the wall on the far side, where a mattress lay vacant.

They kissed again, still standing, their bodies pressed close once more. Carla was very aroused indeed, now, and she devoured him hungrily, her hips moving back and forth as she ground her pubis against his leg. Suddenly she was overwhelmed by a desire to fellate her partner.

'I want to taste you,' she whispered in his ear. 'Let's get down on the mattress.'

The man sat down, and Carla dropped to her knees between his legs. She wasted no time, undoing his fly and dragging his trousers down to his knees. His cock looked inviting in the dim light, standing stiffly to attention, the veins in it pulsing. She lowered her head over it, taking it between her lips at once. He gave a groan, falling onto his back and pressing his hips up at her as she began to suck hard at it.

She ran her hand over the tightness of his ball sack, caressing it gently whilst her other hand worked his foreskin back and forth. Her head bobbed up and down vigorously, her breasts slapping against his legs with every down stroke. She could sense his excitement increasing now, his moans becoming louder as his thick cock throbbed with desire.

Suddenly he sat up, pulling her head up from his groin and throwing her back onto the mattress. Carla smiled in anticipation, spreading her legs wide apart and reaching for him.

His cock slipped into her easily, her own wetness and the saliva that covered it providing maximum lubrication. In no time he was fucking her hard, his body pressed down on hers as his hips pumped back and forth.

Carla glanced across the room. Less than ten feet away a young couple sat watching her being ravished. She wondered what they must think of her, giving herself so willingly to this man. But she was too far gone to care now. She had been hot for him since he had first placed his arms about her on the dance floor, and now, not ten minutes later, he was fucking her, and she was revelling in the sensation.

He came with a gasp, his cock unleashing a steady stream of semen and causing Carla's own orgasm to overtake her almost at once, her cries audible all around the room as the exquisite pleasure of a climax filled her body.

She lay back, watching him as he shot his load, enjoying the look of sheer ecstasy on his face. It occurred to her that she loved nothing better than to satisfy a man with her body. It was as if it was what she was made for, and in that moment, she vowed to give herself freely and to do whatever was asked of her for the rest of the weekend, dedicating herself to the giving of pleasure.

He withdrew with a grunt, rolling over onto his side, his cock already softening. Carla looked down at him with satisfaction, then rose to her feet.

'Where are you going?' he asked.

'Back to the party. See you later.'

And she began picking her way back towards the door.

Outside she blinked in the brightness of the lights. She had intended to go back to the terrace, but as she passed the bar a shout went up. She turned to see a group of young men sitting round a table. Their dinner suits were slightly the worse for wear, and they had obviously been drinking for some time, but Carla reminded herself of her pledge and when they beckoned to her she made her way across to their table.

She stood in front of them, legs slightly apart, hands on hips, allowing their eyes to take in her lovely young body.

'Enjoying the party, boys?'

'Enjoying it much more now you're here, darling. Give us a twirl.'

Carla pirouetted round on one foot, laughing. 'How was that?'

'Great. Here, have a beer.'

The men had been drinking lager straight from the bottle. Carla took the one offered, putting it to her lips and tipping her head back. She took a long swig of the cool liquid, allowing some of it to escape from her lips and trickle down her chin, forming a narrow stream that ran down between her breasts all the way to her pubic hair.

'Whoops,' she said.

She surveyed the men. There were six of them, all in their twenties or thirties and all unable to tear their eyes from her. Suddenly Carla was feeling very reckless. She was here to entertain Gambati's guests, so what was wrong with these? She moved closer to the man nearest to her, placing her hand on his shoulder, her breasts almost touching his cheek.

'So what does a girl do for excitement round here?' she asked.

The man reached out and placed his hand over her jutting mammary, squeezing it and making the nipple pucker into a brown knob of flesh.

'We could go and look at the garden,' he said.

'Sounds like a good idea. You guys coming?'

'What, all of us?'

'Not if you don't want to.'

'Yeah . . .'

There was a scraping of chairs as they rose to their feet. The man who had been caressing her breast still had hold of her and he beckoned to the one next to him.

'Come on, Steve,' he said. 'Give the lady a chair.'

At first Carla didn't understand what he meant, but she

complied quite happily when the men took an arm each and draped them over their shoulders. Then each put one arm behind her and the other on the backs of her legs and lifted her into a seated postion between them. The position left Carla with her legs stretched wide apart, her sex open. She glanced down at herself and saw that her previous lover's spunk was in evidence, clearly visible as it leaked from her.

'Somebody's had her already,' remarked one of the men.

'Yeah, and there's a few more gonna have her before the night's out. Come on.'

They carried her out, the rest of the men following behind, like a group of monks processing after a holy icon. Carla glanced to right and left as they carried her across the terrace, her naked body open for all to see. She was almost shaking with arousal now, her sex burning to be touched and, more importantly, to be penetrated. She was panting with desire by the time they reached the lawn at the side of the house.

They laid her on her back on the grass. It felt cool and soft against her bare skin and she stretched herself languidly, keeping her thighs wide apart as she watched the first man fumble with his trousers.

He took her without finesse or ceremony, falling onto her and ramming his hard cock deep into her whilst his companions urged him on with coarse shouts and comments. Carla came almost immediately, crying aloud at the sheer pleasure of being fucked so dispassionately. His movements were violent, his hips crashing against her own as he rode her whilst his friends grabbed impatiently for her breasts.

He came with a grunt, filling Carla with her second load of spunk in less than ten minutes. But it would be even less time before the next as she was hauled up onto all fours and made to crouch down whilst another cock was slipped into her from behind.

Carla gave a cry of lust as the second man began to fuck her, his stomach slapping against her behind with every stroke. Then something long and hard brushed against her cheek and she realised that yet another of the men was kneeling before her.

She opened her mouth and took him in, thrilled by the musky aroma and salty taste of his organ as he began vigorously to fuck her face. For Carla it felt wonderful, naked amongst a group of horny men all intent on pleasuring themselves in her lovely young body. And here she was satisfying two at once!

The men came almost simultaneously, more spunk pumping into her vagina as she struggled to gulp down the sticky, viscous liquid that was filling her mouth with every twitch of the thick cock between her lips.

Barely had her own orgasm subsided before she was being flung on her back once again and yet another man was pressing his manhood into her, grinning at her cries of pleasure.

They went on taking her, one after the other, in her sex, her mouth and occasionally her backside. She lost count of how many. Certainly more than the original six. It was more than an hour before they finally left her dirty, exhausted, her thighs, breasts and face streaked with sperm, her sex lips swollen and convulsing from their concerted onslaught.

It was another ten minutes before Carla found the strength to pull herself to her feet and stagger off to find a shower and a drink.

Then she was going to rejoin the party.

Chapter Nineteen

The Judge shook his head. 'An extraordinary tale,' he said. 'And you were completely naked all evening?'

'After that cow took my dress away,' said Carla.

'My dress, I think you'll find,' said Lindy haughtily. 'Let's face it, you loved it. Especially the gang bang.'

'Did you?' asked the Judge.

'I was there to do a job,' replied Carla.

'But you enjoyed it?'

'You know I did.'

'I see.'

'But that wasn't the end of it,' said Lindy.

'You mean there's more?' said the Judge.

'Oh yes. Much more. Wasn't there?'

Carla dropped her gaze.

'Is this true?' asked the Judge.

She nodded.

'And are you prepared to tell us?'

'Do I have a choice?'

'It's either your word, or this lady's.'

'Then I'll tell.'

'Good. But first there's another matter to attend to.'

'Another matter?'

'Those ten strokes. You hadn't forgotten, had you?'

Carla stared at him. 'Surely you're not going through with that?'

'I most certainly am. And I think we're about ready.'

He snapped his fingers and Carla heard the sound of footsteps coming up the steps behind her. She craned round to see the two girls who earlier had bathed and shaved her, mounting the stage from either side. In their hands they held long wooden posts from which hung silver chains. As Carla watched they sank the posts into square holes set on either side and just in front of her, securing them in place with sliding bolts. Then they moved round behind her and began fiddling with the cuffs that held her hands.

The moment her wrists were free, they dragged her arms forward and upwards. Hanging from each of the posts was a manacle, and these were snapped about Carla's wrists. Then the chains were tightened, stretching her arms forward in front of her and bending her over slightly.

Carla had barely had time to utter a protest, and now here she was, her legs still wide apart, her arms helpless, her naked body spreadeagled before the watching crowd. And all the time the chain dug into her slit, its rough surface chafing against her clitoris in a way that was both uncomfortable and exquisitely sensual.

The girls tripped back down the steps. The dark-haired one disappeared, but the blonde made her way round in front of Carla. As she emerged, Carla noted that she had picked up a box from somewhere. It was a long narrow box, similar to one that might have been used to contain a snooker cue, but when the girl opened it Carla saw that it contained a bamboo cane about three foot long.

The girl showed the cane to the Judge, who gave a nod.

'Perhaps this lady would care to do the honours,' he said, nodding to Lindy.

The blonde girl turned, holding out the box to Lindy.

'Please feel free to examine it,' said the Judge.

Carla watched, her heart beating fast, as Lindy reached into the box, taking out the cane. It was about as thick as a pencil, and when Lindy held it at both ends and flexed it, it bent alarmingly easily.

'You want me to use this?' Lindy asked.

'Mrs Wilde is due ten strokes on her behind,' replied the Judge. 'Do you feel up to delivering them?'

A smile spread across Lindy's face. 'It would be a pleasure.'

'No!' shouted Carla. 'You're not letting that bitch near me!'

Bang!

Once again the Judge's gavel descended.

'Be quiet!' he ordered sternly. 'Or the punishment will be increased.'

'But you can't.'

'I think you'll find we can do whatever we like,' said the Judge quietly. 'Now, we will either do this as you are, or I can have you gagged. What do you think?'

For the umpteenth time that evening, Carla found herself without a reply, simply glaring at the Judge. She watched as Lindy walked around the back of the stage and mounted the steps behind her.

Carla looked about at her audience. They were quiet now, the air of expectancy almost tangible as they leaned forward in their seats, watching the scene unfold. She could scarcely believe what was happening to her. It was bad enough having to stand up before all these people and confess to her lascivious behaviour. The prospect of a beating, especially delivered by Lindy, was almost too much. She glanced around fearfully as her chastiser reached the platform.

Lindy walked round her tethered captive, clearly enjoying Carla's intense discomfort. She held the cane out in front of her victim, then pressed it against Carla's cheek. It felt cold and hard, and Carla shivered at the contact.

Lindy moved the cane lower. Lifting Carla's breasts with it, then rubbing it over her nipples, she let it drop to her stomach, sliding it through her pubic hair and running it between her legs. Carla gasped at the intimacy of the contact, feeling the muscles in her sex contract as the coarse wood rubbed against her clitoris.

'Always randy, aren't you, darling?' murmured Lindy. She rubbed the cane back and forth, smiling at the effect it had on the hapless Carla. Then she looked up at the Judge.

'Ten strokes, wasn't it, Judge?' she asked.

'Ten strokes,' he concurred.

She placed her face close to Carla's. 'I'm going to enjoy this.'

Carla stood quietly, determined not to betray her anxiety as the young blonde moved behind her. She felt the cane tap against the cheeks of her backside, and gritted her teeth.

Swish! Whack!

The cane came down hard aross Carla's buttocks, the sound of the stroke echoing about the room. For a second Carla felt nothing, then suddenly the pain hit her, like the sting of a thousand wasps across the tender flesh of her backside.

Swish! Whack!

The second blow fell just below the first, leaving a thin white stripe across the cheeks of Carla's behind that immediately darkened to an angry red.

Swish! Whack!

The cane came crashing down on Carla's behind once more with devastating force. She clenched her teeth harder, determined not to cry out, despite the pain of her punishment.

Swish! Whack!
Swish! Whack!
Swish! Whack!

Each blow landed with deadly accuracy, leaving yet another stripe across Carla's previously unblemished flesh. The pain was excruciating, seeming to double in intensity every time the cane fell. Tears were running down Carla's cheeks now, but still she made no sound.

Swish! Whack!
Swish! Whack!

Every time the cane landed, Carla's body was thrust forward, the chain chafing hard against her clitoris, so that she found herself consumed simultaneously by pain and pleasure, her clitoris protruding prominently from her sex lips and weeping with love juice.

Swish! Whack!

Carla's backside was on fire. It seemed unimaginable that she could take any more. Yet she knew there was one more blow to come, and she closed her eyes as she heard the cane descend.

Swish! Whack!

The final blow was the hardest of all, slicing into her inflamed flesh and rocking her body forward. It was all she could do to prevent herself crying out, yet she controlled the impulse, biting her lip and trying to stifle the sobs that wracked her punished body.

She turned her head round to look at Lindy who stood, the cane hanging at her side, smiling triumphantly at her victim. The girl's hair was a mess and there were beads of perspiration on her forehead as she surveyed the criss-cross of stripes that now covered Carla's behind.

Once again Carla heard the two girls mount the steps, and soon the pair were releasing her wrists. Her legs felt decidedly shaky, but she was determined not to show any weakness as they bound her hands behind her.

The Judge banged his gavel. 'Thank you for your assistance,' he said to Lindy.

'It was a pleasure.'

'I suggest we adjourn for fifteen minutes to allow Mrs Wilde to regain her composure. Then we will ask her to tell us the rest of the events that occurred on that island. You will release the prisoner from her restraints during the adjournment and see to it that she gets some refreshment.'

Carla waited patiently as the shackles on her legs were undone. Then they released the chain that cut into her so intimately. The blonde girl retained hold of it, using it like a dog's lead to guide her away. Carla turned to face her chastiser, glaring at the young woman who had wielded the cane with such enthusiasm. Then she allowed herself to be led down the steps and between the rows of tables, where she knew the men and women were craning for a view of her punished behind.

As the doors closed behind her and she followed her young guards down the corridor, Carla's mind was already running back over the events on the island that she knew she would shortly have to relate.

Chapter Twenty

Carla awoke the morning after the party to find the rays of the sun beating down on her face. She blinked into the sunlight. It was beaming in through an open window, from which she could just discern the green and brown of the island's countryside beyond.

She gazed about the room. It was a small bedroom, decorated in the same modern style that was in evidence elsewhere in the house. Hanging from the wall was a watercolour depicting a local scene and on the bedside table was a vase containing dried grasses. The only other furniture in the room was a tall wardrobe and the wide double bed on which she lay, covered only by a thin sheet.

There was a sudden loud snore from beside her and she realized with surprise that she wasn't alone. The man beside her was in his forties, his hair thinning on top. As she watched, he flopped over in the bed, stretching an arm across her.

Carla eased herself out from under the arm and slid quietly from the bed, anxious not to wake the man. She padded silently across to the mirror and examined herself critically.

Considering the night she had had, she mused, she didn't look too bad. Her hair needed brushing, and there were tell-tale marks of dried semen on her thighs and in her pubic thatch. Her sex lips seemed more prominent than before and her breasts appeared slightly swollen, but there were few aches and pains.

She wondered how many men had fucked her the night before. It had been a long evening. After the gang-bang in the garden she had cleaned herself up and returned to the party, where she had danced enthusiastically with a number of partners, some of whom had then taken her off to enjoy the delights of her body. One had simply laid her across a table in the bar and taken her in full view of the other guests. Another had had her in the pool, their naked bodies entwined together underwater as he rogered her with enthusiasm. Even Gambati had taken her again, stretched out across his desk in the privacy of his study.

She gazed once more at the man on the bed. She remembered him now. She had been heading for her own room in the early hours, after the guests had dispersed, when he had intercepted her. He had demanded she return with him to his room, and she had obeyed without question. Once inside he had stripped quickly, making her suck him before screwing her on the bed. He had taken her twice, once in her cunt and once in her backside before finally allowing her to fall asleep in his arms.

Carla tried the doorhandle. It turned and the door opened onto a long corridor. She threw a last glance over her shoulder at her final partner of the evening, then stepped out, closing the door behind her.

She crept quietly through the house, finding her way back to the terrace. There, a group of servants was occupied in clearing up from the night before. They stopped work and stared at the naked girl, who walked past them without glancing to right or left. In the room where the bar had been she heard voices, and peering through the door noticed that a breakfast buffet had been laid out. There were three couples sitting at the table, all still in evening dress, sipping at coffee and chewing croissants. Suddenly Carla realized that she was ravenous, and the food looked very good indeed. She glanced down at herself. She was hardly in any state to join the other guests, but she needed some sustenance.

She took a deep breath and stepped into the room, grabbing a plate and beginning to load it with rolls, ham, cheese and fruit. She did not look at the couples, but noticed that their conversation stopped at once. She picked up a glass and filled it with fruit juice from a jug. Then she headed for the door, clutching her plate and glass. As she mounted the stairs she heard the sound of laughter, but she didn't care. Here, on this island, there was nobody who knew her. Nobody to chastise her for her behaviour. Here she was free to be naked. Obliged to be naked, in fact, given that she had no clothes whatsoever.

Once back in her room she sat down and devoured the food hungrily, washing it down with the fruit juice. When she had finished, she showered and washed her hair. Then she sat down by the window, combing her locks in the sunlight.

The sound of the door opening took her by surprise. Her first instinct was to cover herself with her hands, though she immediately realized what a pointless act that was. She turned as a figure entered the room.

'Here you are. I've been looking for you.'

It was Lindy. She was dressed in tight jeans and a yellow blouse, open at the neck and exposing a great deal of cleavage. On her feet she wore black boots with spurs.

'Been showering, have you? You'd need to after last night. You'll be a week washing the spunk out. That was quite a performance you gave. How many men did you have?'

'I don't know.'

'Lost count, eh? Still, you seemed to be enjoying it. I reckon I did you a favour, stripping you like that. It certainly made you popular.'

Carla said nothing.

'Anyhow, no time to chat now. Come on, you and I are going visiting.'

'Visiting?'

'Just some friends. Daddy says I can have you for myself today. Won't that be fun?'

Carla wasn't at all sure that it would be fun, but she said nothing.

'Let's go then. I've got the syce to saddle a couple of horses for us. You can ride, can't you?'

'Yes.'

'Well then, come on.'

'I . . . I need some clothes.'

'Clothes?'

'Yes. I told you. I've got nothing. The boatman took it all.'

'It didn't seem to bother you last night.'

'That was at the party.'

'I'll see what I can do, then. Come with me.'

Carla followed her down the corridor, the boots ringing on the stone floor. They descended a flight of stairs, then came to a halt outside a room.

'You wait here,' said Lindy. 'Nick's still asleep in there and I wouldn't want you to get him excited.'

She disappeared into the room. A few seconds later she came out again and tossed something to Carla. It was a poncho, no more than a square of material with a hole in the centre.

'Well then, put it on.'

Carla examined the poncho. It was made from thin cotton, the edge decorated with a knotted fringe. She pulled it over her head. It wasn't very large, the front barely reaching her crotch so that the only cover she had over her pubis were the tassels of the fringe, which hid almost nothing. The roundness of her bottom meant that, at the back too, most of the crack of her behind was visible. At the sides it dropped no lower than her elbows, so that her flesh was exposed to well above her waist.

'Haven't you got something more substantial?' she asked.

'That's your lot. Take it or leave it.'

Carla sighed. 'I'll take it.'

Lindy led the way out to the stables. As she walked along behind, Carla realized that the poncho was of even less use when she was in motion. With every step she took it rode up, completely exposing her sex and behind.

The syce was waiting for them, a bridle held in each hand. The horses were large and athletic looking and extremely well groomed. Clearly Gambati had an eye for good horseflesh.

Lindy took the reins of one of the animals.

'Help the lady to mount, please,' she said.

'It's okay, I can manage,' said Carla.

But the groom wasn't going to miss his opportunity, placing his hands on her behind and pushing her upwards as she mounted, his coarse fingers probing into her slit as she did so.

Carla settled into the saddle. Like the day before, the feel of the leather against her sex sent a spasm of pleasure through her and she was careful to sit back to avoid letting her clitoris come into contact with the pommel. Riding was something that had always turned her on, the feel of the powerful animal between her thighs being one of the most pleasurable sensations she knew. Now, with her bare crotch pressed down on the saddle, the effect was doubled, and she gritted her teeth, trying to suppress the erotic images that were starting to fill her mind.

They set off down the drive at a trot, a pace which changed to a canter as they turned and made their way across country, following tracks that ran between the olive groves. At that pace the poncho was virtually useless at preserving Carla's modesty as it blew out behind her, leaving her practically naked. Every now and then they would pass men working in the fields who would stop and stare at the apparition of beauty cantering past.

They rode on for about fifteen minutes, occasionally slowing to negotiate narrow paths or to cross streams, Carla lifting herself up on her stirrups to prevent the delicious sensation of the leather chafing against her crotch bringing her to orgasm. She knew Lindy was watching closely for signs of her arousal, and she was determined not to betray any.

At last they crested a rise and there, beneath them, was the sea. Carla gazed out, almost breathless with the beauty of it. The water was the deepest blue, the waves glinting in the sunlight. Before them was a steep path that wound down to a long golden beach at the end of which was a house, a good deal smaller than Gambati's residence, but large and imposing all the same.

They negotiated the path at a walking pace, the horses picking their way surefootedly between large rocks. In a short time they were on the beach itself, where Lindy spurred her horse into a gallop, with Carla following in her wake.

As they reached the house, Lindy reined in her mount, and Carla did the same. They walked the last few yards to the gate where Lindy dismounted, Carla following suit.

'Enjoy the ride?' asked Lindy.

'It was all right.'

'Didn't turn you on too much?'

'I can cope.'

'So I see.'

The girls hitched their horses to a post beside the gate. As they did so the door of the house opened and a young man emerged. Carla recognized him at once as the man who had picked her up the day before.

'You've met Alex, haven't you?' said Lindy. 'In fact I hear you asked him to fuck you.'

'Not in so many words,' said Carla. But the sight of the virile young Greek brought back memories of the ride, and the way he had caressed her, and she felt a glow rise to her cheeks as she thought about it.

Beside the house was a short drive, and Lindy indicated a white Mini Moke that was parked there.

'I see Mitch has arrived,' she said.

'Yes, Miss Gambati,' replied Alex. 'And his friend, Tom.'

'Good. They'll be glad to see this young lady. Come on.'

Carla felt an odd sensation as she heard the words uttered. Clearly Lindy had something in store for her. It was with a mixture of trepidation and excitement that she followed the girl into the house.

The room they entered was light and airy, the walls painted the same brilliant white as the outside of the building. The floor was laid with wooden blocks that felt cool on the soles of Carla's feet. At the far end was a sofa and a pair of easy chairs. A young man was stretched out on the sofa. He wore jeans and a T-shirt, his long blond hair tied back in a ponytail. He had blue eyes that seemed to glitter when he caught sight of Carla and she found herself blushing under his gaze. To his right, slumped in an easy chair, was a second man of similar age with short dark hair. He too scrutinized the new arrival with interest.

'Hi, Mitch,' said Lindy to the blond man. 'This is her. Says her name's Carla.'

'Hmm, not bad.' The man did not move from his prone position. 'Let's see the rest of her.'

'Take off the poncho, darling, and give Mitch a better look,' ordered Lindy.

Carla looked about her. All three men were watching her closely, as was Lindy. Then her eyes dropped to the piece of cloth that was her single, inadequate garment. It seemed that even this small concession to modesty was to be denied her now. Yet she couldn't dispute the thrill she had felt when Lindy had given the order. Once again Carla had relinquished control to another, and once again the idea was one that turned her on in an odd sort of way.

She hesitated for a second, then grasped the hem of the poncho and pulled it over her head. For a second she clutched it to her body in a final vain effort to preserve what was left of her modesty. Then she let it fall to the floor, standing with her hands by her sides as the other four took in her ripe swelling breasts, the curve of her hips and the thick lips of her sex.

Mitch rose to his feet and approached her, an approving look on his face. He walked all the way round her. Carla remained as she was, standing stock-still whilst he took in her charms.

Mitch turned to Lindy. 'She'll be ideal,' he said. 'Will she do it?'

'Naturally. She'll do whatever I tell her to. She's mine for today. Besides which, she'll probably enjoy it.'

'Good. I'll get my stuff then. The light's perfect at the moment.'

'Is anyone going to tell me what's going on?' asked Carla. 'I have got a voice, you know.'

'Don't you worry your pretty little head,' said Lindy. 'Mitch is a photographer. He was looking for a model and I suggested you.'

'A photographer?' Carla's voice had a note of concern in it. 'He's not going to photograph me like this, is he?'

'Why not?'

'I'm naked.'

'That's precisely the point.'

'But who'll see the photos?'

'I don't see why that should bother you, the way you've been flaunting your tits and cunt.'

'Even so . . .'

Lindy moved closer to her.

'Listen, lady. Who's paying your wages this weekend?'

'Mr Gambati.'

'Then I suggest you do what he asks.'

Mitch re-entered the room, a large bag slung over his shoulder.

'Come on, Tom,' he said. 'We've got work to do.' He turned to Carla. 'In the Moke,' he said.

Carla hesitated. She hadn't expected this. The whole point of this weekend was that she was anonymous, and free to indulge her desires as she wished, with no fear of discovery by her husband or her friends. Photographs were something else. People might get to see them.

'What are the pictures for?' she asked.

'I'm a professional. I'll try to sell them.'

'But what if someone I know sees them?'

'Don't worry. The magazines I sell my pictures to can't be bought in the UK. They'd be illegal.'

'You're not afraid of a bunch of foreigners seeing your tits and cunt, are you?' asked Lindy. 'My god, I think the little slut's scared. Your friends read dirty mags, do they?'

'Of course not.'

'Then you'll be all right, won't you?'

Carla looked at Lindy, then at Mitch. Then her eyes dropped to her own body. Although she was reluctant to admit it, the prospect of disporting her body under the eye of the camera was an idea that appealed to her perverse nature. The thought of men, strange men, seeing her naked charms revealed to them was something she found oddly exciting, and once more she felt her body respond to the idea warmly.

'All right,' she said. 'I'll pose.'

She stooped to pick up the poncho, but Lindy had her foot planted on it.

'You won't be needing that,' she said.

Carla gazed into her eyes for a second, then gave a slight shrug and followed the two men out into the drive.

The Moke was a sort of miniature Jeep, completely open on all sides, without even a roof. When she settled into the passenger seat, Carla realized that the vehicle offered her no cover whatsoever. Mitch seemed oblivious to this, however, as he climbed into the driver's seat beside her and Tom sat down behind with the equipment. Mitch turned the key and the motor came to life. Then he slammed the car into gear and they swung out onto a track that ran up away from the sea towards the hills.

He turned to her. 'Done any posing before?'

'No.'

'Don't worry. You'll be fine.'

'Where are we going?'

'An old ruin up in the hills. Makes a nice contrast; the dead, dusty building and the vitality of young flesh.'

'Sounds almost artistic.'

He grinned. 'Almost.'

The Moke followed a twisting track that ran up into the hills. Carla sat silently, looking out at the dry, barren countryside. The sun was rising higher in the sky now, and the sensation of its warm rays on her bare breasts was a pleasant one. Suddenly the prospect of spending the morning naked with two young men in this lovely spot seemed a very attractive one, and she felt a spasm of pleasure as she comtemplated what might be to come.

They came to a halt halfway up a hill, Mitch pulling the vehicle off the track and killing the engine. He climbed out.

'Come on,' he said to Carla. 'It's just up here.'

She followed him up a path, with Tom bringing up the rear. They came over a small rise and there below them was the ruin.

It had clearly been a large building. A cluster of buildings, in fact, all now reduced to rubble, the stones strewn about the site. What few walls were left standing were no more than five foot tall at their highest, and the whole place had an air of desolation about it. It was rather more exposed than Carla would have liked, overlooking a valley. Down below she could see men working in the fields. They were close enough that she could make out what they were wearing, so she knew they would be able to tell she was naked.

Tom began unpacking the bag at once, pulling out two cameras, a box of film, a tripod and reflectors. Clearly Mitch took his photography seriously. It took Mitch two minutes to load both cameras, then he turned to Carla.

'Right,' he said. 'Let's have you over by that wall. Lean back on it and look at the camera. Try to look as sexy as you can.'

Carla didn't feel sexy at that moment, just very self-conscious. There were butterflies in her stomach as she made her way to the spot he had indicated. She wasn't sure why. After all, she should be becoming accustomed to her nudity by now. But the thought of displaying herself before the camera made her feel strangely under-confident.

'That's it.' Mitch lifted the camera to his eye. 'Lean back a bit. That's right. Now, turn towards me. Lick your lips. Great. Let's see those tits. Push them forward. Fantastic. Now play with your nipples. Make them hard. That's right. Open your legs wider. Now look at me. Tell me you want to be fucked. That's terrific.'

The orders came thick and fast, and they were just what Carla needed. Once again, someone else was in control, and she was able to free herself of responsibility, simply doing as she was told. Soon she began to warm to her task, obeying his every instruction, lying, standing, sitting, climbing onto the walls whilst all the time he snapped away, capturing every inch of her naked charms. Tom, meanwhile, busied himself with the equipment, changing the films in the cameras and running about with one or other of the reflectors under Mitch's instructions.

As they went on, Mitch became increasingly demanding. At first he had been content to pose her as if for glamour shots, but soon he was ordering her to open her legs, lying her on the ground and making her thrust her hips up at him, then moving in close to capture the sight of her open sex as she offered it to the camera. He made her pose on all fours, her breasts pressed downward and her backside thrust back, as if inviting penetration. He made her play with herself, capturing the shiny wetness of her fingers as she frigged herself.

The more the session continued, the more turned on Carla became, positively panting with desire as she pressed her fingers into her vagina. She knew her arousal was obvious, but she was beyond caring. There was something about displaying her body in this completely abandoned way that excited her incredibly, so that whatever pose Mitch demanded she adopt she did so eagerly, revelling in the opportunity to expose herself. Down in the valley the farmers had stopped work and were standing watching, but Carla didn't care any more. In fact the thought of the audience spurred her on to new heights of depravity, small moans escaping her lips as she pleasured herself.

There was a break in the proceedings as Tom reloaded the cameras and Mitch crossed to where he had left his bag, pulling a box from it. Carla watched him as he strolled back towards her. She was lying on her back along a piece of crumbling wall, one leg placed on each side, her fingers buried in her vagina, masturbating hard.

'Stop that for a minute,' ordered Mitch.

Reluctantly Carla slid her fingers out of her vagina and lay watching him as he approached, the lips of her sex twitching visibly as the excitement continued to course through her veins.

'Get up on your feet and lean against the wall,' he said. 'Both hands on the top, bent forward, your legs spread.'

Carla did as she was asked, bending her slender young body over and widening her stance so that her anus and sex were in full view. She glanced back at Mitch. He had opened the box and removed something. As he came closer she saw that it was a long slim phallic object made of white plastic. It appeared to be some kind of dildo, though to her it seemed too slim to be able to satisfy a girl with her needs. He flicked a switch and the object began to hum. Then he placed the box on the ground and moved up to stand immediately behind her.

Carla's sex was positively gushing with wetness as she waited for him to penetrate her, pressing her backside back at him and moaning with anticipation. But when she felt the plastic on her flesh it wasn't her sex it was pressing against.

It was her anus.

Carla gave a gasp as she felt the end of the object against the small star of her rear hole. At first her instinct was to tighten the muscles of her sphincter in order to deny access to it.

'Relax, baby,' said Mitch. 'Let it in. You'll love it.'

With a supreme effort Carla did as she was told, and Mitch slid the vibrator into her rectum. He pressed it deeper and deeper inside until it was buried to the hilt. For Carla it was the most extraordinary sensation, the muscles of her behind forced apart by the buzzing object, whose vibrations were sending the most delicious sensations through her body.

'Use it,' he said quietly to her. 'Use it on yourself.'

Carla took her right hand off the wall, reaching round behind her and taking the vibrator between finger and thumb. Then she began gently to work it back and forth inside her. At once the pleasure that she was feeling increased twofold and she almost cried aloud with the bittersweet sensation of having her backside so perfectly filled, whilst her cunt still ached to be touched.

Mitch began snapping again, capturing the expression of arousal on Carla's face as she gazed back at the camera whilst working the dildo in and out of her behind. He came in closer, concentrating on the smooth white surface of the object as it disappeared inside her, watching as her dangling breasts shook with every move she made.

'Does that feel good?' he asked quietly.

'Mmmm.'

'Making you hot?'

'Oh, yes.'

'Would you like one for your cunt?'

'Mmmm,' gasped Carla again.

Her heart thumped hard against her ribs with anticipation as she watched him delve into the box once more.

This time it was more like a proper dildo, bulging with veins, the tip thick and bulbous. When he switched it on, the end suddenly took on a life of its own, describing small circular movements like the head of a snake following the charmer's tune.

He moved close to her, standing beside her, his back against the wall. He slid a hand up her thigh and tested the wetness of her sex, smiling as he felt the muscles contract about his fingers. Then he brought the dildo up between her legs. When he pressed it against her sex it slid in at once, the wetness inside her ensuring that there was no resistance as it wormed deep into her hot vagina. Carla cried aloud as she felt it twist and turn inside her, the pleasure increased still further by a small protrusion at the base that rested against her clitoris, sending pulses of vibration through the swollen bud.

'Take hold of it, then turn and face me.'

Slowly Carla reached down between her legs, closing her fist about the shaft of the dildo. Then she straightened and turned around, planting her feet wide apart in the dust and pressing her hips forward.

She began to work herself at both ends, sliding the two objects back and forth, forcing each deep inside her then easing it out again. And all the time the camera was snapping away, capturing every moment of her wanton pleasure. Carla wondered at the sight she must make, standing naked and unashamed in broad daylight, pleasuring herself in the most intimate way possible under the cold eye of the camera lens.

'Come on, Carla,' said Mitch. 'Give it all you've got. The men who buy these pictures will see you're not faking.'

'Who'll buy them?' moaned Carla as she worked on.

'Men who can afford them. Men who appreciate the sight of a wanton woman bringing herself off for their pleasure. Men who'll want to look at your image whilst they're masturbating.'

'Ah!'

Carla felt a sudden spasm of lust as she imagined some handsome young stud, his pants round his ankles, his hand vigorously working his foreskin back and forth as he studied her naked body penetrated front and rear. She pictured his spunk, flying from the tip of his thick cock and splashing onto her image, and suddenly her body shook as a powerful orgasm swept though her.

Mitch continued to snap away as Carla rocked back and forth, her knees bent, her hands working in and out, pumping the two whirring dildos vigorously, her mouth open in a soundless scream of relief. The orgasm went on and on, visibly shaking her body so that her breasts bounced up and down with the violence of it.

She came down gradually, still working the sex toys in and out of her as her knees appeared to buckle beneath her. It wasn't until she had sunk to the ground, her body outstretched, the two devices still projecting from front and back, that Mitch finally lowered his camera.

'Wow!' he said to Carla. 'You're the hottest woman I ever shot.'

Chapter Twenty One

Mitch and Tom dropped Carla back at the house in the early afternoon. She had fully expected both of them to fuck her after her session in front of the camera, but neither had made a move, simply packing their gear back into the bag. Mitch had produced a loaf of bread, cheese and a bottle of wine then, and the three had sat about on the grass eating and drinking. During the meal, the two men made idle conversation, but Carla sat silent, embarrassed by her earlier behaviour, her embarrassment increased by her continued nudity and by the stares of the farm workers, who had moved closer for a better look. She was quite relieved, therefore, when, at last, they had risen to their feet and returned to the car.

They left Carla standing in the driveway and headed off up the track. She watched them until they were out of sight, then turned and walked up to the house.

The front door was locked and all the windows closed. There was no sign of anybody about, and the horses were gone. Carla was alone. She sighed. Under normal circumstances this would have been an ideal opportunity to take a long walk and to explore the island a little. But these weren't normal circumstances. She was naked, with no prospect of finding anything to wear. As a consequence she would have to be cautious about what she did and where she went.

She walked down the path at the front of the house, being careful to ensure there was nobody about. The path led straight down onto the wide, deserted beach. Beyond stretched the sea, blue, clear and inviting. All at once Carla realized how hot she was. The ruin where they had shot the photographs had been in a dry, sultry spot in the lee of the hill, so there had been little breeze. Now, the prospect of immersing herself in the cool sea was suddenly very attractive indeed, and Carla set off for the water's edge at a trot, splashing into the surf, then diving full-length, allowing the blue-green water to envelop her.

She swam for more than half an hour, a solitary figure in the wide expanse of water. For Carla it was a wonderful release from the demands of Lindy, Gambati, Mitch and all the others who had used and abused her body that weekend. She emerged feeling cool and refreshed, wandering along the beach to a small rocky cove. Dominating the area was a wide, flat expanse of rock and she climbed onto it, standing atop it and gazing about her. She felt like some sort of savage in the wilderness, wandering naked through the bush, owning nothing, yet the queen of all she surveyed. Suddenly tired, she lay down on the warm rock, stretching her body out in the sun and closing her eyes. In no time she was asleep.

She never heard the two men arrive, nor did she have any idea where they had come from. She just opened her eyes and there they were, standing on the rock and gazing down at her. They looked like peasants, their clothes worn, their faces tanned a deep brown by the sun. She guessed they were brothers, possibly even twins, about eighteen years old and clearly fascinated by the pale skin of the lone, naked girl.

Afterwards Carla wondered why she had felt no fear. After all, she was totally alone and utterly defenceless. But somehow their presence seemed completely unthreatening and she didn't even attempt to cover herself as they took in her plump young breasts and prominent slit.

They dropped to their knees on either side of her and she reached out and took their hands in hers, placing them on her breasts. They squeezed her soft mammaries gently, sending tingles of excitement through her. She in turn placed her hands against their crotches, feeling the hardness that lurked there.

They took her one after the other, there on the rock in the warmth of the afternoon sun. There was no urgency about them. It was as if the whole thing was scripted, first one and then the other stripping off his clothes and prostrating himself on top of her, his eager young cock twitching as he slid it into her. They fucked her with even strokes, coming quickly and filling her with their seed. Then, when both had sated their lust, they carried her down to the sea, bathing her, their strong fingers sliding into her mouth, vagina and anus and bringing another wonderful climax to her before taking her back to her rock and leaving her there, her skin glistening with moisture. Afterwards Carla wasn't even certain it hadn't been a dream, so perfect had the encounter been, and she drifted off to sleep once more, a contented smile on her lips.

She was wakened by a shadow falling across her face. She opened her eyes to see Lindy standing over her, her hands on her hips.

'So here you are,' she said. 'We thought you'd been abducted. Come on.'

She took Carla's hand and pulled her to her feet. Carla blinked, still not fully awake. It was early evening and the sun was much lower in the sky now, though the air was still deliciously warm.

They walked back along the beach to the house without speaking. As they came closer, she saw that the horses were back, as was Mitch's Moke. The sound of rock music reached her ears, coming from the front room.

Inside the room, Mitch and Tom were back in the same positions they had been in that morning. Alex was sitting in the other easy chair sorting through a pile of records. On a table at the side were trays holding sandwiches and pastries, and beside it was a cooler loaded with beer and wine bottles. As they entered Maria came in through another door bearing a tray. She ran her eyes up and down Carla's body, her face expressionless.

Lindy pulled two bottles of beer from the cooler, flipping off the tops and passing one to Carla. Carla swigged it down from the bottle, enjoying the coolness of the liquid. She looked about for her poncho, but there was no sign of it. She guessed that Lindy had decided that she would have no further use of it that night.

'So what have we got planned tonight?' she asked. 'Another party?'

'Something like that,' replied Lindy. 'Not as grand as last night, though.'

'And do I get a party frock?'

Lindy smiled. 'Not exactly,' she said. 'Although you will be something of a star attraction.'

'I thought I might be.'

Lindy turned to her. 'You puzzle me, Carla,' she said. 'You're not like the usual sluts that Daddy brings back.

Most of them have their brains in their arse. And they're not very good actresses when they're supposed to be faking an orgasm.'

'Maybe it was all those years at acting school.'

'You can't fool me. Mitch told me about how you'd reacted to the dildos this morning. This whole thing gives you a buzz, doesn't it?'

'I'm being paid.'

Lindy laughed, shaking her head.

'You don't have to tell me your reasons if you don't want to. Anyhow, it won't make any difference tonight. As you say, you're being paid. And now I think Alex wants you.'

Carla turned to see that the young Greek had risen from his seat and had moved across to stand beside her.

'Hello, Alex,' she said.

'Hello, Carla. You come upstairs?'

'If you like.'

'Looking forward to having Alex's cock in your cunt, aren't you?' said Lindy.

'Why don't you come up and find out?' asked Carla, draining the last of her beer.

'I might just do that.'

Alex took Carla's arm and led her towards the door. Carla felt embarrassed as she followed, knowing that everyone in the room was aware that she was going to be screwed, but determined to hide her discomfort from Lindy. Alex's grip was strong, and his closeness sent a thrill through her as they mounted the stairs together.

He took her to a bedroom at the front of the house. From the window she could see the last of the sunlight glinting on the surface of the sea. The only furniture in the room was a large brass double bed, the mattress covered with a single sheet. She tested the springiness of the mattress then turned to Alex.

'Lie on the bed, please,' he said, his voice slightly hoarse.

Carla sat down on the edge of the bed, then eased herself backwards, positioning herself in the centre on her back. She watched the young man as he gazed down at her.

'Come on, Alex,' she urged, patting the bed beside her.

'No,' he said. He seemed slightly uneasy.

'What's the matter?' she asked. 'I want to fuck with you. I wanted to yesterday.'

'First I must tie you.'

'Tie me?'

'Miss Lindy told me.'

'To tie me? How?'

He reached beneath the bed and pulled out a box. He put a hand inside and extracted a handful of straps, chains and locks. Carla sat up and stared at them.

'Kinky,' she said.

'I'm sorry?'

'Never mind. So Lindy's into bondage, is she?'

She picked up one of the straps. It was made of expensive leather, lined on the inside with soft velvet. It had a metal ring set into it to which a chain was attached, about the thickness and strength of a dog's lead. She fingered it. She had never experienced bondage before, and she wasn't sure what to think. On the one hand, the thought of surrendering herself to the helplessness that the chains would bring seemed a dreadful risk. On the other, she had already surrendered herself completely to the dominance of Lindy and her father during the weekend. This would be merely an extension of the girl's precedence over her. She gave a shrug and passed the objects to Alex, then lay back on the bed once more.

'Better get on with it, then,' she said.

Alex hesitated momentarily before taking hold of her hand. He wrapped one of the straps around her wrist, pulling it tight. Then he took her other wrist and did the same. Once both straps were in place he pulled her arms up above her head, securing the chains to the corners of the bed with the padlocks.

Next it was the turn of her legs, more straps placed about her ankles before he pulled her body taut and fastened them in a similar manner.

For Carla the sensation was extraordinary. She was completely helpless, her body spreadeagled, her breasts and sex totally unprotected. It was at once frightening and exciting to her as she gazed up at her captor, aware that she was totally in his power.

'You going to fuck me now, Alex?' she asked.

'There's more,' he said.

From the box he pulled out what appeared to be a black velvet bag.

'Lift your head, please.'

Carla did as she was told, and he placed the bag over her head. At once Carla realized that it was a blindfold. He pulled it over her face, covering her almost to her mouth and fitting the material snugly against her nose, leaving not a single chink through which light could enter. Then he fastened it at the back of her head with a cord, so that it was quite secure.

Carla had never felt so vulnerable, her hands and feet securely bound, her legs spread wide, allowing her no defence against a potential ravisher, her eyes staring into

Samantha Austen

total blackness so that she could have no idea who could see her or touch her. It was a strange sensation, yet one she found extremely erotic. Ever since she had set foot on the island, decisions as to what she could wear and with whom she could make love had been taken away from her. Now that had been taken to the ultimate extreme, and she felt a shiver of arousal run through her as she contemplated her helplessness.

She waited for Alex to mount her, to feel him slide his cock into her already wet sex, to have him take his pleasure with her helpless body. But nothing happened. Indeed, if she strained her ears she could perceive no sound from him at all. Surely he hadn't left her alone? Surely he wanted her body as much as she wanted his? Yet it seemed he had simply meant to bind and blindfold her, and that she was to lie here frustrated whilst he returned to Lindy and her friends.

A doorbell sounded and she heard voices below. Then a car pulled up outside and more voices wafted up through the open window. The party was apparently beginning, but for the moment there was no part for Carla in it.

For another half-hour Carla lay in the dark, listening to the sounds from below. The music had grown louder, and a general hubbub of voices reached her ears, occasionally punctuated by the shriek of a woman's or a man's loud laughter. She tried to gauge how many guests there were down there. Judging from the noise it was quite a number. She wondered how long she was to be left alone.

Then she heard a footfall. Someone was climbing the staircase quietly, only the occasional creak of the wood betraying their presence. She stiffened, listening hard as a faint whisper reached her.

'Where is she?'

'In there. Take a look.'

'Hey, she's gorgeous. Look at those tits.'

'Take her, then.'

'You sure it's all right?'

'Certain. Come and tell me when you're done.'

Carla could not be certain whose voices she had heard, though she suspected that one was Lindy's. She lay back, her body tense and trembling as she sensed somebody entering the room.

There was a creak of springs as the person sat down on the edge of the bed. Then she gave a start as she felt a hand close over her breast, squeezing the soft flesh. She lay perfectly still as the hand explored her soft globes, making the nipples harden into stiff brown peaks as he caressed them. It felt wonderful. Lying there in her private darkness Carla's mind had been filled with erotic thoughts and to feel herself touched so intimately brought those thoughts flooding back, making the juices inside her sex run anew.

For a second his hands left her breasts, and she gave a little moan of disappointment. Then she felt a thick, hard finger slide down her slit and she gasped as it slipped inside her, probing her in the most intimate manner imaginable.

'You're hot for it, aren't you?' whispered the voice again.

For the second time his hands left her. Then she heard the faint rustle of clothing and something fall to the floor. She bit her lip as she felt him climb onto the bed between her legs and lower his body onto hers.

Something thick and solid nuzzled against the entrance

to her sex. Something that pushed against her insistently. Carla moaned again as she felt the urgency in him. There was no way she could have kept him out, even if she had wanted to, but Carla didn't want to, and she raised her backside from the mattress in invitation as he pressed harder and harder.

All at once he was in her, his cock forcing apart the walls of her vagina as he pressed himself home. He started to fuck her, his heavy body pressing down on her as his hips worked back and forth. Carla groaned with arousal as he plunged his cock into her, his breath rasping against her cheek, his hands massaging her swollen breasts. For Carla the experience was totally unique. She had become accustomed to giving her body to strangers. In fact she got a huge kick out of doing so. But this was different. For a start she was not giving her body, it was being taken, with no thought for her own consent. In the second place the person with whom she was performing the most intimate act possible was hidden from her, leaving her no opportunity to discover who it was that was taking her with such vigour and enthusiasm. The thought sent a powerful surge of arousal through the helpless girl, causing her sex muscles to contract about the meaty organ that was pumping into her.

All at once his rhythm changed, and she sensed a stiffness in his limbs. He seemed to pause momentarily, then there was a gasp and she felt the unmistakable sensation of spunk spurting from his cock as he came inside her, his knob twitching violently.

With a gasp Carla came too, pressing her hips upwards and grinding her pubis against his, small cries coming from her as her orgasm swept through her, every jet of semen renewing her pleasure as she abandoned herself to the joy of her climax.

He collapsed onto her, his breath hissing in her ear as the last dribble of his seed ran from him. Then he was climbing off her, his cock slipping from within her as he rose to his feet.

Once again there was a rustle of material and the sound of a zip. Then she heard him leave without another word.

Carla lay staring into the blackness of her blindfold, contemplating the anonymous fucking she had just received. It almost seemed unreal. And yet it had happened, and the warm wet feeling in her vagina was no longer just her own juices, but a man's spunk as well.

She didn't have long to dwell on what had happened, though. Almost at once she heard someone else mounting the stairs.

'My God, they weren't lying,' gasped a voice.

This man wasted no time at all, climbing straight onto the bed whilst still fumbling with his trousers. By the time she felt his penis pressing against her flesh it was already hard as a rock, and he slipped it in at once.

He screwed her with such urgency she knew he could not last long, and sure enough he came after less than a dozen strokes, gasping and panting as he shot his load. Carla barely had time to begin to feel turned on before he was withdrawing and heading for the door.

Five minutes later someone else entered. He made no sound, simply dropping his pants and pressing his cock against her lips. She opened up at once, taking him inside and sucking hard at him. This time her lover was in no hurry, his strokes slow and measured, his thick weapon sliding almost to the back of her throat as he pumped his hips back and forth. Carla wished that her hands were free so that she could wank him whilst she sucked, but instead concentrated on keeping her lips clamped hard around his shaft whilst flicking her tongue across the tip, enjoying the way it twitched every time she did so.

When he came, the flow of spunk was copious, almost making her gag as it splashed against the back of her throat. She swallowed his seed with relish, consuming every drop, then licking his penis clean.

'Wow, you're a real pro,' he muttered, stroking her breast. Then he was gone and she was alone once more.

This time the break was nearly twenty minutes. Carla lay, listening to the sounds of the party downstairs, wondering who would be her next visitor. Having been deprived of an orgasm from the last two she was starting to feel decidedly horny again and her heart leapt when, at last, she heard someone climbing the stairs once more.

She heard the person enter and stop beside the bed. There was a strong whiff of scent in the air, an odour that smelt decidedly un-masculine. The hand that stroked her breasts was small and soft, and seemed more gentle than her previous ravishers' had been.

Then it struck her. Her visitor was a woman!

More than that, though. There was something oddly familiar about the scent. It was an expensive one, certainly, but it was one she had smelt before, not recently, but not all that long ago.

She sensed the woman leaning over her, and a mouth was placed over hers. Then a tongue was pressing insistently against her lips, and she opened them to allow it inside.

The woman's kiss was as familiar as her scent, and Carla

searched her mind to try to recall the memories it evoked. What woman's kiss could possibly be so familiar?

The answer struck her like a bolt of lightning. There was only one woman.

Phaedra!

She pulled her head away, breaking the kiss.

'Phaedra!' she gasped.

There was no reply.

'Phaedra. It is you, isn't it?'

Still nothing, just the faint rasp of silk rubbing against nylon. Like the sound of a pair of silk knickers being removed.

'Phaedra?'

She felt the pillow pressed down by a weight beside her left ear, and almost at once a similar pressure by her right ear. Then came the smell of female arousal, and she realized with a shock that the woman was straddling her face.

She could feel the heat against her cheeks as the woman crouched lower. Then she felt something soft and damp touch her lips.

Carla realized with a shock that what she could feel were the lips of the woman's vagina. The message was clear. The woman wanted to be licked. Nervously she protruded her tongue, and for the first time she tasted a woman's slit. It tasted odd, slightly bitter and salty, the flesh soft and pliable. She ran her tongue higher and encountered something hard, like a fleshy peanut. She craned her head up and took it between her lips, sucking at it, and the woman gave a barely audible sigh.

Encouraged, Carla began to lick harder, running her tongue downwards again, then sliding it into the girl's vagina, tasting the fluids that were flowing from her. She protruded her tongue still further, probing deep into the pulsating love hole that hovered just above her face.

'Mmmm.'

This time there was no mistaking the pleasure in the woman's voice as she pressed down hard against the captive's face. Carla tried to picture Phaedra, her dress raised about her waist, her sex open as she revelled in the licking she was receiving, and almost at once her juices began flowing anew. She set to with enthusiasm, her little tongue sliding in and out of the woman's vagina and then lapping at her clitoris, eliciting fresh moans from her partner.

And the more she licked, the more excited the woman became, forcing her sex down over Carla's mouth, her hips working back and forth, her breath becoming shorter by the minute.

She came with a moan of ecstasy, her sex lips convulsing about Carla's tongue as her juices flowed from her open sex. Carla lapped and sucked as hard as she was able as she felt the shudders run through her partner's body.

Satisfied at last, the woman raised herself and climbed from the bed. Once again Carla felt the soft fingers run over her breasts, then slide lower, running through her pubic hair and down the open cleft of her sex, where she knew the woman would find the spunk of her previous partners seeping from her.

'Phaedra . . .' she said once again.

But there was no answer, just a pat on the thigh, and the sound of receding footsteps.

Carla was confused. Had she been mistaken? Could it really have been Phaedra? And if so what on earth was she doing here?

But she didn't have much time to ponder the questions. Already a heavy tread was mounting the stairs and she braced herself to receive her next customer.

Chapter Twenty Two

There was silence when Carla came to the end of her narrative. She stood, gazing down at the faces below her, trying to gauge their reaction to this latest confession. Many of the women looked shocked, some tut-tutting as they shook their heads in disbelief at her lasciviousness. Others looked on in fascination, their mouths open as if they were panting. The men were almost all held spellbound, many of them grasping the hand of their partner. Some had their hands out of sight, and at more than one table Carla was sure that mutual masturbation was taking place.

Carla was in the same position as they had placed her originally: naked, her hands tied behind her, legs pinned apart on the floor, the cold hard chain pressing against her clitoris. By the time they had brought her back into the room she had regained her composure and the redness in her backside had subsided, though this had simply exaggerated the contrast between the angry red stripes that criss-crossed her behind and the natural paleness of her skin. Telling the tale of her visit to Gambati's island had been the toughest ordeal yet, particularly with Lindy there to correct her if she missed out the slightest detail of her debauched weekend.

She couldn't say how many men had had her during

Lindy's party. If anything she had had more cocks inside her than the night before, each one totally anonymous, simply a breath on her face and a cock spurting deep inside her. They had released her three or four times to wash the spunk from her and to eat and drink, taking her down and parading her naked through the party, her blindfold still in place. Then she had been taken aloft and tied once more whilst a queue of men waited to fuck her. For one of the sessions they had tied her face down, and a number of the men had taken the opportunity to bugger her, preferring the tightness of her anus in which to satisfy their desires.

At last though, her visitors had become less frequent, and eventually she had fallen asleep where she lay, still spread across the sperm-stained mattress.

The next day Alex had ridden with her back to Gambati's house. She had ridden naked, attracting the stares of passers-by, men who, for all she knew, had fucked her only hours before. Back at the house, Gambati had been waiting and she had spent the rest of the day with him, fucking and sucking him to orgasm a surprising number of times for a man of his age.

The visit had ended as it had begun, riding with Alex down to the sea where Maria was waiting and the boat was anchored just off the beach. She had kissed Alex goodbye and swum with the young Greek girl out to the boat. There, her clothes lay on the deck exactly where she had abandoned them, as if she had been gone no more than a few minutes. She had struggled into them, then sat in the stern and watched as the island sank below the horizon, to become no more than an extraordinary memory.

'There is one charge that has not yet been substantiated,' said the Judge suddenly, shaking Carla from her reverie.

'The matter of whether this lady was present.' He nodded to Phaedra who had sat expressionless through the whole narrative.

'I'm certain it was her,' insisted Carla. 'It felt and smelt exactly like her.'

The Judge turned to Lindy. 'Was this lady present?' he asked.

'Who can say? There were lots of people there that night. It was a long time ago. I can't remember the guest list.'

'But you must remember', put in Carla. 'Why not ask Phaedra herself?'

'She is not the one on trial,' admonished the Judge.

She can still answer, though,' said Carla. 'Come on, Phaedra, it was you, wasn't it?'

Phaedra smiled. 'I don't remember.'

'But you must. Were you or were you not on Gambati's island last summer?'

'I did spend some time in the Greek islands and I attended some parties, but I can't be sure.'

Carla frowned at the woman. 'I don't believe you.'

Bang!

The Judge thumped his gavel down on the table.

'May I remind you, Mrs Wilde, that it is you that is on trial here, not this lady. You would do well to curb your tongue.'

Carla opened her mouth to reply, then remembered the tenderness of her backside and closed it again, contenting herself with a glare in Phaedra's direction.

'Now, young lady,' said the Judge, addressing Lindy once more. 'Have you anything else to add?'

'No,' replied Lindy. 'I think I've established what sort of a woman this is.'

'We will be the arbiters of that, ultimately,' said the Judge. 'Thank you for your testimony. You may go now.'

Lindy threw a final triumphant glance in the direction of the prisoner, then turned and walked out of the room.

'Now,' said the Judge. We turn to a new phase in this sorry tale.'

Carla gritted her teeth. 'Haven't you heard enough already?' she asked. 'How long is this charade going on?'

'It will go on until all the evidence is heard, either from your lips, or from the witnesses,' replied the Judge, tersely.

'Or until everyone in this room has got his rocks off,' muttered Carla.

The Judge banged his gavel once more. 'Call Mitch Stephens!' he shouted.

Carla watched as Mitch strode through the doors. She should have guessed that the photographer would be called to give evidence against her. It was obvious that these people knew every detail of her misdemeanours over the past year, and that no stone would be left unturned in bringing those details to the attention of the court.

Mitch grinned and winked at Carla as he approached. He still wore his hair in a long ponytail at the back, and he clearly hadn't bothered to dress for the occasion, being clad in an old T-shirt and frayed jeans. Over his shoulder was a tassled leather bag.

'Your name is Mitch Stevens?' asked the Judge.

'Certainly is.'

'And do you know the defendant?'

'Sure. Hi, Carla.'

Carla managed a faint smile in return.

'What is your relationship with Mrs Wilde?'

'I'm not having a relationship with her.'

The Judge strummed his fingers irritably. 'Your business relationship, then.'

'She posed for me.'

'Posed?'

'Yeah. I'm a photographer, you see.'

'And it was you that photographed her on the isle of Kofru?'

'That's right. Great set of shots, they were.'

'You have copies?'

'Better. I've got the mag.'

Mitch reached into his bag and fumbled about for a few moments, then pulled out a glossy magazine, which he dropped on the table before the Judge. On the front cover was a picture of Carla perched naked on a crumbling wall in the Greek sunshine. The title of the magazine, scrawled in large red letters across the top, was *Orgasm*.

'May I?' asked the Judge, reaching for the magazine.

'Be my guest.'

The judge opened the pages on the table in front of him. Even from where she stood, Carla could make out the shots of herself, displaying her body to the camera, many shots depicting her with her legs wide apart. As he flipped through the pages she saw the ones of her with the two dildos, an obvious expression of lust on her face as she worked them in and out.

'And Mrs Wilde allowed you to publish these?'

'Naturally. She was quite keen.'

'I wasn't,' put in Carla. 'I didn't even know where you were going to publish them.'

'Is that true?' asked the Judge.

'I told her they'd be published abroad,' said Mitch.

'And they were. Strictly speaking these mags aren't legal in this country.'

'So you knew they were intended for publication?' the Judge said to Carla.

'I suppose so,' she replied. 'But remember I had to do what Lindy told me.'

'Does that mean these photos were taken under duress?' he asked Mitch.

'She posed happily enough for them,' said Mitch. 'Of course, strictly speaking she was working for Gambati then, but I used the shots anyhow. And when she saw them, she seemed quite keen to do some more.'

'You took more shots?'

'Certainly. It was Carla's idea. She called me up and asked me to.'

'And there were a number of these sessions?'

'Quite a few. Look at these.'

He hauled a small pile of magazines out of his bag and placed them on the table. All, like the first, bore lurid titles accompanied by cover photos of nude women. Some of those photos were of Carla.

'Look inside,' said Mitch. 'Even where she's not on the cover you'll find her inside. I tell you she just loved it.'

The Judge flicked through the pages of some of the publications, then passed them on to others. For the next ten minutes the room was a hubbub of noise as the onlookers pored over the photos. At last the Judge banged his gavel once more.

'Well, young lady,' he said. 'Do you wish to give us an explanation for these?'

'Are you likely to believe me?'

'Naturally we will listen to what you say.'

'That's not exactly the same thing.'
'Nevertheless, you have a right to speak.'
'All right,' said Carla. 'I suppose I might as well . . .'

Chapter Twenty Three

It was some six weeks after her return from Kofru that the package dropped through the letterbox. Eric had picked it up, along with the other mail, and had placed it on the breakfast table in front of Carla, before immersing himself in his newspaper once more. Carla had torn it open, reaching inside for its glossy contents. She had the copy of *Orgasm* nearly halfway out of the envelope before she suddenly recognized the naked beauty on the front as herself.

The shock was so great that she dropped the envelope onto the floor, and the magazine fell out under the table. At once she was on her knees, scrabbling to replace it.

Her husband looked up. 'What is it?' he asked.

'Nothing. Just a seed catalogue,' she said, hurriedly.

'A seed catalogue? Since when were you interested in gardening?'

'Oh, just Barbara at the club,' replied Carla, trying to keep the tremor from her voice. 'She kept going on about this seed catalogue and eventually I agreed to send off for it. You know what she's like. Gardening mad.'

'Even so, it's a strange time of year to be sending off for seed catalogues.'

'They do spring bulbs as well. I thought we might plant a few.'

'As you wish.' He stared at her for a moment. 'Are you all right, my dear? You look quite pale.'

'I'm fine,' she said. But when she raised her coffee cup to her lips her hand was shaking badly.

Eric seemed to take an age getting off to work that morning. It was with a sigh of relief that Carla heard his car head off down the drive. She immediately retired to the privacy of her room, locking the door behind her. Then she pulled the magazine slowly from the envelope once more and laid it on the bed.

She began leafing through it, studying each page, her eyes wide with dismay. There she was, in all her glory, displaying her naked form to the camera with abandon. She was shown standing, lying, on all fours and in every pose imaginable. But worse were the shots with the vibrators, close-up pictures showing her grasping them front and back, the arousal showing clearly on her face as she worked them back and forth vigorously.

She began to read the captions. They identified her as Cathy, and the wording was as explicit as the shots.

Here we see Cathy enjoying the sunshine in the way she likes best, showing off her lovely body to full effect. Just look at those stiff nipples!

The only thing Cathy needs now is a stiff cock to fill that gorgeous cunt. But help is on the way, because she's brought some sex toys with her.

One dildo just isn't enough to satisfy a hot little number like Cathy. Here she is, doubly-penetrated and loving every moment of it.

Carla gazed at the images that stared back at her from the magazine's pages. There was no doubt that the photographs were extremely sexy. Just looking at them was stirring her desires, and the thought of strangers picking them up sent a warmth to her crotch that she hadn't felt for some time. She thought of the image that Mitch had conjured up during the photo session. An image of men staring down at these photographs, their fists grasping their erect tools as they masturbated hard. She imagined thick, creamy spunk splashing onto the pages, obscuring her image as the men came, their minds filled with the fantasy of fucking her. Her hand crept down between her legs as the idea filled her brain.

Since her visit to Kofru, Carla had abstained from sexual encounters. The experience had been too much even for one of her desires and she had resolved to behave herself and to return to playing the dutiful wife. Whether Eric had noticed this resolution, however, was open to doubt, as he still spent much of his time away and showed little interest in rekindling his sexual relationship with his lovely young wife. Still Carla stuck to her new celibacy, reasoning that her Greek experience was as far as she could possibly go, and that the game she had been playing was simply too dangerous to continue.

Now, however, the sight of the photographs and the memories they evoked was beginning to arouse those same passions that had driven her to sell her body in the first place, and she found herself flicking back and forth through the pages, her hand toying with the gusset of her panties beneath her skirt, feeling the wetness there increase.

'No,' she muttered to herself, throwing down the magazine and snatching her hand away from her crotch. 'This just won't do.'

She picked up the envelope and went to replace the magazine. Then she noticed there was a piece of paper inside. It was a compliment slip, and as she pulled it out she saw the words 'Mitch Stephens Photography' emblazoned across it. There was a note, written freehand beneath, and she read it, her hand trembling.

Hi Carla. Hope you like the shots. We could do more if you like. You've got a gorgeous body. Call me. Mitch.

Carla replaced the slip, along with the magazine, in the envelope, and placed it in her bottom drawer beneath a pile of clothes. Then she went downtairs and poured herself a cup of strong black coffee.

It was nearly a week before she opened the drawer again. A week during which she had been quite unable to get the magazine out of her thoughts. She had lain awake at night tossing and turning, and her dreams had been filled with images of the camera's lens following her as she strutted naked before it. On more than one occasion she had found herself masturbating beneath the sheets and had had to force herself to stop, and every time she entered her bedroom she found her eyes straying to the bottom drawer where the magazine lay.

She wasn't sure what it was that finally led her to open the drawer once more. She told herself that it was probably boredom as much as anything, but the fact was that she had known all along that she would do so, and it was almost with a sense of relief that she finally slipped the magazine from the envelope and stared once more at its pages.

Half an hour later she was picking up the telephone.

'Mitch Stevens Photography. Can I help you?'

Carla stared at the mouthpiece, unable to speak.

'Hello?' he said.

'Mitch?'

'Mitch speaking. Who is this?'

'Carla.'

A silence.

'Mitch?'

'Hello, Carla. Why are you calling?'

'I . . . I just wanted to ask. About the magazine . . . Who can . . . ?'

'Who can buy it? Almost anybody. But not in this country, unfortunately. The Powers That Be consider the sight of you rogering yourself with two dildos too much for the average British male. But there's plenty of Yanks, Italians, Germans and Belgians probably getting an eyeful of your charms right now. Does that excite you?'

'I . . . I just wanted to know.'

'It does excite you, doesn't it, Carla?'

Carla glared at the phone. Was she really that transparent? Of course it excited her. It excited her more than she cared to admit even to herself. Yet Mitch knew.

'You still there?'

'Yes.'

'You want me to take some more? I've got this great idea for some beach shots. You're there, sunbathing sans cozzy and these two beach bums come along, see you, and it continues from there.'

'There'd be men as well?'

'Sure. I mean the dildos were all very well, but my readership likes to see the real thing occasionally. What about it, Carla?'

'No, I couldn't.'

'Why not? You know you'd enjoy it. And it would sell. Think of all those guys getting their rocks off watching you getting fucked by a couple of studs.'

'It's outrageous.'

'But that's why you like the idea, isn't it, Carla?'

'How much would it pay?'

'It'd pay. But don't tell me it's the money that's important.'

'Stop trying to tell me what to think.'

'I could set up the shoot for the day after tomorrow. What do you think, Carla?'

'I don't know.'

'We could fix another date if you prefer.'

'It's not that.'

Carla knew that the day he suggested was ideal. Eric was operating on that day, and on days when he operated he seldom got home before midnight.

'Come on, Carla. I'll pick you up at ten.'

'No, don't pick me up. Not here.'

'Take a cab to my studio then.'

A pause.

'All right.'

'That's great, Carla. You've got the address?'

'Yes.'

'See you in a couple of days then.'

'Listen, Mitch. About there being two blokes . . .'

But he had already rung off, and Carla was left listening to the dull buzz of the dialling tone.

Chapter Twenty Four

Carla's cab arrived outside Mitch's studio at five minutes to ten. She paid the driver and climbed out, glancing about her as if afraid she might be recognized. The studio was in a small Soho street, between two Indian restaurants. It was on the first floor, the door being marked with a plastic sign announcing Mitch's trade. There was a doorbell with his name beside it and Carla stared at it, hesitating.

It had taken some nerve to come this far. She had lost count of the number of times she had reached for the phone in order to cancel their appointment. Once she had actually dialled his number before slamming down the receiver once more.

She had not slept well, tossing and turning in her bed, her mood fluctuating between fear and total arousal as she contemplated what she was to do. She had almost hoped that Eric would say that his surgery was cancelled for the day, but he left for the hospital at the usual time, announcing that he would be very late.

Carla's actions had been almost mechanical as she dressed and called a cab. She chose a simple white summer frock and comfortable but stylish shoes. She contemplated wearing her bikini underneath but ended up opting for matching white bra and pants.

During the cab ride she remained silent, nervously fiddling with her bag as they made their way through the traffic. By the time they arrived she was thoroughly on edge, and nearly dropped the change when the driver handed it to her. Now, as she stood staring up at the building that housed Mitch's studio, she found herself wondering once again if she really wanted to go through with the photo session.

'Hello. You're early.'

Carla swung round to see Mitch standing just behind her, smiling. He was just as she remembered, tanned and blond, his long hair bleached even lighter by the sun.

'Aren't you going to ring? You've been standing there for ages.'

'How do you know?'

'I was in the café on the other side of the street. I often nip across there for a coffee in the mornings. Go ahead and ring. Tom's inside.'

'Is there anyone else in there?'

'No. Just Tom. Who were you expecting?'

'It's just that, well, you said . . .'

'Two beach bums? Yeah, we're meeting them at the beach.'

'You see I'm not sure that . . .'

'Don't worry. You'll like them. They're friends of mine. Come on, Carla, let's go up.'

He inserted a key in the lock and turned it, pushing the door open. Before Carla had a chance to protest he had ushered her inside, closing the door. Ahead was a steep narrow staircase.

'Up we go,' he said.

Carla climbed the stairs slowly, with Mitch just behind

her. At the top was a door with his name written on it and he reached past her, pushing it open.

'Welcome to my workshop,' he said. 'Tom! Carla's here. I told you she'd come.'

On the other side of the room was a door with a red light above it. The light was on, and a sign saying 'Darkroom. Do Not Enter' hung below.

'I'll be out in a second,' called Tom.

'Make yourself comfortable, then,' said Mitch. 'I'll just get my equipment sorted.'

Carla glanced about her. Apart from the darkroom, the studio consisted of a single large room. At one end a myriad of lights was arranged about a small stage, with a paper backdrop and curtains. The wall beside her was festooned with photographs, many of young women, though Carla could not see one of herself. From the other wall hung his camera equipment, cameras, lenses, tripods, flashguns, all suspended from hooks by leather straps. The sight of the cold eyes of the lenses made her feel uneasy once more.

'Listen, Mitch,' said Carla quietly. 'I'm not completely certain about this.'

'Why did you come, then?'

'I'm not sure. You see, this business of two guys. It's a bit much, isn't it?'

'Do you think so? You've taken on two guys at a time before, haven't you?'

Carla blushed. 'Not in front of a camera.'

'What's the difference?'

'The difference is that people are going to see me.'

'Only strangers.'

'Even so, two guys . . .'

Mitch put an arm about her shoulder.

'Listen.' He said. 'We'll go down to the beach and you can meet the guys. If you decide one's enough, or you want to chicken out, then we'll say no more. Okay?'

Carla looked at him. 'Okay.'

'Good. Now what are you wearing underneath?'

'What?'

'Underwear. What have you got on?'

'Bra and panties of course.'

'Take them off'.

'What?'

'The elastic will make marks, and they take ages to fade. The sooner your skin's right the quicker we can start shooting. Now take them off please.'

Carla hesitated for a moment, then she turned to face away from him and unfastened the buttons that ran down the front of her dress, beginning at the neck and undoing them almost to her waist. She shrugged the dress off her shoulders and reached behind for her bra catch. She slid the garment down her arms and dropped it onto a chair. She stared down at her breasts. The nipples were already stiff with anticipation, and she ran her fingers lightly over them, the sensation sending a tingle through her. Then she pulled the dress back up again and refastened the buttons. Once they were done she reached under her skirt, taking hold of her pants and pulling them down her legs. She stepped out of them and dropped them on the chair beside her bra. Only then did she turn and face him once more.

She was surprised to see that he had been paying no attention to her, busily taking down his camera equipment and packing it into a bag. For some reason this annoyed Carla. As if she had been putting on a show, and nobody had come to see it. Then she was distracted by the sound of the darkroom door opening as Tom emerged.

They travelled to the sea in Mitch's car, Carla seated beside him at the front and Tom on the back seat with the camera bag. Mitch made light conversation during the journey, but Carla wasn't really in the mood to talk, preferring to look out the window and watch the countryside speed past.

At last they reached the coast, and before long Mitch had pulled the car off the main road and was heading down a smaller country lane. They came to a wood with a gate across the entrance, and Tom climbed out and opened it. Soon they were bumping along a small track that ran between the trees.

They came to a halt in a clearing and all three climbed out. Then Mitch led the way through the forest with Carla and Tom following on behind.

Suddenly the track opened into an expanse of beach, beyond which was the sea, the high tide crashing against the sand. Mitch stopped and waited for his companions to catch him up.

'This is the spot,' he said. 'What do you think?'

'Is it safe?'

'You mean is anyone likely to come along? I don't think so. Apart from Doug and Art, of course.'

'Doug and Art being the beach bums?'

'That's right. They're genuine beach bums, too. They've got a shelter just down the beach. They've worked for me before. I think you'll find they're good performers.'

He placed an emphasis on the word 'performers' that brought a blush to Carla's face.

'Right,' said Mitch. 'Let's get started. Might as well get a few shots in whilst we're waiting for them. Carla, lean against that tree and undo a few buttons on that dress.'

Mitch rummaged in his bag whilst Carla walked across to the tree that Mitch had indicated. She stood uncertainly beside it whilst the two men loaded the cameras. All at once she felt very nervous, and she glanced guiltily about her as she waited.

'Come on, Carla,' said Mitch as he approached, camera at the ready. 'Start flashing those tits.'

Carla reached up to her bust and began slowly undoing the buttons one at a time. When she had three undone she stopped, looking questioningly at Mitch.

'One more, I think,' he said, squinting through his camera lens. 'Then lean against the tree and look sexy.'

Carla did as she was told. The dress was open at the front now, barely concealing her plump breasts, and she knew the two men were getting glimpses of her nipples as she moved closer to the tree and leant against it.

'That's right, lean back. Look at the camera. Lick your lips. Good. Press your chest forward. That's right. Now undo another button. Pull back the dress and show them to us properly. That's fine. Play with your nipples. Just like that. Hold it.'

Carla found herself falling under Mitch's spell once more, just as she had on the island. Once again she reflected on how much easier it all was when someone else took charge and she simply had to follow orders. And for the first time she began to feel sexy as she exposed herself to the camera's eye.

Soon all the buttons on her dress were undone and it hung open, exposing the naked flesh beneath. Then Mitch made her discard it altogether, posing her all round the tree as he recorded the contrast between the gnarled old bark and the silkiness of her young skin. And the more he photographed her, the more turned on Carla became, posing her body this way and that whilst Tom ran around with the reflectors and spare cameras.

'Hi.'

So absorbed had Carla been in her posing that she hadn't noticed the arrival of the two men. Now she looked up in surprise as they strolled up from the beach. They were both quite young, in their mid-twenties she estimated, and both wore jeans, with short white vests barely covering their broad, hairy chests. They gazed frankly at the naked beauty leaning against the tree, giving Carla a sudden urge to cover herself.

'Hi Art, hi Doug,' said Mitch. 'This is Carla.'

'Hi Carla.'

'Hello,' she replied quietly, blushing as she felt their eyes roving over her body, taking in her breasts and crotch.

'We gonna do it right here?' asked the one Mitch had referred to as Doug. He was the taller of the pair, his hair long and dark, his eyes icy blue.

'I thought we'd use the beach.'

'There's a good little cove just down the way. Lots of rocks. Ideal, I'd have thought.'

'Show me.'

The four men stepped back onto the beach, leaving Carla on her own. She took the opportunity to get a good look at the two new arrivals. Both had strong, sinewy bodies, their skins tanned dark brown. Art wore his hair short, with a gold earring in one ear. His eyes were dark, set beneath thick eyebrows.

As she watched them chat, the realization that she was about to be fucked by the pair of them sent a shiver of excitement through Carla's body, and she felt the wetness begin to fill her crotch. She eyed the two of them up and down, and as she did so her hand dropped unconsciously to her crotch and her fingers sought out her love bud between the thick lips of her sex. She leant back against the tree, widening her stance and running her fingers over the hard little nodule that was rapidly becoming the focus of her desires as she waited for her lovers to return.

Carla closed her eyes. It was the first time for ages that she had allowed herself the indulgence of masturbation, and it felt good to be stimulating herself once more. She thought of the way the men had looked at her, and of the brazenness of her own demeanour, and her fingers began to work harder, rubbing her clitoris vigorously as her baser instincts took control of her.

Suddenly she felt her fingers brushed aside as a larger, stronger hand closed over her open sex. She opened her eyes to find herself staring into the face of Art. He was smiling, his fingers worming their way into the heat and dampness of her crotch. She tried to pull away, but she was already up against the tree, and he pressed her back against it as he rubbed the sensitive flesh between her legs.

'They told me you were hot,' he said. 'They weren't kidding.'

Carla twisted away from him, aware that the other three were also watching what was happening. She placed a hand over her crotch and wrapped her arm across her breasts.

'What are we doing?' she asked Mitch.

'The guys reckon there's a better spot just down the beach,' he said. 'We're going to walk down. I'd like to take some shots of you on the way, if that's okay.'

'You're the boss,' she replied.

They set off down the beach, Doug, Art and Tom going ahead whilst Mitch and Carla brought up the rear. As they walked, Carla's inhibitions evaporated, and she let her arms drop to her sides once more, though she was still embarrassed by the fact that the men had caught her masturbating. Mitch was back in charge now, circling her with the camera as she walked, the whirr and snap of the instrument accompanied by his incessant directions to his naked model.

It took less than ten minutes to walk to the area about which Doug and Art had been speaking. It consisted of a group of large dark grey rocks close to the sea's edge, a steep cliff rising up behind. Mitch was clearly pleased with the location and immediately set about posing Carla on the rocks and snapping her with enthusiasm whilst the others looked on.

Once again Mitch took control, and before long Carla found herself lying with her legs spread, pressing her open crotch up at the camera with enthusiasm.

'Right,' said Mitch at last. 'Time to introduce you guys. Come on, Doug.'

The two men rose from where they had been sitting on the rocks.

Mitch started by setting up a scene where the sunbathing Carla is apparently surprised by the men's appearance. Then he posed them in front of her, apparently in conversation with them, her legs spread so that her sex was clearly visible in the shot.

'Okay,' said Mitch. 'Let's have some action. Doug, you stroke her pussy like you were doing before, whilst Art grabs her breasts.'

The two men came to sit on either side of Carla, Doug

immediately running his hand down between her legs whilst Art began to caress her jutting breasts. Carla lay prone on the rock, her head lolling back, her eyes closed as she felt her body respond to their intimate caresses. Any inhibitions she had had about being photographed with two men together were rapidly evaporating under the firm caresses of the two beach bums, and she began to moan quietly as Mitch snapped away.

'Now, Carla,' said Mitch. 'I want you to suck Doug's cock.'

Carl didn't need asking a second time. As Doug sat back on the rock she rose eagerly, kneeling between his thighs and reaching for the fastening of his jeans.

She wasn't disappointed. His cock was huge, bulging with veins, the bulbous end flicking up and down every few seconds. Carla took it in both hands and pressed it against her breasts, teasing her already erect nipples and leaving a shiny smear of his lubrication across them as Mitch captured the moment on fim. She pulled back his foreskin, uncovering the purple smoothness of his glans. Then she bent her head and went down on him, taking his thick shaft into her mouth and beginning to suck, whilst she ran her tongue back and forth over the small hole in the end.

As Carla fellated the gasping Doug with relish, she suddenly felt one of her hands being taken by Art. He pulled it towards him, then she found her fingers closing about yet another hefty shaft. She glanced sideways to see that he had stripped completely, and she ran her eyes admiringly over his strong body, his deep suntan covering his entire frame apart from a thin, pale strip across his midriff. His cock was magnificent, stiff as a rod of iron and throbbing with arousal and she began to wank him hard as Mitch's camera closed in to record the act.

Art wasn't content to be masturbated for long, however, and he began to edge round behind the kneeling girl, who kept hold of his cock as he did so, sensing his purpose and anxious to accommodate him.

When his cock was hard against the soft flesh of her vagina he paused, allowing Mitch to photograph the three of them as they were, she with a rampant erection in her mouth, another in her hand whilst the two men revelled in the sheer debauchery of their mutual partner.

'All right, fuck her,' said Mitch.

At once Carla felt the pressure of Art's cock as he pressed himself against her, and she widened her stance to allow him access, still guiding him with her hand. He slipped in easily, bringing whimpers of joy from her as his fat erection forced apart the walls of her sex. He began fucking her at once, his hips slamming against her backside and threatening to dislodge from her mouth the penis she was so greedily devouring. Carla's body shook with passion as the two men rode her. Even in the short time that had elapsed since Kofru she had forgotten what it felt like to have a live, throbbing cock inside her. To have another filling her mouth at the same time served almost to double that pleasure. And to think that images of her satisfying the pair would be available to others! Out of the corner of her eye she could see Mitch manoeuvring about to get the best possible shot, and the sight of the camera lens spurred her to new heights of passion.

Carla wondered at the image Mitch must be framing as she sucked hard at Doug's erection, her pale young body sandwiched between the two hefty, suntanned men, her dangling breasts shaking back and forth with every thrust against her behind.

She came suddenly and unexpectedly, her squeals of delight muffled by the thick rod that filled her mouth. Mitch moved close to record the expression on her face as her cunt muscles tightened round Art's cock, her small body shuddering with passion as wave after wave of lust flowed through her.

'My God,' grunted Art as he continued his onslaught. 'This chick ain't faking. She loves it.'

As the violence of Carla's orgasm began to abate, Mitch shouted an order. At once Carla felt Art withdraw from her whilst Doug pushed her head out of his lap.

For a second the lustful youngster couldn't understand what was happening. Then she realized that Mitch was repositioning them for a new shot. This time he made Doug lie back across the rocks whilst Carla, moaning with pleasure, lowered herself onto his stiff organ, forcing her backside downwards until she felt the solidity of his pubic bone hard against her own. Then he pulled her down onto him, so that her breasts pressed against his strong chest whilst at the same time she felt Art's fingers prising her backside open.

The yelp she gave was half pain, half pleasure as he plunged his cock into her backside, ramming it all the way in despite her protestations. Then both of them were thrusting into her with vigour, bouncing her body back and forth between them as they rogered her hard.

Carla's second orgasm was as strong as the first, the sensation of the twin erections filling her so intimately proving too much for her and bringing new screams from her lips as the pleasure ripped through her, whilst Mitch once again recorded her passion with his camera.

No sooner had Carla recovered than Mitch was once again giving orders, making Doug pin her down on her back whilst Art straddled her, placing his penis between her breasts and squeezing them together as he tit-fucked her.

The session went on and on. It seemed that Doug's and Art's self-control knew no bounds, their cocks remaining stiffly erect with no sign of a climax from either, unlike their lascivious young partner who had two more shattering orgasms during the session. At last, though, Mitch seemed satisfied.

'Right,' he said. 'Let's go for the come shots. You guys ready?'

'Not half,' grinned Doug. 'This is the hottest piece of arse I've had for ages.'

At the time, Carla was arched across one of the rocks on her back, her cunt filled by Art's erection, her head thrown back so that Doug could kneel behind and get his own cock into her mouth. Mitch ordered the two studs to withdraw, then pulled her to her feet and made her lie on her back, half-seated against the rock, her legs spread wide. The two men came round and knelt beside her head on either side, their stiff erections bobbing just in front of her face.

'Go to it, Carla,' ordered Mitch.

Carla stared at the two cocks. Each was shiny with her secretions, one glistening with saliva whilst the other bore a smooth sheen of love juice. It was to this one she turned first, smelling and tasting her own arousal as she took it into her mouth, her hand caressing his tight ball sack whilst her other hand began working Doug's foreskin back and forth.

'Put both of them in your mouth,' said Mitch.

Carla obeyed, opening her mouth wide and guiding the thick rods between her lips, licking and sucking them whilst Mitch clicked away.

Carla continued to work the pair, taking first one, then the other into her mouth whilst wanking both hard. All the time she could sense the tension in the two men increasing, their cocks almost jumping out of her grasp as their convulsions increased.

'I'm going to come,' gasped Art suddenly.

'Me too,' said Doug.'

'Fire it into her mouth,' said Doug. 'Come on, Carla, open up.'

Carla grasped both cocks hard in her hands, pulling them close to her face, her fingers working the shafts frantically.

They came simultaneously, great gobs of spunk suddenly flying from their cocks and into her open mouth. She struggled to catch each spurt as it sprang from them, but their cocks were twitching so violently now that the hot viscous fluid went everywhere, splashing onto her cheeks, her eyes, her hair, whilst all the time Mitch was close by, the incessant rattle of the shutter filling her mind.

'Don't swallow,' ordered Mitch. 'Keep your mouth open. Let me see the spunk inside.'

Carla did as she was asked, managing to catch the last drops as they dribbled from the now spent cocks, then raising her sperm-coated face to the camera, allowing Mitch to see the creamy mouthful before finally gulping it down. Then she flopped back onto the rock, gasping for breath, her chest rising and falling rapidly.

'Seen enough?' she murmured.

Chapter Twenty Five

The room was silent once more as Carla completed her tale. The relating of the photo shoot had aroused her once more, and again she was forced to restrain herself from pressing her crotch down on the rough metal of the chain as she felt the juices flowing inside her.

'And that was just the first photo shoot?' asked the Judge, turning to Mitch.

'One of many,' he agreed. 'I shot her in the studio, in the woods, in a country house. Even on a boat on the Thames.'

'And always with two men?'

'Sometimes three. And occasionally with another woman as well. She'd do it any way I asked.'

'And the payment?'

'I paid her, certainly. But to the best of my knowledge none of the cheques was actually cashed.'

'Did she ever chase the payments?'

'Never. If all my creditors were like Carla I'd be a rich man.'

'So she did it for pleasure?'

'You'll have to reach your own conclusion on that one. All I know is that if she was faking those orgasms she deserves an Oscar. And the way she savoured their spunk!'

'What do you mean?'

'A lot of girls pose with a mouthful of come, then spit it out afterwards. Not Carla, though. She relished the stuff, quite often she'd clean the guys off with her tongue afterwards.'

'I see.' The Judge turned his gaze back on his naked captive. 'Do you have anything more to say about this?'

'What can I say? You've got the pictures. In fact, unless I'm mistaken, there's a guy on table three about to come all over one of them.'

The audience turned to stare at the red-faced man as he fumbled about under the table, obviously trying to squeeze his erection back into his pants whilst his partner looked on in obvious annoyance.

'So you moved from escorting to part-time prostitution, and then to porn modelling?'

'Like I say, you've got the pictures.'

'But it didn't stop there, did it?'

'What do you mean?' asked Carla.

'I mean that you weren't content to stick with stills photography,' said the Judge. 'You wanted to move on to something a good deal more explicit.'

Carla did not reply.

'What can you tell us about Mrs Wilde's next escapade?' the Judge asked Mitch.

'She wanted to get into the movies.'

'The movies?'

'Sex movies. Hard-core stuff. The kind of thing you don't get in this country.'

'And she approached you?'

'Who else? Practically begged me to find her a part.'

'You don't make films yourself?'

'No.' Mitch shook his head. 'I'm a stills man. Never

could get to grips with movie cameras. And then there's the sound. It's a whole new area and one that doesn't interest me. I've got plenty of work without going after that sort of thing.'

'Nevertheless Mrs Wilde asked you to help her?'

'Yeah. Well, I've got plenty of friends in the industry. I knew where to look.'

'And what happened?'

'I got her a part. A pal of mine does a lot of that kind of stuff. I do the stills work for the video covers, so we work fairly closely. Anyhow, he was planning a shoot the following week, so I sent Carla along.'

'And were you present at the filming?'

'No. But I went to the first screening, and that was quite an experience.'

'The first screening?' The Judge raised his eyebrows.

'Sure. The company runs the film privately at a club to gauge the reactions.'

'And where exactly is this club?'

'It varies. They like to try a different one each time. This particular one was in North London.'

'Was it a normal preview?'

'No. This was different from any I had experienced previously. But I suppose I've come to expect that where Carla is concerned. She's not like any normal model, that's for sure.'

'I think we're starting to realize that,' said the Judge, looking pointedly at Carla. 'Nevertheless, tell us what was unusual.'

'Well, for a start, Carla was there.'

'That's unusual?'

'Yeah. These small-time porn stars tend not to face their

public much. I guess they're embarrassed about the whole thing. But not Carla. I reckon she positively loved the attention she got.'

'I see.' The Judge addressed Carla once more. 'Have you anything to say on this matter?'

'I think I've said enough, don't you?' she replied testily.

'In that case, perhaps we should watch the film.'

'Watch it?'

'Certainly. It wasn't easy, but we managed, with this gentleman's help, to secure a copy. I have it here.'

The Judge held up a video box. On the cover was a depiction of Carla, perched on the bonnet of a car, a spanner in her hand. She was naked, her body covered with black grease stains. Above were emblazoned the words *Car Mechanics on the Job* in yellow letters. Once again a murmur of chatter went up from the crowd.

'That's one of my covers,' said Mitch, a note of pride in his voice.

Carla stared, open-mouthed, at the Judge. 'Surely you're not going to show that?' she gasped.

'Certainly I am. This room has a video player and a sophisticated projection screen. We shan't miss any of the action.'

'But that would just be voyeurism. It wouldn't add anything to the case.'

'On the contrary, it would add a great deal. But if you're determined to stop me showing it, there is one alternative.'

'What's that?'

'Tell us the story of the preview night. In your own words.'

'You really get a kick out of hearing me talk dirty, don't you, Judge?'

'I tend to feel it gives you a kick as well,' he said. 'Particularly considering the way you've started masturbating yourself again.'

Carla's face reddened as she realized that she had indeed been rubbing her clitoris back and forth over the chain between her legs. She hadn't even known she was doing it, but looking down she could see the gleam of her love juices on the metal.

'Now, Mrs Wilde,' the Judge went on. 'Do I hand this video over for showing, or do you tell your tale?'

Carla glared at him. She certainly didn't want to have to detail the events at that London film club. But the alternative, to have to stand and watch herself fucked on-screen in front of this particular audience, seemed too much.

'I'll tell,' she said at last.

'Excellent. Now, as I understand it, this was your first venture into motion pictures?'

Carla grinned wryly. 'Motion pictures,' she said, 'makes it sound rather grand. But it certainly wasn't that . . .'

Chapter Twenty Six

What Mitch had said about Carla begging to be found a part in a pornographic film was not exctly true, though it was certainly the case that the idea appealed to her greatly, so that when the suggestion was made she found herself fascinated by the idea.

In a sense it had begun with the video that had dropped through her letterbox on the night she had had her first experience of whoring. The night that had ended with her submitting to the two pimps up the back alley.

She had watched the film over a number of times after that first night, usually naked, with a vibrator nearby to bring herself off with when the arousal in her became too strong. She had bought the vibrator in the hope that it would satisfy some of her desires and act as a substitute for the wanton behaviour that kept attracting her back to the agency and to Mitch's studio, but it seemed to have the opposite effect, often arousing her to such a frenzy that she found herself reaching for the phone and dialling the agency long before it had brought her to orgasm.

But her main fascination had been with the girl in the video, a slim young brunette like herself who apparently shared similar desires. Carla watched over and over again how she gave herself to the men in the film, her manner totally uninhibited. She imagined herself in a similar role, being watched by people in cinemas and clubs as she gave vent to her needs.

Meanwhile she continued with the photographic sessions with Mitch. The pictures taken on the beach had been a great success and it was not long before a second shoot was in demand. Once again Carla had submitted willingly to the demands of the cameramen, enjoying every moment of the attentions of her two new partners.

It was quite by chance that she had spotted the proof for the video cover lying on the table in Mitch's studio. She had just returned from a shoot in a wooded glade where she had enjoyed a three-way session with a young stud and another female model. The bright colours of the picture caught her eye and she studied it with interest. It depicted a young woman stretched naked across the seat of a motorcycle whilst a pair of leather-clad men groped at her body. Emblazoned across the top of the picture was the title, *Bikers' Girl*.

'What's this, Mitch?' she asked.

'Just a cover for a new video,' he replied.

'I didn't know you were into video.'

'I'm not. Just the covers. A friend of mine makes them.'

Carla's eyes widened. 'Really? What's his name?'

He stared hard at her. 'Andy Lang,' he said. 'Why are you so interested?'

'Just curious, that's all.'

He grinned. 'I know you, Carla Wilde,' he said. 'You fancy yourself as a porn star.'

'No, I don't. It never crossed my mind,' she lied.

He moved up behind her and placed his arms about her, reaching up for her breasts, which he squeezed through the thin material of her summer dress. She wore no bra, in fact no underwear whatsoever, and he could feel the hard rubbery teats of her nipples.

She laid her head on his shoulders. She liked being touched in this way, and Mitch's combination of strength and gentleness was a real turn-on to her. She had started screwing Mitch after that second photo session on the beach. Now they would often return to the studio after a shoot and have sex on the couch there. They had even taken to meeting secretly when she wasn't posing for him and the sex he gave her was very good indeed.

The strange thing about what went on between her and Mitch was that it was the only relationship in which she felt really unfaithful to her husband. The other men who fucked her were doing it purely for physical reasons, or because they were being paid. With Mitch there was a real desire, and his experience of watching her with other men had taught him just what it was that she liked, so that their sessions were long and amorous. It was not a serious relationship, though. Mitch had a long-standing girlfriend with whom he lived and to whom he returned each night. But each of them gave the other what they wanted, and Carla grew to look forward to fucking with Mitch even after the rigours and inevitable orgasms of a photo shoot.

He began unbuttoning her dress, starting at the bust and working his way down.

'Mitch,' she admonished. 'We haven't got the time. I have to be back.'

He reached into her now half-unfastened dress and closed his hands over the warm softness of her breasts. 'There's no great hurry, surely?' he murmured as he massaged her gently.

'It's just that Eric said he might be early this evening. We're going to a cocktail party or something.'

'You won't be late. Would you like an introduction to Andy?'

'I beg your pardon?'

'I said would you like to meet Andy Lang?'

'The film-maker?'

'Yes.'

Carla didn't answer immediately, but she knew he must be able to sense the effect his words had had on her, her breath shortening slightly as her nipples became even harder.

'I . . . I don't know.'

His right hand dropped to the remaining fastenings on her dress whilst his left continued to massage her breast. He began to slip them undone one by one. This time she said nothing, simply pressing her body back against him, feeling the hardness at his crotch against her back.

He reached the bottom of the dress, then eased it from her shoulders. She let her arms hang at her sides as it dropped off her onto the floor. Then his hands were at her breasts once more, kneading the soft, pliant flesh between his fingers.

'Oh God, that feels good, Mitch,' she sighed, letting her head fall back as his lips worked their way up and down her slim neck and over her shoulders. 'Tell me more about Andy Lang.'

'He's one of the best. Been in the industry for years. He was one of the first to switch from celluloid to video.'

'What sort of films does he make?'

'Hard core. Full penetration and lots of heavy shagging. A bit of S and M every now and again.'

'S and M? What does that stand for?'

'You really don't know?' Mitch slid his hand off Carla's right breast and ran it down over her rib cage, across the smooth flatness of her stomach. She felt her body tense as his fingers approached her sex, which was already hot and wet in anticipation of what was to come.

'Oh!'

She gave a start as he found her clitoris, his fingers rubbing over the top of it and sending pulses of pleasure through her.

'Oh, that's lovely Mitch,' she moaned. 'Don't stop. Tell me what S and M is.'

'Sado-masochism. The girl gets tied up and whipped. Or maybe gets clamps put on her nipples.'

'Ah!' she gasped. 'Are all his films like that?'

'No. He does mostly mainstream stuff. Why are you so interested, Carla?' He slid his hand lower and penetrated her with two fingers.

'Ahhhh! I'm not sure.'

'I am. You want to do it, don't you? You want to be a porn actress.'

'Mmmm.'

'Was that a yes?'

'Tell me about it.'

'You'd be in a roomful of men. It's not like photography where just me and Tom can handle it. They'd film you being fucked. They'd want real close-ups of you sucking cock or getting a stiff erection in your cunt or arse. You'd be the centre of attraction Carla, giving that lovely body of yours to a couple of studs.'

'Ohhhh,' Carla moaned. Mitch was frigging her hard now, and she was responding eagerly, her legs splayed wide, her knees bent as she pressed her crotch down hard against his hand, his fingers making a squelching sound as they worked in and out. Her mind was filled with the image of the video shoot. All those men watching as she cavorted naked before them, giving herself totally to their desires. Even the thought of being tied and whipped sent an odd feeling of desire through her.

'Then afterwards,' Mitch went on. 'They'll show the film in cinemas all over the place. Just think of all those men watching you get fucked, Carla, then going off and wanking over the idea. Or maybe taking a whore, or their own lover and fucking them hard afterwards. But all the time it'll be you they're fucking, Carla. Hundreds of men, all imagining their cocks are in you. Does that turn you on?'

'Ahhhh!'

Carla's response was to come loud and hard, her small frame shaking as spasms of lust flowed up from her sopping love hole and permeated her entire body. Mitch gripped her body tightly as first she stiffened, then slumped into his arms, panting for breath.

He lowered her gently onto the couch, where she lay gazing up at him as he began to strip. He pulled off his shirt and dropped it to the floor beside her dress. His shoes, socks and jeans swiftly followed, and soon Carla was staring at his stiff cock as he lowered himself onto her.

'Do you really think my body would turn men on like that?' she asked.

'You can see the effect it's having on me,' he grinned.

She reached down and took hold of his cock, closing her fingers about his shaft.

'Your body's not so bad either,' she said, guiding him towards the pink cleft of her vagina.

He slid into her, the expression on his face showing how he loved the way the muscles of her sex seemed to caress his organ.

'Better be quick, Mitch,' she whispered in his ear. 'I really do have to go out tonight.'

'Seems a shame to rush it,' he said. But already he was driving into her, taking her breath away with the force of his onslaught.

'Did you really mean that, about all those men thinking they were fucking me?' she asked quietly.

'Yeah,' he gasped. 'Every one of them imagining his cock is right where mine is now, and about to fill you with spunk like I am. Do you want me to introduce you to Andy?'

At that moment his cock gave a sudden twitch and, true to his word, he began pumping his sperm into her sex. Carla held back for a second, then she screamed as yet another orgasm gripped her and she thrashed about beneath him, her hips jabbing up against his own.

It was a long and delicious orgasm, the pair of them locked together at mouth and groin as they milked their pleasure from one another. When finally they parted Carla relaxed back on the couch, a contented expression on her face, her vagina still pulsing about his cock.

'I'll take that as a Yes, then, shall I?' he said.

Chapter Twenty Seven

Carla's heart was aflutter as she entered the auditorium of the private film theatre and glanced about her. It was smaller than she had expected, and she suspected the low lights were designed more to conceal the shabbiness of the decor than to improve the atmosphere. There was a slightly musty smell about the place as well. Not exactly the Odeon, Leicester Square, she mused.

She studied the clientele. There were about twenty of them, which meant that nearly half the seats in the cinema were filled. Most were men of middle age, though there were none of the dirty macs she had expected. They were sitting alone mainly, but here and there they were in pairs. There were no other women present.

Carla looked about for Mitch or Andy, but could see neither. She had obviously arrived before them. She felt very conspicuous as she made her way to a seat near the middle of the cinema. She wore a short one-piece dress that hugged her curves beautifully, accentuating the shape of her breasts and the curve of her behind, and she knew she looked good. She chose a seat between two men, leaving a gap of at least one seat between them. They stared at the lovely young girl as she sat down and waited for the film to start. The man on her right leaned across and offered her a sweet from a bag, but she declined. She began to feel rather nervous alone in this seedy little picture house.

She might have guessed that Andy would be late. Ever since she had first met him he had given the impression of being slightly scatterbrained, although she liked him very much.

They had met in his office. Mitch had accompanied her there. It was in an old warehouse beside the Thames and was reached by a flight of winding metal steps. Andy had sat behind a desk cluttered with cameras, video tapes and phographs. He was about thirty years old, with close cropped hair and dark glasses. He had grinned in recognition as Mitch had entered.

'Hi, Mitch. These cover stills are excellent. Thanks.'

Don't thank me, just pay my bill on time,' replied Mitch, returning his grin.

'So this is Caroline, is it?' he asked. His accent betrayed a childhood spent somewhere in Essex.

'Carla actually,' she replied.

'Sorry, Carla. That your real name?'

'Well, it's not Caroline.'

He laughed. 'Sit down, Carla, and tell me about yourself.'

She perched on the edge of chair. 'What's to tell? I'm twenty-three, unemployed and I've been doing some work with Mitch here lately. He says you can put me in one of your films.'

'You know what kind of films I make, Carla?'

'Yes.'

'And you don't object to getting fucked on film?'

'No.' Carla felt a flush come to her face as she replied.

'Can you act?'

'I was in the drama group at school.'

'In the drama group at school, eh?' he said, imitating her accent.

'Listen, Andy,' she replied testily. 'If you're just going to take the piss, I'll go.'

'No, don't,' he said. 'Just my way, I'm afraid. Still, I've got to say that you don't sound like the usual girls I get auditioning. Most of them haven't got a brain cell between them.'

'Carla's something special,' put in Mitch. 'I told you that on the phone.'

'And I'm beginning to believe you,' replied Andy. 'Listen, Carla,' he went on. 'Do you mind taking that dress off? I just need to get confimation that your body's okay. You can leave your undies on.'

'I'm not wearing any.'

'Ah.' Now it was Andy's turn to look embarrassed. 'Would you like to go behind the screen or something?'

'What's the point?'

Carla rose to her feet and reached for the zipper at the back of her dress. She pulled it down in single movement, then let the dress fall to the floor, stepping out of it and dropping it onto the chair. Then she placed her feet slightly apart and stood facing him, her arms at her sides, trying to look relaxed, though in reality she felt slightly awkward.

Andy gave low whistle. 'Wow, you're gorgeous,' he said. 'Turn around.'

Slowly Carla revolved on the spot. She knew she looked good, her breasts standing proud from her chest, the up-turned nipples contrasting with the paleness of her young flesh. She had trimmed her pubic bush carefully for the meeting, ensuring that her sex lips were prominent beneath, and as she turned her back on the film producer she knew he would be captivated by the firm roundness of her backside.

Carla loved to be looked at, particularly when she was naked, and this occasion was no exception. By the time she was facing Andy again she could already feel the wetness seeping into her love hole, and she knew Mitch would be aware of her arousal.

'What do you think?'

'Very nice. Very nice indeed. I think you've got what it takes, Carla. When are you free?'

'That's the only problem,' she replied. 'I can't always get away. When do you want me?'

'We're starting a shoot next week. Tuesday and Wednesday. How's that?'

'That sounds okay.' Carla knew already that her husband was off at a conference the following week. It all seemed perfect.

'Great. I'll see you here at nine in the morning on Tuesday, then.'

'Do I get a script beforehand?'

'You won't need one. Just bring along those pretty tits and arse and be prepared to suck some cocks.'

A tremor of anticipation ran through Carla's body as she reached for her dress. She wasn't going to be able to wait until the following Tuesday. She hoped Mitch knew somewhere nearby where they could fuck.

All that had been nearly four weeks ago, and now here she was, sitting in the cinema waiting for the film's first showing. She thought back to the two days of shooting, and the numerous orgasms she had enjoyed in the eye of Andy's camera. Most of the film had been shot in a garage that

Andy had rented for the occasion, so that, as well as the camera crew, the mechanics had been able to watch her as she paraded her body and gave herself to the male actors. Before she had left she had signed a nude photo of herself and had given it to the men. It gave her a real thrill to think of it hanging in their workshop, allowing them to ogle her body any time they liked.

All at once the lights began to dim. Carla had a last glance about her. There was still no sign of Mitch or Andy. Then the screen flickered into life and she concentrated on the pictures before her. The video image was crisp, despite being projected onto the large screen, and a murmur of approval went up as the words *Car Mechanics on the Job* flashed up before them.

Carla watched intently. It was an odd experience to see herself on the screen. It was hard to believe that the sexy young girl in the impossibly short orange miniskirt and tight silk blouse was actually her.

The first few scenes showed her climb into small car and drive off down the road. Even here Andy had managed to make her look remarkably sexy, angling the camera to allow a perfect view down her cleavage as she steered the car down a quiet road.

All at once the car began making a strange squeaking noise, followed by the sound of two backfires. Smoke was seen to pour from the exhaust, as the driver fiddled with the knobs on the dashboard. Then a garage appeared ahead and the car turned onto the forecourt.

The girl climbed out of the car and lifted the bonnet. The camera filmed her from behind as she leant into the engine, her skirt riding up and showing the white flesh of her thighs above her hold-up stockings and the black panties that were pushed so far into the crack of her behind as to be almost superfluous.

At that moment a pair of men appeared, dressed in greasy overalls. Both were tall and good-looking, with slim hips and broad chests. One of them had shoulder-length curly hair and a dark moustache, while the other's was short and streaked blond. Carla licked her lips as she eyed their images on the screen, memories of their firm bodies filling her head.

The pair took up station on either side of the lovely young motorist, gazing at the engine as she explained her predicament. When she straightened up her blouse and skirt were streaked with black oil from the engine and she gave a cry of dismay.

'Don't worry,' said one of the mechanics. 'There's a washroom inside. You steer the car and we'll push it into the workshop.'

The scene switched to inside the workshop, where the two men set about repairing the car whilst the camera followed Carla's character into the workshop. A whistle sounded from the back of the cinema as she began undoing the buttons on her blouse, followed by a cheer as she pulled it off, revealing bare breasts beneath. Carla looked about her at her fellow spectators. All were leaning forward in their seats watching intently as she flaunted her body before them.

The skirt followed, revealing the scantiest of panties beneath. They were black, with a transparent panel down the front through which her pubic hair was clearly visible. At the back they tapered to no more than a thong that disappeared between the cheeks of her backside. Apart from her stockings and high heels, these were all she wore.

The next few scenes followed Carla as she scrubbed her clothes in the sink. Every now and then the action would switch to the two men, still hard at work on the car. At last she was finished, and she hung the garments on a stand in front of a gas heater. At that moment one of the men called to her and, wrapping her arms about her breasts for protection, she stepped back into the workshop.

The man beckoned her to join him at the car's bonnet and she leaned over beside him, one arm still placed across her nipples.

He pointed at something inside the engine compartment, and when Carla's character claimed not to be able to see what he was indicating he placed an arm about her waist, pulling her close. Carla watched with baited breath, remembering the smell and the feel of the man as he had stood beside her, his strong fingers sending thrills through her as he stroked her bare skin.

In no time they were in a clinch, his mouth locked over hers whilst his strong hands pushed her arm away and closed over her breasts. His hands were dirty from the engine, and left dark streaks over her pale skin, but she was apparently unconcerned, kissing him with relish as her nipples visibly hardened.

She dropped to her knees, unzipping his overall and pulling his cock from his pants, going down on his thick weapon at once whilst he gasped with pleasure. At that moment the second of the two mechanics came up behind Carla, taking hold of her panties and dragging them down her legs and off.

Carla was now on all fours, her legs apart and backside thrust back, revealing her shaven sex lips and the pink wetness within. The man began to run his hands over her bottom, leaving black fingermarks as he did so.

The girl on the screen continued to fellate her companion with relish as Carla watched from her seat, becoming more aroused with every minute. Then a sound from her right made her turn. The man sitting only one seat away had his cock in his hand and was rubbing his shaft as he watched the action on screen.

Carla looked on with fascination as the man masturbated himself, clearly oblivious to everything but the naked nymph on the screen whose breasts shook delightfully as she worked her head up and down over the shiny glands. She turned her gaze back to the film, the memory of the taste of his cock sending a shiver through her. Then, almost before she knew what she was doing, she slid off her seat and crawled down to where the man was sitting.

'What the . . .'

He gave an exclamation of surprise as she brushed his hand away from his erection and took it in her own fist, working his foreskin up and down. He stared at her, then his jaw dropped.

'It's you,' he gasped. 'You're her.'

Carla put her finger to her lips. 'Shh!' she hissed. 'Do you want what he's getting?'

The man nodded dumbly, watching in obvious fascination as Carla lowered her head over his rampant tool and took it between her lips, beginning to suck.

Carla fellated the man with enthusiasm, her head bobbing up and down, her hair flying about as she worked his foreskin back and forth with her hand. The man simply sat, gasping with delight, his penis stiff as a ramrod, his gaze alternating between the naked image of Carla on the screen and the real thing crouched between his legs.

The studs in the film were practised in restraint, able to hold back for as long as was necessary during filming. Not so the man in the cinema, though, and Carla was suddenly rewarded by a gush of spunk filling her mouth as he came with a grunt. She stayed where she was, her lips locked about his shaft as she wanked him, swallowing every drop of the hot viscous fluid that spurted from his cock.

When he was finally spent, Carla lifted her head from his lap and turned to return to her seat. Then she stopped short. Another man had occupied the spot where she had been sitting a short time before and was beckoning to her, his penis projecting straight up from his trousers.

Carla threw a glance at her alter ego on the screen, who was now sucking at the second of her two companions, who had stipped naked, his athletic young body rippling with muscles, whilst the first one kissed and stroked her breasts. Then she silently moved along the row.

The man pulled her to him, dragging her up onto her knees and planting his mouth over hers whilst his hands went to her breasts, squeezing them through the thin fabric of her dress. She reached down for his cock, grasping his shaft in her hand and beginning to masturbate him gently. When he began undoing the buttons on her dress she made no move to stop him, a small moan escaping her lips as his fingers found her nipples.

He pulled back from the kiss, then dropped his eyes to his cock. Carla glanced behind her at the screen, where her alter ego was kneeling before the two seated mechanics, her mouth alternating between their erections whilst both gasped with pleasure. Then she lowered her head over the man's lap and began to fellate him.

Scarcely had Carla found her rhythm with her new

partner, than she felt a hand on her backside. A third member of the audience had seen what was happening and had slipped into the seat next to the man she was sucking. Now he was sliding his fingers under the hem of her dress and up the soft flesh of her inner thigh. He pressed against the gusset of her panties and she knew he would be able to feel the wetness there.

He hooked his fingers into the waistband and pulled down the silky garment. Carla raised her knees, then her feet, allowing him to take them all the way off. Then she gave a start as he sought out her slit, running his fingers down the slippery pink furrow and finding the hard little nut of her clitoris.

Carla's moans were muffled by her mouthful of male flesh as he slipped two fingers into her vagina and began to work them back and forth. She tried hard to concentrate on the job in hand, slurping and licking the man's erection whilst thrusting her backside hard against the fingers that penetrated her so deliciously.

The man's orgasm took her almost by surprise, and it was all she could do to gulp down his spunk as spurt after spurt filled her mouth, accompanied by the hoarse gasps of the man in front of her. Once again the wanton young girl relished the taste of his seed as her second helping of come slid down her throat.

No sooner had she raised her head from the man's lap than she felt the third man remove his fingers from inside her and lift her dress to her waist. Moments later she felt something hot and hard pressing insistently against her from behind. At once she dropped onto all fours, moaning quietly as he slipped his weapon into her.

Carla braced herself against the seat beside her as the man

began his onslaught, jabbing his hips against her backside with undisguised urgency. On the screen the other Carla also had a cock inside her, draped face down across the bonnet of her car whilst the naked stud behind her pounded away at her, the camera clearly showing the shiny wetness of his tool as it slid in and out of her shaven love hole. The sight of herself being rogered so publicly sent a new thrill coursing through Carla's body, and she bit her lip to stop herself crying out under the onslaught from behind her.

When the man came in her, she came too, her breasts shaking as her body was racked with spasms of pleasure. She stayed where she was, gripping the seat hard, until her new lover was spent, groaning as he withdrew from her.

'Over here.'

The whisper came from the row of seats in front, and Carla looked up to see yet another member of the audience beckoning to her. She rose, climbed over the back of a seat and dropped into the place beside him. He reached for her breasts, which were still projecting plump and inviting from the front of her dress. On the screen the picture showed one of the mechanics seated on a chair with Carla on his lap, facing away from him. His cock was firmly embedded inside her and her breasts rose and fell with a fascinating elasticity as she bounced up and down on his erection.

'Like that,' the man whispered to her.

Carla felt for his fly, pulling down his zipper and releasing yet another rampant cock. His was long and veined, and she could feel the blood coursing through it as she closed her fist about it. He took hold of her dress and pulled it over her head in a single movement. For a second

Carla glanced about, concerned as to who might see her naked. Then she almost giggled as she remembered that, above her on the screen, her naked body was exposed for all to see.

She rose from her seat, still gripping the man's erection, and moved across until she was poised above his lap. Then she slowly lowered herself, at the same time guiding him into her vagina.

It was all she could do to prevent herself crying aloud as he slipped deeper and deeper into her. By the time her bottom came into contact with his lap she felt completely filled.

He placed an arm about her, grasping her breasts and kneading them gently. His other hand dropped to her crotch, burrowing down through her pubic hair and finding her clitoris. His touch triggered an instant and unexpected orgasm in the excited girl, sending convulsions through her vagina that made him gasp aloud. Then she was moving, working her body up and down as his cock slipped in and out of her burning cunt.

The rest of the screening was something of a blur to Carla, as she found herself passed from seat to seat, sucking and fucking with the audience whilst on the screen the action was as hot as ever. By the time the final scene appeared, with a grease-streaked Carla kneeling on the floor of the garage whilst the two studs came over her breasts and upturned face, Carla was exhausted, her sweaty body covered in spunk, her hair a mess. As the lights came up the sound of her umpteenth orgasm rang around the room.

There was silence for a moment, then the men broke into applause, though Carla never knew whether it was for her performance on-screen or in the auditorium.

Chapter Twenty Eight

The makeshift courtroom was hushed once again as Carla finished her narrative. She gazed about her at the audience, many of whom had been on the edge of their seats during the narration. Mitch too was silent. He had perched himself on one of the tables and now sat, his face cupped in his hands, staring up at the chained girl.

The Judge turned to him.

'Was that how it happened?'

'I couldn't have told it better myself, Judge,' he said. 'Me and Andy arrived about ten minutes after the film began, and she'd already started. I reckon she managed to bring off all twenty of them in that audience. I never met such a game woman.'

'Some would call her a slut.'

'Only because they didn't know her. Carla's no slut. She's a woman with a lovely body who's not afraid to share it. Carla loves giving pleasure to men and getting it herself. That's all there is to it.'

'But she's a married woman.'

'In name, yes. But he never gives her what she wants. That's why she goes to men who appreciate her for what she is.'

'So you wouldn't condemn her?'

'Condemn her? Hell no! There's nothing to condemn. Carla's not guilty of anything more than being herself.'

'Are you still seeing her?'

'No.'

'Why not?'

'My girl found out something was going on. And I wasn't going to leave her for Carla.'

'So despite what you've said, you don't back up your words with actions?'

'It's not that. Carla's not a one-man woman. With us it was nothing more than good sex and a genuine friendship. So I gave her up and went back to my girl. There were no bad feelings, were there, Carla?'

Carla smiled at him. 'None,' she said.

'All right,' said the Judge. 'I think that's about all we require from you. Thank you for attending.'

Mitch paused, still staring up at his former lover. 'You gonna be okay, kid?'

'Yeah. Don't worry.'

Carla watched him as he departed. She wondered if she should have asked for his help to get out of this mess. But somehow she sensed there was nothing he could have done. If the Judge had considered him in any way dangerous he would never have allowed him into the court. Besides, he had been the first person really to speak in her favour, and that must have been a help in itself.

'Mrs Wilde,' said the Judge. 'Are there any other aspects of your life over the past eighteen months that you wish to confess to?'

'So you've run out of witnesses then?'

'Answer the question!'

'I think you've heard enough, don't you? There's a

couple of guys out there who'll bust a blood vessel if I say any more.'

'And what of your present escapades? Did you make any more films?'

'Three, actually. The latest has lots of bondage and whipping in it. It'd be right up your street. We were going to make another next month, but I guess that's off now.'

'And the agency?'

'I saw my latest client three days ago. Eric was out for the evening, fucking Phaedra, I guess.'

'Phaedra?'

'Why else would all this have happened? I've been thinking it through, and it has to be her. She led me into all this, and now she's going to take my place. Well, you're welcome to him, dear. Those two pimps who screwed me up that alley had more integrity than him.'

'But that first evening, when all this started. You claim you saw him with another woman, whilst Phaedra was downstairs.'

'That was probably some floozy. That was when she got the idea that maybe she could get Eric from me. So she planned the whole thing. And I was stupid enough to fall for it. Well, you can do your worst to me, Judge. Frankly I'm past caring.'

Carla glared defiantly down at the Judge, then round the rest of the room. Nobody spoke. Her eyes fixed on Eric, but he wouldn't meet her look, keeping his gaze fixed on the table in front of him. She turned to Phaedra, but the woman was writing fast, apparently oblivious to what had been said.

Bang!

The Judge's gavel came down hard.

'Does anyone else have anything to say before the jury considers its verdict?' he asked.

Still the room was silent.

'The accused may step down,' he said.

'Don't I get to listen to this lot slagging me off?' asked Carla angrily, as her two handmaidens appeared on the stage beside her and began undoing the shackles on her ankles.

'The jury will deliberate in private,' replied the Judge.

'Meaning everybody gets to hear but me.'

'You will find out the verdict in due course.'

'And I wonder what it'll be? I've heard of kangaroo courts but this one takes the biscuit.'

'Take her out,' ordered the Judge.

The youngsters undid Carla's leads and led her down from the stage, her wrists still fastened behind her. She looked neither right nor left as she walked from the room, oblivious to the stares of the onlookers.

Instead of taking her back to the room in which she had previously been kept, they took her along a narrow, poorly lit corridor, and down a steep flight of stairs. They stopped outside a stout wooden door and unlocked it, then took her inside. The room was bare apart from a metal bed in the corner and a sink against the wall. The blonde girl undid Carla's wrists, then the pair of them left, banging the door behind them.

Carla stretched her arms above her head, glad to be free of the cuffs at last, then rubbed her wrists where the metal had been chafing against her skin. She gazed about the cheerless cell. The bed had no blankets or sheets on it, just a thin mattress, and when she sat down on it, it felt hard. She wondered what was going on in the room above, what they were saying about her. She wished she could hear the debate. Down here in the bowels of the building she felt suddenly quite helpless, destined merely to sit and wait whilst her fate was decided elsewhere.

She got up and paced the room a couple of times. Then, on a whim, she tested the door. To her surprise it was unlocked.

Carla's mind raced. Had the girls forgotten to lock her in? Had the lock failed? Or were they merely so sure of her that they hadn't seen the necessity to lock her in? Whatever the answer was, she didn't intend to stay in the room for a moment longer than necessary. Easing the door open she peered out.

There was nobody about. She stepped silently into the corridor and looked up and down. She listened hard, but could hear no sound from either direction. She hesitated for a moment, gazing down at herself. If only she had something to wear she would have felt more confident. Being naked simply increased her feeling of vulnerability. But there seemed nothing she could do about it so, taking a deep breath, she set off in the direction from which they had brought her.

She climbed the stairs as quietly as she was able, listening hard for the sound of anybody approaching. At the top of the flight was a door and she turned the handle.

It was locked.

Damn! She descended the stairs once more. There was nowhere else to go but back past her cell, so she made her way in that direction. Just beyond her cell door the corridor swung left, and she peered round the corner. Once again there was nobody about. The passage was about twenty yards long, with a door in the middle on the left hand side and another at the end. Carla padded towards the one at the end. It was a thick wooden door with a heavy handle, which she tried.

Locked.

She gave a little cry of despair and turned. There was only one door left, now, and she made her way silently towards it.

She paused outside, noticing for the first time that the door was open a crack. A thin sliver of light emerged from it. She put her eye close to the opening, but could discern only a wall. She pushed gently against the door, opening it a little further. Then she heard a sound.

It was a soft, rhythmic, hissing sound. For a second she couldn't place it. Then she realized with a shock that it was the sound of someone breathing hard. She almost ran at that point, but checked herself. After all, where was there to run to? Back to her cell, to await the return of her captors? She pushed on the door once more, opening it a little further, then peered inside.

What she saw made her stifle a gasp. The room was quite large, and brightly lit. There were no doors or windows, other than the entrance she had used. A lone man was standing in the room, his back to the door, facing a wide table. Laid out on the table were a number of magazines. They were all open and he was studying the pictures. He seemed to be trembling, and he was breathing heavily.

Carla recognized him at once. It was one of the waiters. He was quite a young man with a freckled face and flaming red hair. She had first noticed him when he had wandered into the room whilst she was recounting one of her adventures. Such was his surprise at seeing her naked and trussed that he had dropped his tray, smashing plates and glasses and momentarily bringing proceedings to a halt.

After that he had been unable to take his eyes off her, and had blushed brightly whenever she caught his eye. But what was he doing now?

Unable to contain her curiosity, Carla slipped into the room behind him and moved silently closer. She peered over his shoulder, and her heart leapt as she realized that the magazines he was studying were the ones that Mitch had brought into the court. Spread out across the table were images of Carla, quite naked, in various poses with a number of young men. The photos were totally explicit, depicting her with cocks in her mouth, vagina, backside, between her breasts and in her hands.

It was only then that she realized that the man was masturbating, his long pale cock grasped in his fist as he worked his foreskin urgently back and forth.

Her initial reaction was one of shock and surprise. In all her sexual escapades she had never come across a man wanking alone like this. The shock soon gave way to a feeling of excitement, however, as she realized that it was her image that was arousing him. It occurred to her that this was precisely the scenario that had filled her head when she was posing for the shots with Mitch.

She wondered if she should withdraw. Leave him to his fantasies. But she was too fascinated by the sight he made, and besides there was clearly no escape from this part of the house. She watched, her arousal increasing with every moment, as he masturbated hard, his hand flying back and forth.

Then she could contain herself no longer. Reaching round him from behind she placed her hand over his, feeling the way his cock pulsated under his fingers.

He gave a jump, spinning round to face her. Then his

face glowed crimson as he realized he had been caught in the act. He tried to hide himself, placing his hands over his erection, but she pulled them away, wrapping her fingers round his twitching shaft.

'Enjoying the pictures?' she asked.

'I . . . I'm sorry. I was just looking . . .'

'That's what they're for, isn't it?'

'What?'

'The pictures. They're for looking at. And for turning men on. That's why I posed for them.'

'I suppose so . . .'

'What's your name?'

'Peter. Listen I have to be going.'

'There's nowhere to go. We're locked in. Didn't you know that?'

'No. I just came down here for . . .'

'For a bit of privacy?'

He blushed again. 'Yes.'

'Well, it looks like just the two of us now. I'm waiting for the verdict and you're . . .' she broke off, glancing down at his cock which she was still grasping.

'Look,' he said. 'I'm sorry about this.'

'You've said that already. What are you sorry about?'

'You know,' he said, indicating the pictures.

'They're good, aren't they?' She ran her fingers up and down the length of his shaft. 'Which do you like best?'

'I don't know.' His face was redder than ever.

'Yes, you do. Tell me, Peter.'

He hesitated, then pointed to one of the shots. It depicted Carla lying on her back across a table, her legs spread wide, a stiff penis probing at her sex.

'Would you like me to pose like that?'

He didn't answer, but the sudden twitch from his rampant organ told her all she wanted to know.

She released his cock and turned her back to the table. The hard cold edge of the wood pressed against her backside, but she didn't mind, letting her body fall back until she was prostrate on the table's surface, her firm breasts falling apart slightly as she did so. Slowly she spread her legs, revealing the pink flower of her sex in all its glory. She gazed down between her twin mounds at him.

'You can touch me if you like.'

For a few seconds Peter simply stood and stared at her, as if rooted to the spot. Then he slowly stretched out a shaking hand, placing it on the inside of her thigh. At once Carla felt her sex lips convulse, and a small bead of moisture escape from within her.

'Move it higher, Peter,' she urged.

Gradually he moved his hand up over the smooth flesh of her thigh. She could sense it trembling, but the continued stiffness of his erection told her that his desires had not diminished.

'Ah!'

Her hips jerked forward as he touched the soft leaves of her sex, making the lips twitch once more. For a second she thought he might withdraw his hand, but then she felt it creeping up towards her clitoris.

He slid his finger up her crack, bringing a fresh gasp from her. Then he was touching her where she loved to be touched most, and she thrust her hips upwards, moaning aloud.

'Do you want me, Peter?' she murmured.

He nodded dumbly.

'Then take me, for Christ's sake. Slide that lovely cock of yours into me. Fuck me like that stud in the picture, Peter.'

He took his cock in his hand, guiding the tip towards her gaping love hole. She groaned as she felt the hard bulbous glans brush against her. Then he pushed, and she cried aloud as he slid into her.

He took hold of her thighs on either side and began to fuck her, hesitantly at first, then with increasing boldness as he saw the effect it was having on her. Carla lay prostrate across the hard wooden surface, her feet planted firmly on the ground, her backside raised clear of the table as she thrust her pubis up at him, as if urging him ever deeper within her.

She looked up at his face, and realized suddenly that his eyes were fixed on the open magazine beside her. She reached out, taking hold of his chin and pulling his face round to hers.

'Look at me, not at her,' she urged. 'She's just an image. An object of men's fantasies. Something forbidden. I'm real, Peter, and I'm the one you're fucking. And your cock feels better than any of those studs' did.'

Once again she felt his penis throb at her words. Then his hands were on her breasts, squeezing and kneading them whilst his hips continued to pound against her own. She was almost screaming with pleasure now, her backside slapping against the table top with every stroke as he brought her to new heights of delectation. Then she sensed a tension building in him as his breath shortened, and she thrust against him all the harder, urging him towards his climax.

The pair of them came simultaneously, shouting in chorus as his thick weapon unleashed its load of thick spunk deep inside her vagina. Carla panted with lust as she continued to match him thrust for thrust, revelling in the sensation of being filled by his seed. The table legs creaked as it crept back across the floor, each jab of his hips moving it further towards the wall, such was the violence of his orgasm.

They came down slowly, each reluctant to allow the moment to pass, their pubes grinding together as each extracted every possible ounce of pleasure from the other. At last though, they were still.

'That was good, Peter,' she breathed.

'As good as those studs?'

'Better. Those bastards never came in me. And that's what I like best.'

He grinned sheepishly. 'I never thought of myself as a great lover.'

'More of a wanker?'

He looked at her sharply, then saw she was grinning.

'Maybe I should concentrate more on the real thing.'

'Maybe you should.'

At that moment there was a sound outside in the corridor, and Peter sprang back from her, hurriedly tucking himself back into his trousers. Moments later Carla's handmaidens entered, stopping short at the sight of her spreadeagled on the table, the spunk oozing from her sex.

'So there you are,' said the blonde.

'Where did you think I'd be? After all, you locked all the bloody doors.'

'Better come back to the cell and clean up,' said the girl.

Carla rose to her feet. She turned away from the girls and took Peter's hand. Then she kissed him on the mouth.

'So long,' she said. 'It seems I've got to go.'

'Come on,' said the blonde impatiently.

'What's the hurry?' asked Carla. 'I'm not going any-where.'

'Oh yes, you are,' replied the girl. 'You're going upstairs again.'

'Upstairs?'

'Yes. They've reached their verdict.'

Chapter Twenty Nine

Carla stared down at her jurors, her glance going from face to face, meeting their eyes and holding their stares for an instant before moving on. Once again there was no sound from the onlookers as they looked up at the naked young beauty who stood before them, her hands cuffed behind her, her legs apart, her breasts thrust proudly forwards.

She heard the sound of a door opening, and glanced across to see the Judge as he entered the room. There was a scraping of chairs as all those in attendance rose to their feet in deference to his presence. He strode along, grim-faced, looking neither right nor left as he made his way to the table where he had sat throughout the trial. Eric and Phaedra were already there, and he nodded to each before taking his seat between them. As soon as he sat, the rest of the room followed suit.

He called forward one of Carla's young escorts, who walked hesitantly into the centre of the room, clearly overawed by the Judge's presence.

'You were a long time bringing the prisoner back up,' he said. 'Please explain why.'

'She wasn't ready.'

'Not ready?'

'She had to get cleaned up.'

'What do you mean?'

'We'd found her with one of the waiters. He'd managed to get into the cell area.'

'What was she doing with this waiter?'

'He was having her.'

'Having her?'

'He was fucking her. That's why she had to get cleaned up. She was full of his spunk.'

The Judge shook his head. 'Even in that short time she manages to find a man to satisfy her desires,' he said. 'It's really quite incredible.'

Carla said nothing.

There was a pause as the Judge arranged his papers in front of him. Then he turned to Phaedra.

'Has the jury reached its verdict?'

'Yes, Judge.'

'And is it a unanimous decision?'

'Yes, Judge.'

'Stand and deliver that verdict please.'

The room was totally silent as Phaedra rose to her feet. She turned to face Carla, who stared back at her, her face calm.

'Carla Wilde,' said Phaedra. 'Do you understand why you are here?'

'To entertain this bunch of perverts,' replied Carla defiantly.

'You are here to stand trial before your peers on charges of wanton and lascivious behaviour, of infidelity to your husband, and of bringing yourself and your neighbourhood into disrepute. Charges to which you pleaded not guilty.'

'If you say so.'

'The jury has heard the case against you, and has reached a verdict.'

'And how does the jury find the defendant?' asked the Judge. 'Guilty or not guilty?'

'Guilty.'

A murmur went up from the crowd as Carla gazed about her. Guilty! She hadn't expected anything else. Now she watched in silence as the Judge rose to his feet once more.

'Carla Wilde,' he began, his voice a flat monotone. 'You have been found guilty on all charges. Have you anything to say?'

'I'd have thought you'd heard enough from me today,' she said. 'At least that waiter's reaction was honest. He was wanking, you see. I just gave him some relief.'

'Have you no remorse for the way you have behaved?'

'Why should I have? That bastard of a husband of mine couldn't give me what I wanted. He was too busy giving it to that bitch Phaedra. So I went and found it elsewhere. I don't know why you're being so pious. There isn't a man in this room who wouldn't slip me a length given half a chance, including you, Judge.'

Bang!

'That's enough,' barked the Judge.

'Well, you asked,' murmured Carla quietly.

'Carla Wilde,' he said again. 'It is the sentence of this court that you be taken from here to a place of correction. There you will be taught obedience and prepared for your new role. When you are successfully trained, you will begin a period of servitude, during which your sole responsibility will be bringing pleasure to men in any way they desire.'

'You mean I'm to become a whore?'

'There are many who will say you are that already.'

Carla did not reply. There was no point. The whole of the trial had been no more than a sham, and the verdict a foregone conclusion. She reflected on the Judge's words. Training. What could that possibly involve? She thought of the caning they had given her, and of the stripes that now decorated her behind, and an unexpected shudder of lust shook her body.

It looked as if her life was about to change beyond measure.

Chapter Thirty

Carla stared around at the four grey featureless walls of the cell in which they had left her. She had been here for more than an hour now, her arms held above her head by steel manacles that surrounded her wrists, her back resting against the cold wall. She was naked, the chill air making her shiver as she stood there, unable to move. The cell was the same one she had been left in whilst awaiting the verdict. It was lit by a single naked light bulb that illuminated her pale flesh, contrasting it with the dull grey of the walls.

Once the sentence had been handed down she had not remained in the court for long. Even as they were leading her out, the room was already emptying as the couples headed out to their cars and home. There had been no prospect of that for Carla, however. She had been led straight down the stairs and into this small room, where she had been secured to the wall and then left alone.

Since then she had been surrounded by complete silence, the only sound that of her own breathing. With nothing else to occupy her mind she had had ample time to contemplate her fate, and the Judge's words had gone round and round in her head.

A place of correction, they had said, in a remote part of

Africa or Asia, where recalcitrant girls were sent to learn obedience under a cruel master's whip, followed by a year or two in a brothel or harem in one of the less enlightened parts of the Dark Continent. It was an extraordinary prospect. Unimaginable. To be made the naked slave of some unknown man and be expected to satisfy his sexual whims.

Yet the idea, dreadful though it was, was having another, and quite unexpected effect on her. It was making her horny. The thought of being used as a sex slave was a fantasy that had often haunted her. And now, apparently, it was about to become a reality. She imagined herself in a harem, chained and naked as she was now, awaiting a beating from a strange man who would surely fuck her afterwards, and all at once she felt the wetness inside her increase and she longed to be able to touch her clit and to relieve the sexual tension that was building inside her.

Suddenly she heard the sound of footsteps outside the cell, the clicking heels telling her that it was a woman's tread. They stopped at the door and the jangling of keys reached her ears. It must be one of her jailers, she thought, returning to check on her.

The door opened, but the brightness of the light outside the cell temporarily prevented her from seeing anything more than a dark silhouette of the female figure framed in the doorway. Then the woman stepped inside, under the lone bulb.

'Phaedra!' Carla's jaw dropped as she recognized the woman. Her enemy. The architect of her current situation. She had imagined Phaedra long gone, heading home with Eric to the house they could now share without fear of interruption from Carla. Yet here she was. Had she come to gloat? If she had, Carla had no intention of showing any remorse or distress.

'Hello, Carla.'

Carla said nothing, glaring at the woman.

'Are you angry with me?'

'Of course I'm bloody angry. This whole thing was your fault.'

'My fault?'

'Yes, yours. Right from that day at the party, where you frigged me in the hotel room. You had the whole thing worked out. The men, the whoring, the photos and videos, everything. That was you on the island, wasn't it? Getting me to lick your cunt. The entire situation was your doing.'

'Nobody forced you to climb into that first car. Or to streetwalk that night. Or to join the escort agency. You went of your own accord to Mitch's studio. And to Andy's.'

'But you were behind it all, egging me on. I bet it was you that sent me the video and the magazines. You've been behind everything that's happened to me over the past year. And now look at the mess I'm in. I'm off to this so-called training camp whilst you're about to move into my house and my bed and to start fucking my husband.'

'Is that what you think?'

'Of course. What would you think?'

Phaedra laughed. 'Listen, Carla, I wouldn't get into bed with that cheating rat of a husband of yours for all the tea in China. He's a wimp and a fool, and he doesn't deserve you. Christ, he's the last person I'd want to move in with.'

Carla stared at her in confusion. 'Then what the hell was it all about, Phaedra?'

The woman moved closer to the naked captive and,

reaching out a hand, placed it on Carla's breast. She began to caress it gently, teasing the nipple to erectness

'Carla, you're one of the most beautiful women I've ever seen,' she said quietly. 'And you have the desires of ten women. I've never known a woman with such sexual stamina, and who so clearly enjoyed being fucked. Most women would be finished after two men, yet I've seen you still having orgasms after a dozen men have had you. That is a rare and unusual quality, a girl so sensuous, and with such an appetite for sex.'

'Yes, and look where it's got me.'

'But I don't think you fully understand where it has got you.'

'What do you mean?'

Phaedra transferred her attentions to Carla's right breast, caressing the soft flesh and rolling the ever-hardening nipple between finger and thumb.

'What was going on out there was not exactly what it seemed,' she said.

'I don't understand.'

'There were a lot of people who wanted a closer look at you, and confirmation of your lascivious nature. They wanted to hear from your own lips about your escapades. To get confirmation of what I had been telling them.'

'You . . .?'

'Yes. You see, Carla, we've been watching you for some time. Ever since that party, in fact.'

'Why me?'

'Because you're unique. And we wanted to let you show us, and yourself, just what you're capable of.'

'But why?'

'Because we believe in sexual freedom. And we also

believe in a woman's right to use her own body as she wishes, and to profit from that usage.'

'Profit?'

'Certainly. How much were you paid by that escort agency? Or by the tricks you pulled?'

'It depended. A couple of hundred usually.'

'A couple of hundred. That's peanuts.'

'Yes, but I wasn't doing it for the money.'

'You'll need the money now, though, won't you?'

'I suppose so.'

Phaedra moved closer, her fingers still toying with Carla's nipples.

'Listen, Carla. All that stuff about training camps and whorehouses in North Africa wasn't strictly true.'

'It wasn't?'

'No. There's a training camp, all right, and that's where we want you to go. But all that slavery business was nonsense. We think you're pretty damned good at using that body of yours already. All we want to do is hone some of those skills and maybe teach you a few new ones. In about two months you'll be a complete expert at satisfying men.'

'You want to turn me into a trained whore?'

'Kind of. Maybe give you a higher pain threshold, although I must say you responded pretty well to that whipping. We'll teach you a few more erogenous zones, as well, and train you to pace yourself a bit better. Then you'll be ready to really start using your body.'

'How?'

'There are men out there who will pay well for the kind of services you can provide, Carla. Not just two hundred a night, but thousands. Men who will keep you in the lap of luxury. Who will pander to your every whim just to be allowed the use of this gorgeous body. All they want is that you be totally free of inhibitions and prepared to play out their fantasies.'

'Who are these men?'

'Rich men. Millionaires with more money than they could possibly spend in a lifetime.'

'And where do you fit in?'

'As a kind of escort agency. Not unlike the one you were using, except they rented you out for a night, or maybe a weekend, whereas we'll sell you for six months. A year, even. And the money will be big. In three years we can make you a millionairess in your own right.'

Phaedra moved her hand down Carla's body, sliding it towards her crotch, watching the anticipation on Carla's face as she did so.

'Ah!'

Carla's body gave a lurch as the woman's fingers found her slit, and felt the wetness of her arousal.

'So what do you think?' asked Phaedra.

'I . . . I don't know. I don't understand how all this happened.'

'I spotted you back at that party. I could see you had the right temperament for what we needed right away, and that you were wasted on that creep Eric. So I started putting temptation in your way. You took the bait, Carla, and confirmed what I suspected all along. So we set up the trial. That allowed us to confirm your suitability as well as to ensure Eric was taken out of the picture. He's filing for divorce, by the way. Don't bother to contest.'

'You keep saying "we". Who are you?'

'About a third of the people in that room today were part

of our organization, as well as one or two of the witnesses. We find the right girls, train them and sell them, then take a percentage. The rest goes to the girl. It's an honourable trade, and everyone wins in the long run.'

'But how did you get involved in this thing?'

'Haven't you guessed? I was once one of the girls. Lots of the women there tonight have been through the training. I spent nearly seven years shagging some of the richest men in the world. As did every woman from the organization who was there tonight.'

'What, even some of the women I knew?'

'Certainly. Take that tall blonde at the back. The one who runs all the bridge parties.'

'Lucinda?'

'That's her. She spent two years as the sex slave of an Eastern European president. When she left he gave her a Ferrari, a wardrobe full of designer clothes and an apartment in Monaco. And that was just extras.'

'Wow!'

'So you see, once you're trained, we'll place you with the right person. You can carry on with it as long as you want. There's no shortage of men out there who'll want to take you. Then, in a few years' time, you'll be the one seeking out new recruits. Meanwhile, though, just enjoy what you've got.'

Phaedra slid her fingers into Carla's vagina, bringing another gasp of pleasure from the tethered girl.

'So what do you say? You want to go and find some crummy PA job in the City, or become a high-class escort, devoting your life to satisfying men's and your own desires? And ending up rich into the bargain.'

'When you put it that way . . .'

Carla was writhing with pleasure now as Phaedra worked her fingers back and forth. Suddenly the prospect of doing what the woman suggested seemed extremely attractive. The thought of spending her life giving and receiving pleasure, with no guilt attached and no need to hide her deeds from her husband, was a thrilling one.

'All right, I'll do it,' she moaned as she thrust her hips forward against Phaedra's fingers.

All of a sudden, Phaedra's hands left her body. She gave a little cry of disappointment as the woman moved away from her towards the door.

'Phaedra . . .'

Then the door swung open, and another figure entered the room.

It was the Judge.

He had changed from his evening suit into a dressing gown, and looked a good deal less imposing than he had in the court.

'She's agreed then?' he asked.

'Yes,' replied Phaedra. 'She's agreed.'

'You were right, as always.' He eyed Carla up and down. 'She'll be a valuable asset to us.'

'She certainly will.'

He addressed Carla. 'So, my dear, you're going to put those talents of yours to good use.'

'When do I start?' she asked.

'You'll be shipped out to the training camp in the morning. There you'll be kept under a strict regime until your training is complete. During that time your body will be entirely under our control. Do you understand that?'

'Yes, Judge.' Carla felt a frisson of pleasure run through her at these words. Once again the idea of abdicating power and responsibility to another was one that turned her on.

'Meanwhile you'll remain here for the night,' the Judge went on. 'And whilst you're here, I shall take full advantage.'

Carla stared down at his gown. There was no mistaking the way it stuck out at the front.

'Yes please, Judge,' she said.

He smiled, and turned to Phaedra. 'Is she wet?'

'Very. I saw to that.'

'Good. My gown.'

Phaedra moved forward. She took the cord that tied his gown shut and pulled. The knot came undone and the gown fell open. He shrugged and it fell to the ground.

Carla studied his naked body. His chest was broad and hairy, his stomach showing no signs of a bulge. His cock was beautiful, soaring up from his loins thick and meaty, the glans shiny with his secretions.

Phaedra dropped to her knees in front of him and took it into her mouth. Carla watched the expression of ecstasy on his face as Phaedra sucked him, and wished that it could be her.

'Enough,' he said at last. 'I want her now.'

Phaedra rose to her feet and, taking hold of his thick erection, took him across to where the younger girl hung in her chains. She nodded to Carla, who spread her legs and thrust her pubis forward.

As he slipped his cock into her, Carla reflected briefly on what was to come. She wondered how many more men would have her in the near future, and in what ways they would want to use her lovely young body.

And as the Judge started to fuck her, the most violent orgasm of her life shook her small frame, making her scream aloud with sheer pleasure.

Lust and Lady Saxon

LESLEY ASQUITH

Pretty Diana Saxon is devoted to her student husband, Harry, and she'd do anything to make their impoverished life in Oxford a little easier. Her sumptuously curved figure and shameless nature make her an ideal nude model for the local camera club – where she soon learns there's more than one way to make a bit on the side . . .

Elegant Lady Saxon is the most sought-after diplomat's wife in Rome and Bangkok. Success has followed Harry since his student days – not least because of the very special support lent by his wife. And now the glamorous Diana is a prized guest at the wealthiest tables – and in the most bedrooms afterwards . . .

From poverty to nobility, sex siren Diana Saxon never fails to make the most of her abundant talent for sensual pleasure!

FICTION / EROTICA 0 7472 4762 5

A Message from the Publisher

Headline Delta is a unique list of erotic fiction, covering many different styles and periods and appealing to a broad readership. As such, we would be most interested to hear from you.

Did you enjoy this book? Did it turn you on – or off? Did you like the story, the characters, the setting? What did you think of the cover presentation? How did this novel compare with others you have read? In short, what's your opinion? If you care to offer it, please write to:

> The Editor
> Headline Delta
> 338 Euston Road
> London NW1 3BH

Or maybe you think you could write a better erotic novel yourself. We are always looking for new authors. If you'd like to try your hand at writing a book for possible inclusion in the Delta list, here are our basic guidelines: we are looking for novels of approximately 75,000 words whose purpose is to inspire the sexual imagination of the reader. The erotic content should not describe illegal sexual activity (pedophilia, for example). The novel should contain sympathetic and interesting characters, pace, atmosphere and an intriguing storyline.

If you would like to have a go, please submit to the Editor a sample of at least 10,000 words, clearly typed in double-lined spacing on one side of the paper only, together with a short outline of the plot. Should you wish your material returned to you, please include a stamped addressed envelope. If we like it sufficiently, we will offer you a contract for publication.